SECRETS

— OF THE —

OAK

LYNN WHITSITT

SECRETS OF THE OAK

First edition. February 27, 2024.

Copyright © 2024 Lynn Whitsitt.

ISBN: 979-8224621859

Written by Lynn Whitsitt.

Disclaimer

This book is a work of fiction. Names, characters, places, and incidents are either the products of the author's imagination or used fictitiously. Any resemblance to actual persons, living or dead, businesses, companies, events, or locales is entirely coincidental.

While this novel draws its inspiration from historical events and figures, the author has utilized artistic license in the portrayal and interpretation of these elements. The narrative and character development are the results of the author's imagination and are not to be construed as real. The author has made every effort to ensure historical accuracy, but certain liberties have been taken for the sake of the narrative.

This novel contains material that may be disturbing or triggering for some readers, including scenes depicting suicide and sexual assault. These scenes may not be suitable for all readers, particularly those who have been personally affected by such events or are currently struggling with related issues. If you or someone you know is in distress, we strongly encourage you to reach out to a mental health professional or trusted individual in your life. For those in the United States, the National Sexual Assault Hotline offers 24/7, free, and confidential support at 1-800-656-HOPE (4673), and the National Suicide Prevention Lifeline provides support at 1-800-273-TALK (8255).

This novel is meant to entertain and inspire, and it does not aim to glorify or promote harmful behavior. It hopes to raise awareness of historical events and human resilience in the face of adversity. Reader discretion is strongly advised.

To my wife, Brandi, my guiding light and unwavering support. To my parents, who taught me the strength of character and the power of dreams. And to the courageous soldiers and their resilient families-those who have served, those who were lost, and those who continue to serve now-your bravery and sacrifice do not go unnoticed. This book is dedicated to all of you.

"The line separating good and evil passes not through states, nor between classes, nor between political parties either-but right through every human heart." ~ Aleksandr Solzhenitsyn

Prologue

On a pleasant spring morning in May 2005, a red convertible Corvette sped down Highway 81. The driver, his silver hair glinting in the sunlight, reveled in the wind rushing past.

With the car's top down, the fragrant aroma of blooming flowers filled the air, and the warm sun bathed his weathered face, evoking a profound sense of nostalgia.

As he passed the old, abandoned cotton mill with the rusted Harrington Industries sign, he knew he was nearing home. *Home?* he mused with a chuckle, a place he hadn't visited in years since relocating to Atlanta. He remembered the tranquil days spent in the small Georgia town of Warrenton, a stark contrast to the bustling city life he now led.

As he navigated the well-known streets, *They're all staring. Not that it matters*, he thought, noticing the curious glances he drew from onlookers. *I don't know them anyway.*

The sight of the massive oak tree on the hill as he turned left onto a dirt road confirmed he was nearing his destination. He slowed down, admiring its ancient limbs reaching towards the sky. Allowing himself a moment to savor the sight before accelerating again.

He spotted the sign announcing, 'Estate Sale Today - 1:00 pm,' and turned into the dirt driveway, noticing another car already there. *The house still looks the same*, he thought, as he pulled into a stop. Memories flooded his mind as he stared at the white wooden structure, its paint peeling from years of exposure to the elements.

He gathered himself and stepped out of the car. As he walked up the steps to the porch, a short, middle-aged brunette with a confident demeanor emerged to greet him. She wore a tailored outfit, and her chestnut hair framed her face in soft waves. Her eyes met his with a warm, understanding gaze.

"Mr. Anderson, I presume. Right on time. I hope the trip wasn't too bad. I'm Sharon Morris, we spoke on the phone yesterday."

He nodded, the memory of their phone conversation still fresh. *I expected someone younger based on her voice*, he thought, but quickly dismissed it. "Thank you for seeing me so early," he said.

"No problem, come on in," she remarked with a smile as she held the door for him. *It's still technically my house*, he thought, as he followed her inside without voicing his thoughts.

"I've gathered all the items from the safe as you requested. I put them in a box together. It's in the back room. I'll go grab it for you," she said, before disappearing around the corner.

The sun filtered through the dusty windows, casting a golden glow on the worn furniture. In the corner, the grandfather clock ticked softly, counting the seconds of his long-awaited return.

Ms. Morris returned, carrying the box. "Here you go," she said, handing it to him. "You sure it's all you want?"

"I'm sure," he responded, feeling the weight of the box as he accepted it.

"Will you at least stay for the sale today?".

"I don't believe so. I need to get back to Atlanta before rush hour hits." It was a white lie. The journey was only two hours, but this trip was more about appeasing his wife than anything else.

"As you wish," she replied, escorting him to the door. "Be careful on your way home, and I'll call you tomorrow with the final sales results."

Offering his thanks, he sauntered back towards his car, cradling the box in his arms. "Take care," he said softly, more to the box than anyone else. He gingerly set it on the passenger seat, handling it as if it were as fragile as the memories it carried.

With the box secured, he allowed himself a final look back at the house, imprinting the image in his mind. Then, settling himself behind the wheel, he guided the car away down the driveway and onto the open road, leaving the house and its memories in his rearview mirror.

As he neared the familiar silhouette of the grand old oak tree, he gently brought his car to a stop. The engine's soft hum was the only sound piercing the tranquil silence of the surrounding countryside.

He lingered for a moment, captivated by the tree that harbored so many memories. Standing tall and resolute, the oak's knotted branches stretched out like ancient arms, each crevice narrating the passage of time. Its thick bark, etched with the marks of countless seasons, stood stark against the vibrant green leaves rustling gently in the breeze.

Memories of his youth came flooding back, blurring the lines between past and present. He could almost see his younger self playing hide and seek among the oak's roots or lounging under its shade on lazy summer afternoons with his girlfriend and friends.

Overwhelmed with nostalgia and immersed in serenity, he remained motionless, absorbing the sight of the old tree. To him, it was more than just a tree; it was a guardian of his past, a symbol of time's relentless march, and a silent witness to his life's journey and that of many others.

Turning off the engine, he opened the car door and stepped out onto the grassy roadside. Behind him, the door closed with a soft click, the noise almost lost in the rustle of leaves in the soft wind.

He made his way around to the passenger side, opening the door to retrieve the box nestled on the seat. The box, filled with its precious cargo, felt heavier than it actually was, its weight representing the memories it contained. He held it securely, his fingers brushing against the cardboard, rough and slightly worn at the edges.

With a deep, steadying sigh, he closed the passenger door and turned to face the hill. The grass rustled beneath his shoes as he began his ascent, his heart beating in rhythm with the quiet cadence of his surroundings.

Reaching the oak, he settled down against its sturdy trunk, the box placed beside him. *What am I doing here?* he pondered, closing his eyes to bask in the warmth of the sun and the gentle rustling of leaves above. The familiar sounds and scents of his childhood wrapped around him, allowing, for the first time in years, a brief reconnection with his past.

The box, unassuming in appearance, held no visible clues of the secrets it contained. His hand hovered over the lid, momentarily lost in a sea of memories and emotions. Taking a deep breath, he surrendered to the moment and gently lifted the lid of the box.

As it opened, the box extended a silent invitation, revealing its contents long hidden from the world. His hand, etched with the marks of time and experience, reached in with a blend of care and curiosity.

Inside, each item emerged as a puzzle piece, offering keys to unlock long-haunted questions that had gnawed at his mind's corners over the years. His fingers traced the contours of each object, each carrying the weight of untold stories and forgotten narratives.

In that moment, time seemed to pause, the world outside fading into irrelevance as he delved deeper into the box's depths. Every careful examination, every tender touch, brought him closer to truth, inching towards unraveling the enigma that had remained shrouded in mystery for too long.

Chapter 1

Innocent Encounters

On a sweltering summer afternoon in 1936 near Warrenton, Georgia, 10-year-old John Anderson and his best friend, Timmy Griffin, were up to no good as usual. Their mischief today was led by the overwhelming allure of the plump watermelons in a nearby field.

John, a farmer's son, was often seen with a worn-out hat atop his mop of unruly brown hair, shielding his deep forest-green eyes. These eyes, filled with wonder, hinted at dreams much bigger than the farmland he worked on daily. Yet, they also held an innate timidity.

Timmy, a stout young black boy and a year older than John had a strength which belied his size, with an infectious laugh and a heart full of courage. He was always by John's side and was the shield in their adventures, often going to lengths to protect his friend, even if it meant courting a little trouble.

Crouched on a knee at the edge of the woods, John's stomach rumbled with hunger as he surveyed the vast watermelon field ahead. Beside him, Timmy hesitated, his eyes dancing with mischief even as he whispered apprehensively, "John, you sho' 'bout this?"

"Scared?" John teased with a smirk.

"Scared? No suh!" Timmy said, puffing out his stout chest. "Don't wanna be messin' with Ol' Man Crawford, is all."

The allure of the ripe fruit proved too tempting. Pushing aside their nerves, they darted into the field, eyes widening in delight at the sight of the plump watermelons. Moving with stealth and speed, they quickly chose a particularly ripe, juicy specimen and, clutching their prize, made a hasty retreat, hearts pounding with exhilaration.

However, their celebration was short-lived. A shout echoed across the field. "You boys! Get off my damn property!" It was Old Man Crawford, the mean farmer, storming towards them, shotgun in hand.

Fear spiked through them, running faster than they ever had. The sound of a shotgun blast followed, filling the air with a noise which seemed to vibrate through their bones. Trailing Timmy, John yelped, feeling a sting on his backside.

They ran towards the safety of the woods, their laughter echoing as the thrill of their successful mischief overcame John's discomfort of the non-lethal, yet painfully memorable, salt-rock shot. It was a common, non-lethal way of deterring trespassers, painful but usually not seriously harmful.

"Next time," John panted, a hand clutching his stinging backside, "let's stick to the peach orchard."

As they caught their breath, the woods seemed to come alive with the sound of nature and distant laughter. John's gaze landed on a large oak in a small clearing where he recognized the spirited and curious Sarah Carter, daughter of the wealthy general store owner.

Her bright blue eyes sparkled like the ocean, and her golden hair flowed like a sun-kissed river. Dressed in a green sundress, which fluttered in the gentle breeze, her bare feet were caked in dirt and moss from her own adventures in the woods. Her laughter filled the air as she twirled around, chasing after a butterfly which had caught her eye. Her friend, Emily Branson, watched with an amused expression from a nearby log.

Emily had long, curly brown hair bouncing around her face as she laughed, her nose freckled. Dressed in a simple cotton dress, her bare feet also bore the marks of their woodland escapades. She lived in a small cabin on the outskirts of town. Having lost her mother to pneumonia at the tender age of 8 and with her father resorting to the bottle over the years, she found solace in the woods with Sarah, escaping her difficult home life.

Their shared laughter drew the boys closer. Upon noticing them, Sarah turned with a bright smile, her dimples becoming more pronounced. She greeted them warmly, sparking a conversation about their shared love for adventure and exploring the woods.

They traded stories on the vibrant colors of autumn leaves and the scent of pine needles in the summer heat. Sarah's voice was soft and musical, as she led them to her secret hiding spot behind the massive oak, the refreshing coolness of the shade and the earthy scent of the moist soil enchanted them.

Upon reaching the secret spot, Emily hopped off the log and bounded over. "Hey there," she greeted, her gaze pausing on Timmy. "I think I've seen you around town."

Timmy nodded, a touch shyly, but before he could speak, John interjected, "This here's Timmy. He lives near my place."

"And this is John. He loves exploring the woods like us!" Sarah said.

As they relaxed under the shade of the old oak, John raised the watermelon. "Y'all want some?" he asked.

Sarah and Emily exchanged a glance before Sarah responded with a bright smile, "Sure!"

Timmy reached into his pocket and pulled out a small, sharp pocket knife his father had given him. With practiced ease, he cut into the ripe melon, revealing its juicy red fruit. The sweet scent wafted through the air, enticing their senses and making their mouths water in anticipation.

John then took over, carefully slicing the melon into even portions. He handed a slice each to Sarah and Emily, who smiled brightly at the sight of the refreshingly juicy treat.

Taking bites from their slices, sweet juice dribbled down their chins, causing a fit of giggles. The flavors seemed to add a spark to their escapade. As they savored the treat, they spat out the seeds, dotting the ground with scattered black specks Their laughter resonated in the tranquil woods, the shared enjoyment of the melon amplifying the charm of their journey.

"We all be enjoying this melon, don't we?" Timmy chuckled, his hand already sticky with juice.

"Yes, we surely are," Sarah responded, grinning widely.

"Yeah, it sure was worth it," John added, trying to sound casual.

"Worth what?" Sarah asked curiously.

"Nothin'," John replied, swiftly changing the subject.

With their hands sticky and faces smeared with juice, Emily looked at John, asking, "We were talking about going on an adventure to find the hidden stream. Do ya'll want to come with us?"

John's ears perked up at the mention of a hidden stream. "Wait, what hidden stream?"

"It's a secret. But I heard an old man talking 'bout it in town. He said it's hidden deep in the woods, and only the bravest can find it," Emily said.

"And we are the bravest adventurers around, right?" said Sarah.

They laughed while Emily continued. "We've been trying to find the darn thing for weeks now. We think we're close, but shore could use ya'll's help."

Timmy spoke up with his cheeks a tinge red and his eyes on Emily. "Could'st I come along?"

Emily's cheeks tinged with a soft blush, and she offered a shy nod. "Of course," she murmured, her voice barely above a whisper.

John smiled, happy his best friend was getting to spend time with the girl he had liked from afar but was too shy and scared to ever speak to.

"Well, let's go then," Sarah said, taking the lead. Her golden hair swayed with each step.

John couldn't help but observe the way her dress fluttered in the breeze, revealing her bare legs and feet. Occasional rays of sunlight pierced through the canopy, catching her features and making her glow with natural beauty. As they walked, the leaves rustled underfoot, their soft crunching filling the air. He was grateful most of the path was cloaked in the cool shade of the trees, shielding them from the sun's intense rays.

On the winding forest path, Sarah inquired about John's favorite outdoor activity. "Wanderin' the woods, I reckon,'" he replied, appreciating the peace of nature. Emily voiced her love for river swimming, and Timmy boasted on his fishing exploits.

They delved deeper into the forest, sharing observations of the flora and wildlife around them. The sun's rays pierced the canopy, casting a golden glow on the forest floor, accompanied by the harmonious sounds of birds and rustling leaves.

As the hidden stream drew nearer, the tranquil murmur of flowing water intensified. The cool breeze carried the fragrance of wildflowers and the earthy scent of the forest, enveloping them in an exhilarating yet calming embrace.

When the stream revealed itself, they stared in wonder. Sunlight danced on the water's surface, creating a sparkling spectacle and casting a spectrum of colors over the glistening rocks and pebbles beneath.

"This is incredible!" John said.

"I told you it would be worth the journey," Sarah replied, smiling.

They waded into the refreshing stream, water lapping at their toes and creating playful ripples. With each stone skipped, droplets were sent flying into the air. Despite the cold causing shivers, they were lost in the enchantment of the moment, surrounded by nature's breathtaking beauty.

As the sun started to set, painting the world with its warm glow, they returned to the old oak, weary yet content with their adventure. The leaves of the surrounding trees shimmered in the fading light, creating a magical aura around them.

"This was the best day ever ya'll!" Emily said. She collapsed onto the ground, her body relaxing in fulfillment as she let out a long, satisfied breath. "I can't wait to do it again."

Timmy grinned, "Yeah, we sho' should be doin' this more."

Sarah turned to John. "What do you think? Want to join us on more adventures? Maybe we can go on a treasure hunt next time, or explore the old abandoned mill on the edge of town."

A thrill of excitement coursed through him at the thought of more adventures with her. "I'm up for 'bout anything," he said with a wide grin.

Timmy stood, dusting off his pants. "Well," he said, looking at the sky where the sun had begun its descent, "I best be getting home. Pa be wondering where I off to."

John nodded, rising to his feet and offering his hand to help Sarah up. "I should probably be heading back too. Ma will be worrying."

Sarah and Emily agreed, a touch of sadness lingering in their expressions at the end of their adventure. Emily, especially, seemed reluctant to return home, her gaze lingering on the forest as they started their journey back.

"I wish I could up and live out here forever," she confessed to Sarah, her eyes not once leaving the fading sunlight filtering through the canopy above. "I ain't much in the mood to head home, but I got to."

Sarah, looking down at her own dress, the fabric now smeared with grass stains and streaks of dirt. "My ma's gonna raise a ruckus about this dress, ain't she?"

Emily glanced at Sarah, a smile tugging at her lips despite the situation, "She sure is."

Understanding each other's predicaments but unable to provide any further comfort, the girls gave each other a reassuring hug. After a final wave and promises to meet up again soon, they all parted ways, each carrying with them memories of another day spent in the embrace of the forest and their newfound friendship.

Walking back home, Timmy felt a mix of happiness and apprehension. He knew his father, Jerimiah Griffin, would ask him where he'd been all day.

As he approached his home, a small but cozy cabin, he spotted his father on the porch in his rocking chair. He was a tall man with a strong build from years of working on the ranch. His dark skin was weathered, and his hands were rough, but his eyes were kind and wise.

"Where you been off to, boy?" he asked, his voice deep but gentle.

"Was out with John, Pa, and that Emily girl from town. We been explorin' the woods, done found us a stream," Timmy responded.

Jerimiah narrowed his eyes, "You ain't been stirrin' up no trouble has ya?"

"Naw, suh," he assured him, "We been foolin' around, stumbled upon a watermelon too."

Jerimiah's stern face softened into a smile. "John, ya say? His pa's a good man. And Emily Branson, she's a strong little lady. Heard 'bout what happened to her Ma a bit ago, tragic thing it wuz."

Timmy's shoulders relaxed, and a tentative smile found its way to his face. He met his father's gaze and nodded. A moment passed before he summoned the courage to continue, his voice a touch softer. "And Sarah Carter was there too, Pa. She be real nice."

Hearing the Carter girl's name, his father's face took on a grave expression. He was silent for a moment, carefully choosing his words, "Ain't got no issue with you keepin' company with the Anderson boy or the Branson girl. They wouldn't hurt a fly. They's good country folk, like us. But you got's to see it clear, son. Them Carters, they's well-off. Got the general store in town. Folks of their kind...well, they might not take kindly on a colored boy spendin' time with their little girl, no matter how innocent it be."

Timmy met his father's gaze, his young face a mirror of his father's seriousness. "I hear ya, Pa," he said earnestly, "I ain't lookin' to make no trouble. Want to have friends is all?"

"Alright, son," he said, patting Timmy's shoulder, "Now, you best get in an' clean up. Your ma's got supper almost ready, an' she ain't gonna appreciate you comin' in all covered in dust an' dirt."

Timmy nodded, his excitement from the day's adventure dampening. He understood the caution in his father's words. He respected him, a hardworking man who had faced prejudice and adversity and taught Timmy the importance of respecting boundaries in their small Southern town. He also knew the societal expectations of their world, as tricky to navigate as the densest parts of their beloved forest.

Promising to be careful, he hugged his father, an exchange which held all the unspoken understanding between them. As he turned towards to enter their small house, he cast a final, lingering glance back at the forest, the woods which held the memory of the day's adventure. His heart was full of hope for many more adventures to come and how to balance his simple joys with the complex realities of their lives.

THE NEXT MORNING FOUND John at the breakfast table, squirming uncomfortably in his chair. His left buttock still stinging from yesterday's encounter, but he tried his best to mask his discomfort.

His father, noticing his son's unusual restlessness, looked at him curiously. "Everything alright?" he asked, taking a sip from his coffee.

"Yeah, Pa. A bit stiff, I reckon' didn't sleep right," John replied.

His father raised an eyebrow but said nothing more on it. Instead, he turned to his wife, who was busy tidying the kitchen. "Believe I'll mosey into town for a spell, grab a few items," he said casually.

John's eyes lit up at the mention of going to town. "Can I come too Pa?" he asked eagerly, the discomfort momentarily forgotten.

His father looked at him, taking a moment before responding, "Well, I reckon', long as you're up to hitchin' the wagon."

"Yes, sir!" he said, leaping from his chair and practically sprinting out the door. His ma watched him go, a smile playing on her lips, while his pa took another sip of coffee, winking at her over the rim of his cup.

As they pulled in front of the general store, John's gaze found Sarah. She offered him a shy smile, her eyes briefly meeting his before looking away. In response, he raised his hand in a subtle wave. They then focused on their task at hand, busily gathering their supplies and loading them into the wagon. As they were about to pull away, Old Man Crawford ambled up, his approach slow but determined.

"That melon your boy snatched, how'd it taste?" He asked.

His pa's eyebrows furrowed in confusion. "What's that, Crawford?"

"Came across your boy and his colored friend helping themselves to a melon from my patch. Recognized the lad, so I gave 'em a touch of salt instead of the usual buckshot."

His father turned to John, "Is this true, son?"

"Yes, sir," John admitted, head bowed.

His father nodded, looking back at Crawford. "Well, how much we owe you?"

Crawford waved it off. "No need this time. Probably the colored boy put him up to it. But hear me now, you best stay out of my field, you hear?"

John responded, chastened, "Yes, sir."

As they rolled away from the general store, his pa broke the silence, "So, it wasn't a crick you found last night, was it?"

"No sir," John admitted.

His pa chuckled, "Well, I reckon' I caught my fair share of salt at your age."

"You ain't mad?"

His father shook his head, "Not mad, son. Jus' a mite disappointed. But maybe that lick of salt taught you somethin'. You gotta respect what's other folks. Don't be taking nothing you ain't paid for or ain't yours. Understand?"

"Yes, sir."

"And we best not mention this to your ma. Let's keep it between us men, how's that sound?'

"Thanks, Pa!"

"Timmy your best friend, ain't he?"

"Yeah, Pa," John replied, his voice laced with a touch of worry.

His father nodded, taking a moment before speaking again, "Ain't nothin' wrong with that, son. Some folks might raise an eyebrow, 'cause he's colored. But in my book, it don't make no never mind. What counts is if they a good man. Jus' gotta remember, we all got our own row to hoe in this here world."

John looked over at his father, nodding his understanding of the quiet wisdom his pa was imparting to him.

"An' the Carter girl, Sarah?" his pa asked.

John hesitated for a beat before responding, "Well, we met her an' Emily in the woods yesterday, shared the melon with them."

"Looked like she took a shine to you. Noticed the smile an' wave. You take a shine to her too?"

John's admission sent a warm rush to his cheeks, a telltale blush he couldn't hide from his pa, "Yeah, Pa. I reckon' I did."

His pa chuckled, giving his head a good-natured shake. It was these straightforward father-son talks John held dear, simple and full of unspoken understanding.

From that day forward, John, Sarah Emily and Timmy all became inseparable, spending hours exploring the woods together, their laughter echoing through the forest. They would chase after butterflies and search for hidden streams, imagining themselves on wild quests and daring adventures.

During their numerous excursions, Timmy found himself gravitating towards Emily more and more. They had a shared sense of curiosity which seemed to pull them together. They could spend hours debating the best way to catch a frog or discussing the peculiarities of a newly discovered insect.

Sarah loved John's unwavering composure and steadiness, even when confronted with danger. And he in return, loved her boundless energy and enthusiasm. Their connection was a perfect balance: her energy complemented his calm demeanor.

But, in the midst of all this camaraderie, they were all aware of the invisible line they were treading. The friendship which had been born in the purity of childhood grew in complexity as they approached their teenage years. Yet, they continued their adventures, cherishing the bond they had created, and hoping it could withstand the pressures beginning to encroach upon their carefree world.

Chapter 2

Whispered Promises

As the years passed, Sarah and John's friendship evolved, maturing from a childhood companionship into something more profound. Often, they retreated to their special haven, the secluded spot beneath the towering, ancient oak-it was their world away from the rest of the world. One warm afternoon, they found themselves reunited under its familiar embrace. Sunlight filtered through the canopy, casting patterns of dancing shadows across their youthful faces. They shared a companionable silence, understood only by those as close as they were.

As they sat together, enjoying each other's company, John broke the silence, his voice laced with a hint of nervousness which was unusual for him. "Sarah..." he began, fumbling with an acorn which had fallen nearby, his eyes focused on the ground.

"Yes?" She turned to him, noticing the seriousness on his face.

"Well...we've been stickin' together for a spell," he continued, shooting a quick glance at her before his eyes returned to the acorn in his hands.

"Yes, we have," she said smiling.

He took a deep breath and set the acorn aside lifting his eyes to hers. "I ... well, I reckon' I've grown a real liking to you. More than a friend, mind you," he admitted, cheeks flushing under the summer sun.

Surprise registered in her eyes, rendering her momentarily silent. John mistook her silence for rejection and overwhelmed by embarrassment, he began to stand, intending to put distance between them, perhaps to salvage what remained of their friendship.

But after a heartbeat, she grasped his hand, her fingers wrapping around his in a gentle but firm hold. Pulling him back down beside her, she whispered, her voice barely audible yet laden with unspoken emotion, "John, don't go."

He hesitated, looking at their entwined fingers, then back at her. In her eyes, he saw a reflection of his own vulnerability and hope. "John," she continued softly, allowing her emotions to thread through her words, "I like you too."

Relief spread across his face as he broke into a warm, genuine smile. The nervousness was replaced by an unmistakable glow of happiness. He leaned in, eyes locked with hers, as if asking for her permission. She responded by closing the distance between them, their lips meeting in a sweet, tender kiss, a natural progression of their shared affection.

The kiss was soft and inexperienced yet filled with the purest emotions they harbored for each other. Underneath the old oak, their bond was sealed with this new shared secret, their young love blossoming in sync with the onset of summer.

After, their relationship deepened and solidified, facing not only the intrinsic challenges of a budding romance but also navigating through a labyrinth of societal and family expectations. Together, they vowed to create a life interwoven with love, laughter, and happiness, even in the shadow of adversity.

Sarah's sanctuary beneath the sturdy branches of the old oak, once a simple refuge, now cradled a dearer memory, potent enough to elicit a smile with each reminiscence of their first kiss and the warmth of John's embrace.

Yet, her family's disapproval cast a persistent shadow over their relationship. Her parents, wrapped in their wealth and social standing, perceived John as nothing more than a disruption in their meticulously curated social circle.

He was a boy from a humble background, lacking the refinement and sophistication they demanded in a suitor for their daughter. They dreamed of Sarah sustaining the family's stature through a prosperous marriage, thereby fortifying their position in a society punctuated by wealth and reputation.

Contrastingly, John hailed from a family of modest, hardworking farmers, familiar with the societal rift which often isolated the working class from the affluent. His parents, particularly cognizant of the challenges embedded in the convergence of contrasting social divisions, harbored reservations regarding his relationship with Sarah.

John's father, a World War I veteran, had returned to a life tilling the land post-service, while his mother managed their household with steadfast resolve.

They had lived through the realities of a society where wealth and status often played a pivotal role in shaping one's life, a truth they feared their son and his beloved might have to confront.

They knew many in their small town would frown upon a relationship between the two, including her parents, who would disapprove of their daughter's association with a boy from a poor farming family who's best friend was a negro.

One day, while working silently alongside John in the field, his father broke the stillness. "You know, Sarah's kinfolk got a whole heap of money. They own the general store in town and they swing a big stick 'round here."

"Yeah, I know. But I ain't much concerned 'bout no money. I'm sweet on her for who she is, not for her money," John responded earnestly.

"Good to hear, son," said his father with a nod before continuing. "Keep in mind money can bring along a heap of expectation and pressure. She comes from a different world than yours, with different ways of thinking. It's mighty important to recognize them differences and to have open and honest talks."

Tipping his hat, John responded, "Yeah, but I don't reckon' she's that type of gal. She's got her feet on the ground and ain't no pretender."

Firmly, his father patted him on the back. "I trust in your judgment. But sometimes even the most genuine of folks can be swayed by their surroundings and what's expected of 'em. It's right important to be mindful of those influences and not let 'em muddle your clear sight or change who you are."

"What are you getting at?"

Choosing his words carefully, his father explained, "She might have herself some expectations on courtin' and such, what with her family's high status and all. She might be wantin' certain things from you or the relationship you ain't comfortable with."

"I understand. But I don't aim to change myself or step over my own boundaries jus' to make her or her folks happy."

His father's face softened into a smile. "That's the spirit, boy. It's crucial to stay true to who you are and yer own moral compass. Make sure yer having them open, truthful talks with her and findin' places where you both see eye to eye."

"I'll keep it in mind, Pa."

Laying a hand on John's shoulder, his father continued, "I jus' want you happy and makin' smart choices for yourself and for what's ahead." He took a deep breath before continuing. "Now, I've watched you grow up, puttin' others before yourself, sometimes to your own hurtin'. It's a fine trait, but you gotta be mindful.

He looked off into the distance, then back at John. "Life ain't gonna be like this here field forever, where you and me work shoulder to shoulder. There'll come a time when I won't be 'round, nor will your Ma or even Timmy."

John's gaze stiffened, a soft defiance in his voice. "I do stand up for myself."

His father, looking earnestly into his eyes, responded, "Standin' tall ain't jus' 'bout them times you gotta holler loud. It's in every turn you take, each bit of give-and-take, and in them quiet moments when you set your pride aside. It's 'bout makin' sure they hear your voice, even when it's shaky, 'specially against those who might wish you ill, or even them folks you care for deeply."

John nodded, his eyes lingering on the horizon. His jaw set in quiet defiance; he was unwilling to accept his pa's observation.

Feeling the weight of the moment, his father gave John's shoulder a firm squeeze. "I'm wishin' nothin' but joy for you, son. Jus' be certain joy don't come at the price of losin' your voice or yourself. I'm here, guidin' you best I can, 'til the day rolls 'round when you gotta walk that path on your own two feet."

As the day waned and dusk cast long shadows across the fields, John found his father's words lingering in his mind. He stared at the sun-hardened earth beneath his boots, his emotions tumbling like leaves in the wind. A feeling of foreboding tightened in his chest. Steeling himself and pushing away his doubts, he recalled his promise to meet Sarah by the old oak later that evening. After bidding his father farewell, he set off.

As days melded into weeks, the weight of his father's words rested heavy on his mind. He often wrestled with the tension of being true to himself while navigating the challenging waters of his relationship with Sarah. Despite the disapproval of her family, they refused to let their love falter.

They continued to steal moments, meeting at their secret spots like the old oak or the creek, where they could be alone, away from the judging eyes. Their love was unwavering and pure, and together they were determined to overcome any obstacle which stood in their path.

LATER ONE AFTERNOON, without warning, Sarah's parents sat her down at the dining table, their faces etched with disapproval. "We need to talk about John," her father said.

"What about him?" she asked, feeling a knot form in her stomach.

"We've been hearing some disturbing news," her mother interjected. "We don't believe he's the right match for you, dear."

Sarah bristled at the implication. "What news?"

Her father exhaled, the weight of his frustration and disappointment evident in the way his shoulders slumped and in the look in his eyes. "Well, darlin', for starters, he's doesn't come from money or influence, and he's friends with the colored boy, Timmy."

Sarah's heart faltered at her father's words; the bitter sting of his prejudice sharply felt. "But father, he's a good soul. John's kind and caring, and he's shown me nothin' but love. And Timmy is a good friend to him... to us. Why does it matter where either of them comes from?"

"It matters!" her father said with a firm voice. "You hail from a lineage of wealth and influence in this town. His kin don't share the same social standing or financial resources we do. This isn't only regarding money, it's about the upbringing you've had, the manners and values ingrained in you since you were no more than a babe. It's about belonging to a certain social class and upholding the traditions and expectations tied to it."

With a disbelieving shake of her head, she responded, "That's not fair. His kin might not possess the same wealth or high standing, but they are good people who work hard and are honest. They have good hearts, and their family values are strong."

Her father hesitated for a moment before speaking again. "I understand your feelings, but there's more to consider. What of your future? Your place in society? It's not only about the two of you, it's how this could impact your entire life."

Sarah grappled with her emotions, torn between her deep affection for John and her family's unwavering expectations. While she understood her father's concerns, she believed them to be rooted in a narrow-minded view, perhaps unjust. She was determined to make it work with John no matter what challenges they may face.

"Why does it even matter?" Her voice rose in anger. "He is a good person and makes me happy. Isn't that what counts?"

"Sarah, you need to consider your future," her mother said. "Do you want to marry someone who can't provide for you the way you deserve?"

Sarah shook her head. "I don't care about money or status. I love him."

"We only want what's best for you. We don't want you to make a mistake you'll regret," her father said.

"I understand your concerns," she said, her frustration mounting. "But my feelings for him are real, and I can't ignore them because you don't approve." Afterwards, she stood and stormed out of the house with a mixture of anger and sadness.

As Sarah sat under the oak waiting for John, her mother's words echoed in her mind. *He's not right for you, dear.* She understood the implications of her mother's words, yet her heart rebelled against them.

When John arrived, he was struck by the sadness in her eyes. "What's wrong?" he asked, his voice filled with concern.

She looked at him, tears threatening to spill from her eyes. "It's my parents. They don't approve of us. They say you're not right for me because of your background."

His heart clenched at her words, his worst fears coming to life. He had known their relationship would be fraught with difficulties, but the reality of it was more painful than he had anticipated. "I reckon' I saw this coming. But I can't stand the thought of bein' without ya."

"I don't want to be without you either. I love you, no matter what my parents say."

Looking deep into her eyes, he reached out and took her hand, offering it a reassuring squeeze. "I love you too. Ain't no storm we can't weather, long as we're side by side."

Their promises resonated in the quiet of the afternoon, as lasting as the oak which sheltered them. United, they pledged to face their challenges together, their commitment unyielding in the face of adversity.

The ancient tree was more than a meeting spot. Its proud, tall figure and sky-brushing branches were symbols of their steadfast love, existing in a realm separate from the demands and expectations of their families or surroundings.

As the sun began to set, long shadows crept around them, fashioning an intimate bubble for the two of them. Under the protective arch of the oak, they found a place where they could be true to their feelings, undisturbed by the world outside.

John cleared his throat, breaking the peaceful silence. "Sarah," he began, turning to her with a serious expression, "What're your dreams?"

Her eyes widened in surprise, momentarily pausing before a shy smile gently curved her lips. "You mean like my aspirations in life?"

Taking a deep breath, her eyes briefly clouded with daydreams. "I've always imagined traveling, discovering new places. Maybe, eventually settling down, getting married, having a family," she said. A self-conscious chuckle escaped her, "It sounds a bit silly, doesn't it?"

"Nah, ain't nothin' silly 'bout it. Fact is, sounds plum wonderful. You'd be a great wife and ma, I'm certain of it."

His words warmed her from within, the feeling of acceptance and understanding washing over her. She beamed at him, asking, "And you. What are your dreams?"

"Well... I've a hankerin' to own a cotton farm like my pa. Not any ol' cotton farm. I aim to have the biggest cotton farm in Georgia."

Over time, their connection deepened, with the oak standing as a witness to their love. Sarah deeply loved John, but her family's persistent disapproval weighed on her. Dinner conversations hinted on marrying within their social class, and disappointed glances from her mother became frequent. Whispered criticisms from relatives regarding John's background and his friendship with Timmy, a local Black boy, didn't help either.

Yet, each rendezvous with John under their tree restored her hope. In her most trying moments, the memory of his reassuring presence would lull her into peaceful dreams, where they faced the world united.

John too grappled with the disdain of Sarah's family and the town's judgment. The disapproving glances, chuckles from wealthier farmers, assumptions on his intent with Sarah, and criticism over his friendship with Timmy cast a pall. Yet, his determination remained unshaken. For John, Sarah was irreplaceable, the only one he envisioned beside him in life. The idea of letting go of their love was unfathomable.

In moments of doubt, the old oak became his anchor. Its towering branches, reaching skyward, represented hope and limitless potential. This fortified his resolve to face the hurdles ahead. Often, even without Sarah, he found comfort under its vast canopy.

Beneath it, he allowed himself to dream of their future. Aspiring to own Georgia's largest cotton farm wasn't only ambition; it signified his genuine affection for Sarah, dispelling notions of him chasing her family's wealth.

He envisioned her laughter filling their fields, their children playing amidst the cotton, the sun casting a radiant glow on the fluff. He yearned for a life steeped in love and simplicity, far from the current societal scrutiny. While his dreams seemed audacious, they grounded him, fueling his determination to persist.

Despite the doubts and fears that at times clouded their minds, the old oak was their sanctuary. It was a place where they found peace and reaffirmed the depth of their love.

As sunlight filtered through the leaves, casting dappled patterns on their faces, and the gentle rustle of the wind played a soft melody to their whispered conversations, they knew their love could surmount any obstacles which may lie ahead.

However, little did they know a wealthy and conniving young man would soon have his eye on Sarah as well, and he was not one to give up easily.

Chapter 3

Tangled Desires

The town had enjoyed a period of tranquility until whispers of a newcomer disrupted the calm. Speculation surged among residents: was he a famous artist or perhaps a wealthy businessman?

The mystery was soon unveiled when Richard Harrington, a man of significant wealth from the Northeast, made his entrance. He had recently acquired the town's large cotton mill, a massive red-brick structure which had been idle for several years. Located on the outskirts, its towering smokestacks dominated the landscape, serving as a poignant reminder of the town's industrial past when the mill had once provided employment to generations of local families.

With Harrington's arrival, expectations soared among the townspeople, hoping he would revive the mill, bringing jobs and economic stability back to their community. With the town abuzz regarding the Harrington's potential ventures, some families were more personally affected by their arrival.

The Carter's household was a flurry of activity. The grand old house, typically calm and quiet, was now buzzing with anticipation. The occasion? They were expecting the Harringtons, the newly wealthy family who recently moved to their small town. The news of their arrival had caused a stir among the town's gentry.

Sarah's parents had seen an opportunity and seized it. The Harringtons had a son, Billy, who was a year older than Sarah. He was a handsome young man, and according to local chatter, he already had a bevy of young women from town vying for his attention.

The Carters, ever astute, saw the potential of introducing their daughter to him, hoping a connection would form which might lead to more than just friendship. By inviting the Harringtons for dinner, they aimed to provide a casual and welcoming setting for this introduction, thereby possibly fostering a beneficial connection between the two families.

Their house was filled with the delicious aroma of various dishes being prepared in the kitchen, the staff bustling around to make sure everything was perfect. Mrs. Carter was overseeing the arrangements, meticulously ensuring each detail, from the table settings to the menu, was impeccable.

"Sarah," her mother's voice echoed through the house, pulling her from her reverie. She appeared at the entrance of the parlor where Sarah sat, with a stern look on her face. "I hope you understand the importance of tonight."

"I do, Mother," Sarah replied, meeting her mother's gaze, trying her best to hide her apprehension.

"I want you to make a good impression on the Harringtons," she instructed her with a firm tone. "Especially Billy."

"But Mother," she began, her heart heavy.

"I know," Mrs. Carter interrupted, her expression softening for a moment. "I know about John. But you must understand, this is concerning our family, our reputation."

"I understand," Sarah said quietly, though her heart felt heavy in her chest. "But I love John. I don't want to be with Billy or anyone else."

Mrs. Carter replied sharply, "I know about your feelings, but sometimes we have to make sacrifices for the betterment of our family." Feeling her throat tighten, she nodded, biting back the urge to protest. She retreated to her room, closing the door gently behind her.

Leaning against it, she felt the cool wood press against her back. *Why can't they understand? Why is the idea of being with Billy more appealing to them than my happiness?* The ache in her heart intensified at the thought of betraying her feelings for John, just to appease societal expectations. She moved to the window, her gaze searching the horizon as if hoping to find John's comforting presence. She knew tonight was going to be challenging, but she had to stand her ground. Despite her personal apprehensions, the house was already transforming in anticipation of the Harringtons' arrival.

Her parents spared no expense in creating the lavish dinner party. They adorned their dining table with the finest linen tablecloths and exquisite porcelain dinnerware. The flickering light of the candles added an elegant touch to the already impressive display.

The room filled with the aroma of savory dishes cooked to perfection as the scent of roasted meats, fragrant spices, and freshly baked bread wafted through the air, tantalizing the senses.

Her mother had spent hours in the kitchen, preparing each dish with meticulous care, while her father had raided his wine collection to select the perfect vintage for the occasion.

The Harringtons arrived in style, driving up in a new sleek black car. Dressed in their finest attire, Billy, their son, was tall and wiry, with a smug grin on his face. As soon as he laid eyes on Sarah, he was smitten with her. Her beauty and poise were unlike anything he had ever seen before.

After exchanging initial pleasantries and admiring the luxury of the Carter home, the Harringtons settled into their seats.

"We're delighted you could join us," Sarah's mother said, pouring wine into Richard Harrington's glass.

The pleasure is ours," Richard replied, taking a sip of the wine. "This dinner is exquisite. Each dish a masterpiece."

Her father beamed. "We're glad you're enjoying it. We wanted everything to be perfect for tonight."

As the adults continued their conversation, Billy leaned towards Sarah. "I've been looking forward to meeting you since my parents told me about you. And you're even more stunning in person."

Sarah, taken aback by his bold compliment, managed a polite, "Thank you, that's kind of you to say."

Billy, unfazed, continued his confident chatter. He dominated their conversation, boasting of his travels, hobbies, and his family's wealth and influence. As the evening wore on, his arrogant demeanor became increasingly pronounced, making Sarah more uncomfortable.

Despite her unease, she kept up a polite facade, recognizing full well what her parents expected. Lost in their hopes of forging ties with the affluent Harringtons, they seemed blind to the underlying tension.

"Billy," Mrs. Carter interjected at one point, her eyes twinkling, "I've been told you're quite the adventurer. Is it true?"

"It's true, Mrs. Carter. I've seen many different places and experienced a lot."

"How thrilling!" she replied, turning to Sarah. "Our Sarah also has a spirit for adventure. I can only imagine the stories you both could share!"

Throughout the evening, the implication of her parents' words hung heavy in the air, leaving her with a sinking feeling in her stomach. She knew this was only the beginning and it was bound to escalate.

There were chuckles around the table and approving nods from the adults. "They would make a charming couple, wouldn't they?" her mother mused. A knot tightened in Sarah's stomach at the blatant matchmaking attempts. Despite the uncomfortable suggestion, she chose to maintain a polite façade.

Engaging in conversation, laughing when appropriate, she kept a cordial front throughout the evening, though it deepened her discomfort. Her heart belonged to John, and no cordial conversation with Billy could change her mind.

Yet, she wanted to avoid disappointing her parents and thus continued to navigate the evening with grace. While she smiled and nodded at Billy's tales, her mind lingered on John and the moments they shared under the old oak.

Billy, carrying the arrogance of someone who believed any girl in town would be thrilled to have him, mistook her silence for interest. Seizing the moment, he saw this as an opportunity to ask her out to the upcoming dance.

"I heard the annual town dance is soon. Would you like to have the honor of being my date?" he asked with a self-assured smirk. Her heart sank as she glanced around the table, feeling the weight of her parents' expectations on her.

While she didn't want to come off as impolite, the idea of attending the dance with anyone but John was unbearable. "Thanks for the invitation, Billy. But I already have plans to go with someone else," she replied, trying to maintain her composure. Her parents exchanged a look of disappointment, but Billy, accustomed to having his way, wasn't one to be dissuaded easily.

He was surprised by her refusal- a rare occurrence, indeed. Yet, he knew he needed to try a different approach if he wanted to win her over. He continued to engage her in conversation, peppering her with compliments, trying to charm her with tales of his exploits and adventures, making it sound as though he was the most interesting man in town. Billy's intrigued gaze lingered on Sarah as the evening drew to a close. Little did she realize dinner would mark the beginning of his relentless pursuit.

In the following days, she couldn't help but notice Billy seemed to be everywhere she turned. She couldn't shake the feeling he was intentionally following her. Whether at the local market, the library, or even church, he was there, lurking out of direct sight.

Her initial discomfort around him deepened into genuine concern. Yet her parents, seemed oblivious to her unease, were thrilled and frequently commented on the prospect of her getting to know him better.

One afternoon, with the sun casting long shadows across the town square, Sarah found herself amidst the usual hustle and bustle. Vendors peddled fresh produce and children played around her. The old church tower chimed in the distance, marking the passage of time. She moved gracefully through the crowd, her thoughts preoccupied with plans for the upcoming week.

She was approaching Mrs. Angela's bakery, her favorite spot for fresh muffins, when a familiar voice called out, "Hey there, beautiful!" It was unmistakably him, his voice echoing louder than the hum of conversations around her. She looked up to see Billy, yards away, approaching her with an overconfident strut she had come to recognize.

A sinking feeling gripped her stomach as she recognized she was trapped in the openness of the square with nowhere to hide. Every part of her wanted to turn around and flee. Trying to maintain her composure, she swiftly pivoted on her heel and began walking at a brisk pace. Yet, with his long strides, he closed the distance with ease.

She stopped, took a deep breath, and turned to face him. "What do you want?" she questioned, her voice betraying a hint of annoyance she couldn't suppress.

Apparently enjoying the chase, he responded with a broad grin, "Only wanted to say hello. Been hoping to cross paths with you again." He tilted his head, eyes narrowing a bit as if studying her reaction, before adding, "And to see if you've had a change of heart regarding the dance?"

Under his intense gaze, she could almost feel the weight of his unspoken expectations bearing down on her. Her mind raced as she searched for the right words. Struggling to keep her voice steady, she replied, "It's a small town, Billy. Crossing paths was inevitable. As for the dance, my answer remains the same. No! I have other plans."

He was taken aback for a moment but quickly regained his composure. She seized the opportunity, turned, and walked away, determined to put distance between them.

However, as she moved further, she couldn't shake off the looming dread. Knowing her parents were fond of the Harringtons, and the resulting likelihood of having to interact with him more often, weighed heavily on her.

As if the day's events weren't challenging enough, earlier in the morning, an argument with her mother had added to her emotional turmoil. Within the walls of the Carter household, tensions had risen. Her mother tried to persuade her to reconsider her decision not to attend the dance with Billy. The weight of the confrontation still clung to Sarah, its remnants lingering.

"Sarah," her mother's voice had strained as she began, "I've heard you refused Billy again. Why are you being so stubborn? He's a good boy from a decent family."

Sarah had stared out of the window, mulling over her mother's words. The phrase *decent family* echoed in her mind. Why had John's humbler background made him any less decent in her mother's eyes?

She remembered the simpler times of her childhood when she and John would laugh and play without a care in the world. But as they grew older, societal expectations and the town's hierarchy started to cast a shadow over their relationship. *Why does growing up come with such burdensome expectations?* she'd wondered.

As the whispers about her and John had started circulating in town, attempting to drive a wedge between them due to the town's prejudices, she'd subsequently taken a stand, summoning all her courage to respond. "Mother, I don't like Billy the way you want me to. I can't force feelings which aren't there."

Her mother's eyes had flashed with displeasure. "Billy doesn't spend his time associating with negroes and causing trouble like John does. You need to think of what's best for you."

Sarah hadn't held back her response, "And you think Billy is what's best for me? Just because he doesn't hang out with Timmy or doesn't share the same values as John does, it doesn't make him a better choice. You need to respect my decisions too, mother."

Her words had hung in the air, and the unmistakable tension between them had remained. With no resolution in sight, Sarah had needed a break from the stifling atmosphere of her home and had sought the familiar embrace of Mrs. Angela's bakery.

As evening approached, she found herself wanting to confide in John. They sat at their familiar spot, under the comforting shadow of their tree. As she shared her anxiety regarding Billy and her sense of entrapment due to her parents' expectations, he listened with undivided attention.

Feeling a surge of anger towards Billy, John endeavored to keep his emotions under control. He didn't want to add to her worries. "Haven't had the pleasure of meetin' this fella yet," John said, his voice tinged with irony. "But from what I hear 'round town, he ain't the kind of man who understands the meanin' of 'no.'"

Sarah nodded, grateful for his understanding. "I wish my parents could understand my feelings and stop pushing me towards him. I love you, and I can't bear the thought of losing you."

His hand clasped hers. "And I love ya too. We'll sort this here mess out, together," he reassured her, his voice soothing her frayed nerves. She gave him a radiant smile of relief, reflecting the comfort she found in his presence. While the path they were embarking on was fraught with challenges, having John at her side fortified her resolve.

As they sat beneath their tree, the setting sun casting a gentle glow around them, Sarah found herself deeply admiring John. He was so much more than a boyfriend to her; he was her steadfast pillar, her confidante, and her guiding light amidst the swirling uncertainties.

The calm before the storm was about to be disturbed as the town's annual dance loomed, an event which promised to jolt the peaceful rhythm of their lives even more.

Chapter 4

A Night to Remember

The town buzzed with excitement for the much-anticipated annual dance. As Sarah prepared to join the festivities, her heart raced with anxiety. She nervously adjusted her long, blonde hair, styled with an elegant bow. Her sparkling blue eyes betrayed her worry, and her expression was one of apprehension.

She donned her finest, a sky-blue gown, adorned with delicate embroidery which shimmered in the moonlight. The dress highlighted her petite frame, and even amidst her evident unease, her natural beauty shone through. The thought of seeing Billy stirred a churning sensation in her stomach, compounded by her parents' evident disappointment over her declining his invitation.

As she made her way toward the dance, her palms grew sweaty and her heart beat faster. While part of her wished she could escape the situation, another part was excited about spending time with John.

Meanwhile, John and Timmy strolled together towards the square. As they neared the bustling town square, they could already hear the music, a joyous melody filling the evening air. As they approached the designated dance area, John noticed the newly constructed wood dance floor, split into two distinct sections.

"Looky there," John remarked, pointing, "they done gave y'all a proper floor this year."

Timmy grinned, "Guess they done got's tired of us tearin' up they fancy grass."

They shared a good-hearted laugh, but their amusement was cut short as they approached a sign reading "Colored Folks", indicating where Timmy was supposed to attend the dance.

John turned to Timmy saying, "I reckon' we'll be meetin' up 'fore long, you hear?" His tone was heavy with regret. "Ain't right, you not bein' able to twirl Emily 'round with the rest of us."

"It jus' the way of things," Timmy replied. "You go now. Enjoy the dance."

John watched Timmy walk away, feeling a surge of frustration at the unfairness of it all. He then made his way to the punch bowl, quickly filling a cup and downing its contents in one swift gulp.

As Sarah stepped into the lively square, the sound of music filled the air, filling her ears with a melodic tune. She looked around nervously, scanning the sea of people, their bodies swaying in time with the beat.

Across the dance floor, murmurs of admiration followed Sarah, her sky-blue gown dancing in the breeze. John, spotting her amidst the crowd, couldn't help but smile. He caught her gaze and beckoned her over with a wave of his hand. Relief washed over her as she made her way over to him, standing well-dressed in a suit and tie by the punch bowl. The lantern light accentuated his chiseled jawline and dark hair.

As Sarah approached, John took her hand and pulled her close. "You're lookin' right purty tonight.," he whispered in her ear, making her blush.

"Thank you. I was so nervous about tonight, but being with you makes me feel so much better."

"I'm right glad to hear it. Remember, we ain't gotta dance with nobody we don't take a shine to. We're here for a good time and to enjoy each other's company,"

"You're right. Let's dance," she said, taking his hand and leading him onto the dance floor.

As they swayed to the music, soft notes from the band intertwining with nearby laughter and chatter, tranquility enveloped her. Closing her eyes, she leaned into his embrace, feeling an implicit promise of safety in his arms. He gently squeezed her hand, and her grip tightened in response - their shared silence a rich tapestry of understanding and comfort. Lost in each other, they reveled in a profound, wordless contentment.

Meanwhile, Emily, dressed in a lavender dress adorned with white lace trimmings, was tucked away behind the tall bushes lining the square's edge. The dress, reminiscent of a spring blossom, flowed down to her ankles and complimented her rosy complexion. She had styled her curly brown hair into a loose bun, with a few wavy strands framing her radiant face. Her brown eyes sparkled in the moonlight as she hid, filled with hope, on the outskirts of the colored section.

Her gaze found Timmy, who seemed oblivious to her presence. Mustering some courage, she attempted to call his name, but her voice barely rose above a whisper. Frustrated but undeterred, she gathered a few small pebbles from the ground.

Her first toss fell woefully short. "Dang it," she muttered to herself. Gathering her resolve, she flung the second pebble with more force, but it veered left, startling a girl standing nearby. "Ouch!" the girl shouted, drawing a few glances. Emily covered her mouth in surprise.

Upon hearing the commotion, Timmy turned and scanned the crowd. His gaze eventually landed on Emily by a bush near the edge of the dance, who was grinning and waving at him. He glanced around to make sure no one was watching him before breaking away from the crowd.

"You the one who hit that poor girl, ain't ya?"

"Well, I didn't mean to! Can't help it if my aim's as crooked as a dog's hind leg," Emily replied, her face reddening. They both chuckled, their laughter barely audible over the sound of the music beginning again.

"Em, what you doin' here, girl? You know we both could be in a heap o' trouble if someone catches us together."

"I don't give a hoot. I only want one dance, Timmy. Now come on, before this song ends," she said, extending her hand towards him.

His initial hesitation melted away at her earnest plea. With a nod, he took her hand and they swayed together behind the big bushes, their bodies moving to the rhythm of the music, stealing a moment of shared happiness in the midst of their divided world.

Timmy pulled back, the magic of the moment making his throat tight with nerves. "Em, does this here mean...we goin' steady now?"

Emily gazed at him, her eyes reflecting the soft glow of the moonlight. A gentle smile formed on her lips. "Well, I reckon' it does, Timmy." A wide grin spread across his face as he took in her words with relief and happiness.

"Well Miss Emily, I suppose I'm the luckiest fella in town tonight."

Pulling her closer, they swayed, their movements a harmonious dance, their hearts finding a shared rhythm in the celebration of something beautifully new.

As the tune reached its conclusion, John's attention was drawn away from the lively throng of dancers. He noticed a subtle movement near the dance segregation line where the tall bushes rustled suspiciously. Emerging from behind the greenery were two familiar figures-Timmy and Emily, sharing a moment with their hands clasped together and smiles wide.

Guiding Sarah away from the dance floor, John discreetly gestured with a subtle nod towards the pair. "Looky there, darlin.'"

Sarah followed his gaze and a broad grin spread across her face. "Well, I'll be! Look at those two! Enjoying their own little dance away from all this ruckus."

Timmy's eyes met John and Sarah's as he shared a silent, triumphant moment with Emily, squeezing her hand reassuringly before parting. Their silent understanding guided her to melt first into the vibrant dance.

First, Emily slipped back into the crowd, seamlessly avoiding attention. As Timmy watched her meld into the swirl of dancers, a strong connection resonated within him, as if she was a singular heart amongst the crowd, yet irreversibly linked to his.

After lingering for a moment, Timmy subtly embarked on his own journey back, edging along the dance floor, navigating the visible boundary marked by a rope, from which signs hung bearing: 'Whites' and 'Coloreds.'

Finally, he navigated his way to where John and Sarah were waiting. "Hey ya'll," he muttered, his voice low with restrained excitement. After casting them a meaningful glance he whispered, "Well, I got somethin' I think y'all should be knowing. Em and I, we decided to go steady!"

As he finished his announcement, a rustle of fabric announced Emily's arrival. She had walked a cautious path through the crowd, trying to avoid any suspicion. Her eyes were glowing with a secret happiness mirroring Timmy's.

"So, did he spill the beans already?" She asked with a smile.

John and Sarah exchanged a glance of delight and surprise. "Well now, ain't that somethin' grand! We're right happy for both of ya," John said with a grin.

Sarah embraced Emily. "Y'all make a fine couple," she said.

As Emily smiled, her cheeks tinged with a blush, she looked down at her feet. "Thanks, y'all."

Sarah leaned closer to John, her voice a soft whisper. "Seeing her this happy, especially after losing her family...and with her brother's whereabouts in the Navy still unknown, it's heart-wrenching. Aunt Jean has done what she could by taking her in. It's been so tough for her. Despite everything, it's wonderful to see her find some joy."

David, Emily's older brother, left home six years ago due to their mother's demise and their father's alcoholism. His departure to join the Navy left Emily alone to deal with their father's downward spiral and eventual death. Afterwards, her Aunt Jean took her in, eventually becoming her legal guardian and raising her alone.

As they chatted and caught up, feelings of belonging and happiness swept over Sarah. She was surrounded by people she loved, filling her with gratitude for the love and support they provided. Even Billy's unwanted attention couldn't spoil her mood. So, she assumed. But her happiness was short-lived when he approached them, his eyes fixed on her.

"Hey there. You look beautiful tonight," he said with a grin, his voice laced with a hint of arrogance. "So, are you having a good time with your friend here?" he asked, nodding towards John.

Her cheeks flushed with anger, a visible sign of her growing frustration as she struggled to find the right words. At that moment, John stepped in, placing a protective arm around her waist. "Yep, we're havin' a right good time. Thanks for askin'."

John's presence did not deter Billy as he continued to engage Sarah in conversation. His voice, smooth and overly confident, filled the air. "Come on, Sarah, let's dance," he proposed, offering his hand with a cocky grin.

She shook her head, trying to maintain her composure. "No, thank you. I'm content here."

"How about a walk then?"

Although a bit of annoyance flickered within her, her voice remained steady. "I appreciate the offer, Billy, but I'm comfortable here."

His smile didn't waver, but his persistence intensified her discomfort. With each passing moment, the pressure increased, and she longed to escape his attention. Despite her polite refusals, he wouldn't take no for an answer.

"No girl has ever turned me down," he said while forcibly grabbing her hand, pulling her towards the dance floor.

Sarah, using her free hand, forcefully pushed him away, freeing herself from his grip. "I told you. I'm not interested," she said as her eyes flashed with a mixture of anger and determination.

John's voice cut through the music. "You heard her, now. Keep your hands off!"

He approached John, stopping inches from his face. "What are you gonna do, farm boy? My dad owns the cotton mill. I'll just tell him not to purchase any more cotton from you, and you'll be even poorer than you are now," he taunted. John's fists clenched, but he held his tongue.

Billy's gaze shifted, landing on Emily who stood next to Timmy, watching the scene with concern. "And what about you, Emily? Still chasing after scum like Timmy?" his words dripping with disdain.

Emily's face reddened as she stepped forward, her stance and expression ready for a confrontation in defense of herself and her friends. Timmy, feeling a surge of anger boiling within him, held her back firmly. He had reached his limit, his anger barely contained.

"Ya need to be movin' on now." he said, each word measured, betraying the effort to keep his anger in check.

Billy smirked and asked, "Or what nigg..."

It was the last straw for Timmy. Unable to restrain himself, he stepped over the rope dividing the two sections, even as gasps of shock from those nearby were drowned out by the loud music.

"Timmy, no..." Emily's plea fell on deaf ears. With his jaw set, Timmy interrupted Billy's rant mid-sentence with a powerful swing of his fist. It connected with Billy's face with a sickening crunch, barely audible over the lively music. The impact sent him flying backwards, landing hard on the ground. Blood trickled from his broken nose.

As he struggled to regain his senses, Timmy leaned over him and said, "Bad luck fo' you, good luck fo' me. See, my pa deals in cattle, not cotton," he said, grinning down at him. "Don't think he be worryin' 'bout losin' no business from you. But here's a warnin' - you disrespect

Emily again, or mess with my folks here, you'll regret it." With a wink, he stood and stepped back over to his side of the rope.

John, casting a worried glance at Timmy, leaned in to whisper, "You best skedaddle quick. We'll meet up in a bit at the train depot." Timmy nodded, recognizing the gravity of the situation.

Billy's fury was evident as he watched Timmy stride away with a victorious air. Sarah, John and Emily passed the fallen Billy, a smile of satisfaction gracing their faces. He had reaped what he sowed in their minds.

They distanced themselves from the turbulent square, heading several blocks to the relative safety of the train depot. Settling on a deserted bench, they each took deep breaths, seeking to calm their heightened nerves.

After what felt like an eternity, Timmy approached, his walk feigning casualness. Relief washed over them; their friend was safe, and they were together once more in the quiet solitude of the train depot.

"That was... something," Sarah said, breaking the silence.

"I reckon' it might not have been the smartest move though." John said.

Timmy cast them a humble smile. "I couldn't jus' be standin' there, lettin' him treat y'all that way," he said.

Emily looked up at Timmy with a smile. "We owe you a heap of thanks for standin' up for us. It was real brave what ya did."

Sarah leaned her head on John's shoulder, feeling a bit of relief. "I'm glad it's over now."

John's gaze dropped as he sat there. *Dad always said, defend your honor and those you cherish.* The weight of those words pressed on him now, accompanied by a pang of guilt. *I should have been the one to confront Billy, to protect Sarah. Instead, I just sat there, paralyzed by my fears. What would Dad think of me now?* As John wrestled with his internal turmoil, the night pressed on, time slipping away unnoticed by the group.

Emily cast a glance at her wristwatch and blinked in surprise. "Well, butter my butt and call me a biscuit, would ya look at the time," she said, rising from the bench. "Guess I oughta be headin' on home now. Timmy, would ya mind walkin' me?" she asked, looking at him with an expectant smile.

He stood up, nodding in agreement. "Sho' thing," he said, extending his hand towards her. "Ain't nothin' I'd rather do, Em."

John watched them as they walked away, feeling happy for his friends. He turned to Sarah, taking her hand in his. "Reckon' it's 'bout time I walked you on home as well. It's gettin' a bit late."

The night air was cool and crisp as John and Sarah walked through the quiet streets, the moon casting a soft glow on their path. Only the sound of their footsteps echoed off the surrounding buildings, fostering an atmosphere of intimacy and seclusion in the otherwise deserted streets as they walked hand in hand.

As they turned the corner onto her street, the familiar houses and streetlights came into view, their warm glow casting a welcoming light on their path. He led her towards her house, taking the path which wound through a small park, the rustling of leaves and chirping of crickets creating a peaceful atmosphere.

As they neared the house, he pulled her close, the world contracting to their shared space under the moonlight. He cradled her face and pressed a tender kiss to her lips. A silent connection, rich with memories and unspoken words, flowed between them.

Her heart fluttered, emotions threatening to overwhelm. She wrapped her arms around him, drawing comfort from his presence. Pulling back, he brushed a stray strand of her hair from her face, creating a soft blush across her cheeks under his gaze. Their eyes met, love evident in each glance.

While no words were needed to convey the depth of their love, John whispered, "Remember, darlin', I'll always be right here for ya."

A wave of warmth washed over her, feeling reassured by his steadfast support and love. She offered him a lingering look, a silent thank you, before she turned to head inside.

As for Billy, they knew he wouldn't forget what had transpired between them. His broken nose and wounded pride would leave a lasting impression, and they couldn't help but wonder if he would seek revenge in the future. Or, if he had genuinely learned his lesson. Only time would tell how he would react, but Sarah and her friends were determined to stay strong and not let him intimidate them again.

AFTER THE INCIDENT, it had been quiet for the last few months regarding Billy. He had kept his distance from Sarah and her friends, avoiding any direct encounters. Yet, they often felt his watchful gaze whenever they were in the vicinity, serving as a silent reminder, he had not forgotten past events.

The Harringtons had ceased all social contact with Sarah's family. They were no longer invited to their social events, and the town gossip made it clear the incident at the dance had caused a rift between the families.

Unfortunately, her parents seemed to blame John for the fallout in the days following the incident, believing he had goaded Billy, causing unnecessary trouble by letting the negro boy assault him. At home, the tension had been unmistakable, eventually one evening, her mother couldn't hold back any longer.

"Sarah," her mother began, a stern look in her eyes, "this mess with Billy is all because of John and his negro friend."

Struggling to contain her frustration, she replied, "Mother, that's not true."

"Indeed, it seems so," her father added. "He shouldn't have interfered. Billy was only being friendly."

"Friendly? He was making me uncomfortable."

"You must understand, dear," her mother continued, "Billy comes from a prominent family. John and the negro boy... well, they don't."

"Respect is what counts! And in my eyes, both John and Timmy have shown more respect towards me than Billy has!"

Despite her efforts, her parents were set in their views. Their disappointment in John was clear, and they seemed intent on pinning the blame on him for the mishap. However, she knew better, and she was determined not to let their misguided opinions tarnish her image of him.

Beyond her family's disagreements, the broader reality told a different story. Despite Billy's initial threat to cut off John's father's cotton supply at the mill, there had been no consequences as the Mill continued to buy their cotton. John and his family had continued with their work with no problems, proving he had no control over them.

It was a victory for them and a lesson for him in which one's status and power could not always be used to intimidate or control others. In fact, John's father had even received a commendation from the Mill for the quality of his cotton, which only further solidified their standing in the farming community.

During the first week of December, the cooler weather settled in, bringing with it a much anticipation for the holiday season. John had celebrated his 16th birthday in mid-November, and he and Sarah had been spending more time together than ever before.

Throughout the years, they frequently sought refuge beneath the old oak. The tree, tall and proud, stretched its bare branches towards the cold, clear sky. Beneath its canopy, wrapped in a warm blanket, they would share stories and laughter. This tranquil spot provided unmatched comfort, a retreat from the world's complexities.

As winter's chill began to set in, the usual pace of life seemed to slow down. Each moment spent together felt infinite, with memories engraving themselves into their hearts. They cherished these moments, drawing strength from one another.

But even as they left their sanctuary, they could sense the winds of change brewing, hinting at challenges on the horizon. While the world was vast and filled with uncertainty, together, they believed they could face whatever might lie ahead.

Chapter 5

Between Love and Duty

John sank into the worn armchair, letting the soft melodies from the radio envelop him like a warm, comforting blanket. The scent of freshly baked apple pie wafted through the air, tantalizing his senses and making his mouth water with anticipation. This lazy Sunday afternoon was a rare moment of rest from the grueling hours of farm work, and he cherished the chance to unwind in this familiar, soothing ambiance.

Closing his eyes, he let the peaceful sounds transport him to the lazy afternoons of childhood when the world seemed boundless and worries were a distant concept. The familiar creak of his father's rocking chair on the floorboards melded with the music, a gentle, rhythmic reminder of these consistent, unchanging, and cherished Sundays.

Unexpectedly, the comforting lull of the radio sputtered and crackled, grabbing both their attention. An eerie quietness from outside seemed to seep through the walls, as if nature itself was holding its breath, awaiting the imminent shift in the air.

The voice which sliced through the silence was unfamiliar yet unmistakably important. It belonged to Franklin D. Roosevelt, the President of the United States. "Yesterday, December 7th, 1941, a date which will live in infamy, the United States of America was suddenly and deliberately attacked by naval and air forces of the Empire of Japan," the President's voice echoed through the room, cutting through the tranquility like a knife.

John's mind raced as the President continued, the news shattering the peace of the Sunday afternoon and replacing it with a resonating fear and uncertainty. He felt a firm hand on his shoulder - his father, offering silent support amidst the shock which had punctured their world. The music had served as a reminder of an untroubled past, but now, the abrupt reality of the announcement cast a shadow upon their present and future.

John turned to his father, his expression one of confusion and concern. "What does this mean? What's going to happen?" he asked.

"We're headed to war again, son. Brings back memories of the Great War."

John's heart dropped, grasping the gravity of the situation. "But why? Why would they attack us?"

His father's gaze drifted off to a distant point, his expression turning introspective as if he were visualizing scenes from a distant past. The subtle softening of his features hinted at memories long tucked away. "Well, son, sometimes things be the way they are, ain't no good reason for it. But we all gotta do our part, protect our folks, and our way of life, you know?"

"What can we do?" John asked.

"We do what we always do. We work hard, we stay strong, and we support each other. And if it comes to it, we fight for what we believe in."

John considered his father's words, recognizing the history and sacrifice which laid behind them. A subtle mix of admiration and contemplation quietly lingered in his eyes.

He wasn't ready to fight, but he was beginning to understand the depth of what it meant to stand for something, to protect those you cared for. His father's solemn demeanor was a silent testimony to the hardship and loss which came with such sacrifice.

Rising from the chair, a mixture of respect, apprehension, and budding determination stirred within John. He gazed down the road leading into town, where a once-peaceful Sunday had morphed into a prelude to chaos. Closing the door behind him, he inhaled the crisp winter air. With tentative steps he gained assurance as he moved, he headed toward the bustling square.

The earlier soothing silence now hung heavily, evolving into distinct, anxious murmurings as he neared, where the former peace was supplanted by a rising cadence of disturbance. As John walked toward Sarah's house, snippets of conversations from the townspeople whispered fears and futures into the chilly air.

"We must prepare for anything," insisted a gruff voice, which belonged to a determined-looking man, his eyes filled with determination.

A woman, her hands wringing a delicate handkerchief, voiced her fear with a tremulous, "What if they come here next?"

A young boy, no older than eight, his eyes wide, confided in his friend with a barely audible, "My cousin is at Pearl Harbor."

Pausing momentarily, John's ears tuned into another conversation where a young man, his posture upright yet shaking with adrenaline yelled, "I'm going to sign up, I have to fight!"

The streets filled with people, each trying to comprehend what had recently occurred. John felt unease washing over him as he realized the world as he knew it was no longer safe or predictable. Despite the surrounding chaos, his mind was on Sarah. He quickened his pace, determined to see her.

As John rounded the corner onto her street, he noticed Sarah sitting alone on the front steps, her posture one of sadness, an inconspicuous silhouette against the turmoil of the neighborhood. Bypassing various clusters of worried neighbors along the way, he headed straight towards her.

When he arrived, her face was pale and drawn. "I'm so glad you're here!" she said.

He felt a wave of relief as he wrapped his arms around her, holding her close. They drew comfort from each other's presence. When they pulled away, she looked at him, her eyes filled with tears.

"I can't believe this is happening. Everything feels so uncertain," she said, her voice trembling. He took her hand, giving it a reassuring squeeze.

"We'll get through this," he said.

A gentle breeze whispered through the barren branches above them, casting sporadic shadows on the cold ground. They both glanced upwards momentarily, as if the stark, intertwining limbs might offer some answers. Her eyes lingered there, while he stared into the distance, as he grappled silently with the uncertainty which lay ahead.

It was only the subtle movement in their periphery view which drew their attention back to the present. Turning towards the disturbance, they noticed Timmy and Emily approaching, their expressions etched with deep concern.

"Y'all hear 'bout the news?" Timmy asked.

John nodded and replied, "We heard it over the radio."

Emily, normally full of life and vivacity, looked drained. Her eyes, normally bright, were now bloodshot and filled with anxiety. "My brother...ya'll know he's servin' in the Navy. I'm beside myself." Her fear for her brother hung heavily in the air, casting a gloomy shadow over their gathering. "I cain't bear the notion of losin' him too."

As the chilling silence set in, John finally broke it. "Well now, ain't no reason to believe he was at Pearl Harbor," he suggested, injecting a sliver of hope into the situation.

Timmy, attempting to provide comfort, slipped his arm around Emily, drawing her close. "We gots to hold our heads high, ya'll," he said firmly.

Sarah, brushing away her tears, felt a surge of gratitude. "Thank you all for being here," she said.

Together, they withdrew from the chatter and made their way towards the old oak, discussing the day's events and grappling with their implications. Upon arriving, John and Sarah nestled together beneath the tree, seeking warmth in each other amidst the crisp December air. Timmy and Emily, expressions somber, soon joined them, settling in quietly.

"Ain't gon' be the same 'round here no more," Timmy said with a firm edge to his voice.

John nodded in agreement. "Reckon' I feel the same way."

Sarah glanced between the two, a confused expression clouding her face. "What do you mean?" she asked.

Timmy's face grew stern, a spark of anger tingling in his words as he retorted, "It's 'bout time we stand tall. Them folks done gone and bombed us, without no cause!"

John hesitated as he gazed at the ground. "I hear ya, Timmy. I'm only 16. Can't enlist even if I wanted to." He paused, raising his eyes to meet Timmy's, "Can't we help without needin' to fight?"

Sarah, laying a gentle hand on his shoulder, looked at him sympathetically. "What are you suggesting, John?"

"We could support those who are fightin', help their families, or work here for those who'll return broken. Being a patriot ain't only 'bout fightin'." He replied.

Timmy exhaled, shaking his head, "John, I understand the fear, but sometimes we gots to confront fear head-on. Ain't no progress gonna be made sittin' back."

After a moment of silence, John gave a slight nod, though a hint of hesitation lingered in his eyes. "Alright, we prepare. For fightin' or otherwise."

"Well then, let's get ourselves ready. We'll do whatever it takes, y'all. Whatever it takes." Emily said, her gaze sweeping over everyone with a fiery determination in her eyes.

In agreement, they pledged to do all within their power to be prepared, whether the path led to battle or different forms of service. Training, studying, supporting one another - they knew the journey would be fraught with challenges. Yet, their resolve to protect their land and way of life, whatever the cost, remained unshaken. As day gave way to night, they walked back towards town, their minds filled with intertwining thoughts and plans for an uncertain future. United by a shared commitment, they knew they were in this together.

America's involvement in the war deepened. Germany declared war on the United States on December 11, 1941, four days after the Japanese attack on Pearl Harbor. John and his friends watched as the world plunged into a global conflict, one which would shape the course of history for years to come.

John spent the ensuing two years in a state of contemplation. His 18th birthday loomed, presenting the imminent decision of whether to join the military and engage in the battle for his nation.

These years, drenched in uncertainty and trepidation, nonetheless fostered growth and enlightenment. It became a period during which John explored his own depths and grappled with the world's complexities more profoundly than he'd ever anticipated.

His choice to fight or forge another path of contribution hung persistently in the balance, awaiting resolution.

Since Warrenton was such a small town, John and his friends found other ways to contribute to the war effort. They organized drives to collect supplies for soldiers overseas, such as socks, toiletries, and non-perishable foods. They also held fundraisers to purchase war bonds and stamps, encouraging their fellow townspeople to invest in the war effort.

In addition, he and his friends worked on a victory garden project, planting and maintaining a large vegetable garden to be used to supplement food rations for the town.

They also helped with rationing efforts, educating people on how to conserve resources like gas and food, and encouraging everyone to do their part to support the war effort.

John dedicated the subsequent days to both physical and mental fortitude, albeit amidst a backdrop of indecision regarding potential military service. He engaged in rigorous daily exercise, running and lifting weights while gradually increasing the intensity.

Yet beneath his exterior, tremors of fear and self-doubt seeped through. The apprehension of disappointing Sarah in an unready moment plagued him. Nonetheless, he endeavored to subdue these anxieties, channeling his focus into aspects within his control, whilst the question of enlistment perpetually lingered.

Even with the dark cloud of war hanging over the world, he found moments of happiness and joy. He continued to spend time with Sarah, the two of them growing closer with each passing day.

They would still meet under the old oak, and would sit on its sturdy roots, leaning against its trunk, talking of their hopes and dreams for the future. At times, they would spread out a checkered blanket and unpack a basket filled with their favorite treats, enjoying a simple picnic. They would watch the changing seasons and the leaves rustling in the wind. And when the night sky was clear, they would lie on a soft quilt under the tree's canopy, staring at the stars twinkling above.

It was on one of those picnics when John's eyes subtly lingered upon Sarah, whose laughter painted a delicate picture more vivid than any photograph. His mind wrestled with the chaotic tumult of war, providing a stark contrast to the serene family life he envisioned with her, her hair now flowing in the gentle breeze. *Would I ever return to see her hair dance in the wind again, should I decide to join the fight?* he wondered. *How can our love survive the harsh challenges and separations brought by war?*

Her hand touched his cheek, "I see the storm within you, John," she whispered, "Your love for peace and your sense of duty are at war within you. I won't tell you what to do. But know this, whether you go or stay, my love remains." Her words hung heavily between them, a tender challenge enveloping his tortured resolve.

Their eyes met, sharing a silent conversation, and the oak seemed to shield them from the impending chaos for a fleeting moment longer. They talked quietly, forgetting the world around them-until Timmy and Emily emerged suddenly from the trees, snapping them back to reality.

They were both beaming with excitement, and it was clear they had something to share. "Hey, y'all!" Timmy called out, waving his arms. "We gots some fine news to spread 'round!" he said. John and Sarah exchanged curious glances, attempting to determine what had their friends so excited.

As they approached, Emily's ear-to-ear grin was visible. "We're fixin' to get hitched!" she said.

They were thrilled for their friends, congratulating them with warm hugs. "It's hard to believe it!" Sarah said, her voice full of excitement.

John grinned. "Well, it's 'bout dang time! Congratulations, you two."

Laughing, Timmy and Emily shared a look of pure joy. "sho took a good while, didn't it?" Timmy joked.

Once they settled, Emily shared their wedding plans. "We're ponderin' on holdin' it this fall," she said, looking excited.

"Sounds perfect!" Sarah responded.

Emily's smile broadened. "We'd be mighty pleased if the two of y'all could help us with the arrangements."

John and Sarah looked at each other before answering together, "We'd be honored."

Turning to John, Timmy said, "Now listen here. I gots a favor to ask. Would you stand by me as my best man? Ain't no other, I'd want at my side."

Surprised, John quickly recovered and gave him a firm handshake. "Well, I'll be... I'd be right proud, Timmy. I appreciate it."

Emily turned to Sarah, "And would ya do me the honor of being my bridesmaid?"

A smile broke across Sarah's face, "Of course. I'd love to."

The remaining hours of the afternoon saw them lost in a world of wedding musings and exchanged tales. The sun dipped lower in the sky, signaling the day's end, yet each step homeward, each shared laugh, seemed to hold the promise of infinite more. As the path forked, Emily and Timmy bid their farewells, veering away with promises to reunite soon.

Alone together, John and Sarah walked hand in hand, basking in a comfortable silence. It was a moment of peace. Their leisurely walk eventually brought them to Sarah's house, which stood warmly lit against the backdrop of the fading daylight. After exchanging a soft smile and a whispered goodbye, Sarah stepped inside.

John, left standing outside, found himself stuck at a crossroads. One path led towards the loud, demanding call of war, and the other towards his peaceful dreams. Under the darkening sky, he pondered, *Is it more honorable to fight for peace, or simply to live peacefully?* The question hung unanswered in the night air as he turned toward home.

Chapter 6

A Solemn Promise

The fall of 1943 had arrived, bringing with it transformation and anticipation. As the country found its stride in the war and the cotton mill hummed with activity, life in their small town pulsed with a renewed sense of hope and purpose. Amidst this backdrop, the event everyone had eagerly awaited came to fruition: Timmy and Emily's long-anticipated wedding day.

It was a bright Sunday morning, beneath a brilliant sky painted in pastel hues, the small, whitewashed chapel on the hill was readied for the event. Wildflowers from Aunt Jean's garden adorned the quaint building, their vibrant colors mirroring the joyful atmosphere.

Standing on the wooden stage, John adjusted his best Sunday suit. His eyes turned to his side, where Timmy, dressed in his new groom's suit, stood. Timmy's face was a picture of calm determination, yet underneath it, he could see a trace of nerves. And it was only natural. Today, his best friend was embarking on a beautiful journey of love and commitment with Emily.

The organist, stationed near the altar, started to play the familiar strains of the Wedding March, and all heads turned to the chapel's entrance. Sarah, with the weighty role of being the sole bridesmaid, dressed in a soft pink dress, moved gracefully down the aisle, setting the stage for Emily's arrival.

John's father, a sturdy figure in his well-worn suit, stepped into the chapel with Emily on his arm. She was radiant, her simple white dress seemed to glow in the church's diffused light, and her face was lit up with a mix of joy and expectation.

A hush fell over the gathering as he and Emily made their way down the aisle. John noticed Timmy's eyes glistening as he watched her approach. Reverend Fisher, the local black Baptist preacher from Timmy's church, stood at the altar waiting for them. His face was solemn as he prepared to unite the young couple in holy matrimony.

When they reached the altar, John's father took her hand and looked at her with a tenderness, making her eyes well up. "Yer pa sure would've been burstin' with pride," he whispered before placing her hand in Timmy's. He stepped back, nodding to the Reverend to proceed.

"Dearly beloved," he began, his voice echoing through the silent church, "we gathered here today, in God's watchful gaze with these here witnesses, to join together Timmy and Emily in holy matrimony..."

As the ceremony progressed, Aunt Jean, seated in the first pew, watched with a proud smile. She had given Emily her blessing to marry before her eighteenth birthday. Clutched in her hand was a handkerchief she intermittently dabbed at her eyes with.

Beside her were Timmy's parents. Their radiant faces were a testament to the strength of love, overcoming societal prejudices pressing against the church doors. They were there, unwavering, to witness their son's union with the woman he loved, irrespective of racial differences.

When the Reverend said, "Son, you may now kiss yo' bride," the chapel burst into applause, and Timmy leaned in to give Emily a gentle kiss. As they turned to face their friends and family, their beaming faces said it all.

As the reverberations of jubilant cheers echoed in the quaint church, a newfound sense of hope and optimism took root. However, outside those walls, the couple knew they would face a different tune.

In the old South, still recovering from the Great Depression and grappling with the tides of war overseas, people clung tightly to the old ways. Being a married mixed-race couple in this time and place, they would face unique challenges, not only from outsiders but also from within their own community.

Yet, bolstered by love and support from their close-knit circle, they stood unwavering. Their union was proof love's power could surmount even the most deeply seated biases.

As days turned into weeks, and the newlyweds adjusted to married life, their connection with their friends continued to be as strong as ever. John and Sarah stood by their side, supporting them in navigating the intricacies of their shared life.

One evening, as the sun began to set, painting the sky with hues of orange and purple, John found himself sitting beside Timmy by the creek which meandered near their homes. The gentle babble of the water over rocks and the rustling leaves created a soothing backdrop to their conversation.

After a spell of silence, as the first stars began to twinkle in the dusky sky, Timmy cleared his throat, breaking the tranquility. "John," he began, his voice curiously hesitant, "There's somethin' Emily an' I... well, we been holdin' on to a lil' secret." John turned to look at him, a question in his eyes.

"We expecting... Em's pregnant," he managed to say, a soft smile playing on his lips as he looked at John for a reaction.

There was a moment of surprised silence, and a grin began to spread across John's face. "That's fantastic news! Congratulations!"

"Much obliged. Ain't no soul else knows 'bout this. Wanted to tell you an' Sarah first, then my folks. Mind keepin' it under your hat 'til then?"

"Of course! You got my word," John said. This was yet another milestone for his friends, and he was grateful to be a part of their journey.

"I'm gonna be a daddy!" Timmy said excitingly.

John nodded and burst into laughter. "You're gonna be a daddy." The two friends shared a moment of laughter and excitement, reveling in the joyous news which would forever change their lives.

As the laughter ebbed away, replaced by a reflective silence, John's mind ventured towards the multitude of paths his and Timmy's lives would soon take. Timmy, now on a journey to fatherhood, yet still planning signing up for the war, and John himself, entwined in his internal battle over joining the fight or maintaining the peaceful life he had always known.

He looked at Timmy, whose eyes now held a mingling of joy and unspoken fears for the future. After a deep breath, he voiced the question which had lingered between them for a while. "Timmy... ya still plannin' to sign up?"

Timmy turned to him. "Ya, I is. With a lil' one comin', I can't sit back. I gotta stand up, not jus' for me and Emily, but for the babe too. I want our child knowing they daddy did somethin'."

John nodded, the war within him coming to a silent resolution. The time had come for him to rise, not only for himself, but for others like Timmy and Sarah, and for the future they all hoped to build. "Timmy, it's gonna be hard without seein' Sarah each day...but I'm thinkin' it's time for me to take a stand too."

Timmy's eyes met John's as he remained silent, prompting John to continue. "Would you wait 'til my 18th birthday? We can sign up together. Stand side by side, like we always have."

Timmy's gaze searched John's eyes for a moment, contemplating the sincerity reflected within them. "Sho 'bout it?" he asked, "It what you really want to do?"

"Yes," John replied, his voice firm and eyes unyielding.

"A'right. I'll wait," he said, smiling as he reached out to pat John on the back. "But jus 'cause it's you askin'."

The two men, friends since childhood, now stood at the cusp of a new, uncertain chapter, bound by a commitment to each other and to the others they held dear. Though their paths were going to deviate from the tranquil life they had known, their bond stood unbroken, ready to weather the storms awaiting.

As they gazed out over the flowing creek, the encroaching darkness seemed a little less daunting with the assurance knowing they would not face it alone.

Days turned into weeks and weeks into months in the little town, where life ticked by with a subtle, but noticeable tension in the air. John, with his enlistment looming, found himself counting each passing day, his anticipation twinged with a growing unease regarding Billy. The latter's infatuation with Sarah showed no signs of diminishing; his stares lingered too long, and his smiles were unsettlingly warm, despite her obvious devotion to John.

Whenever John and Sarah were together, Billy's watchful eyes constantly lingered, igniting a protective instinct in John. The continuous tension from Billy's ambiguous intentions weighed on John. His vigilance around Sarah grew, his fists often clenching and mind swirling with unwelcome scenarios upon each of Billy's challenging stares. Yet, despite the tension, Billy kept his distance, offering John hoped his unsettling focus might eventually shift.

John, inherently peaceful, found comfort with Sarah, a refuge from the weight of Billy's gaze. Their love, a beacon in challenging times, offered respite amid the storm. But time, with its relentless march, was driving him toward the demands of war.

WHEN HIS 18TH BIRTHDAY arrived, John awoke with the sun, donning his best clothes, a mix of eagerness and solemnity coloring his actions. Today, he would walk into the recruiting office and commit himself to the military, solidifying his path with a signature. Stepping out of his house, a cool breeze brushed against his face as the sun ascended over the horizon. The weight of the world pressed on his shoulders, but he was resolved, ready to play his part.

He met up with Timmy, who was waiting for him outside his house. They walked side by side, speculating on what they might face once they joined the military. They had heard the stories from veterans of the Great War and knew it was going to be tough. But they felt they were ready for the challenge.

When they arrived, they noticed the sign read "U.S. Army Recruiting Office." Below, a smaller sign directed to a side tent labeled "Colored." Timmy headed towards the tent, with John opting to wait outside to try and coordinate their enlistment better.

Inside the tent, the atmosphere was quieter, less bustling. A man in a Sergeant's uniform rose from behind a simple table. "Mornin', son," he greeted. "I'm Sergeant Jenkins. What brings you here today?"

Timmy introduced himself, explaining his desire to join the military. Jenkins raised an eyebrow, sliding a stack of paperwork Timmy's way. As Timmy diligently filled out the forms, the weight of commitment filled the tent.

"Look like you got some strength in you," Jenkins remarked, glancing at Timmy. "Ever thought 'bout bein' a loader in the Armor Corps? We're forming a Black tank unit, the 761st Tank Battalion. They call themselves the "Black Panthers.""

Taken aback, Timmy asked, "What that 'bout?"

Jenkins detailed the role of tankers, emphasizing the significance of their role in the war and admitting the demands of the job. Absorbing the information, Timmy nodded assertively, "Put me on the list."

Exiting the tent, Timmy found John still waiting. "How'd it go?" John asked.

"Signed up in the Armored Corps. Gonna be a loader," Timmy answered, a note of thrill in his voice. John gave a nod, acknowledging the need to align his own assignment with Timmy's. After exchanging a few more words with Timmy, he made his way into the recruiting office.

John pushed open the door, stepping into a room abuzz with chatter and cigarette smoke. Soldiers were scattered around, anticipation evident in their voices and postures. A man in a Sergeant's uniform approached, his smile easygoing. "Good mornin', son. I'm Sergeant McCain. How might I assist you today?"

"Mornin'. I'm John, and I got a mind to join up. Been thinkin' 'bout the Armor Corp."

"The Armor Corp, huh? It's a tough job, can you handle it?"

John responded with a nod, earning an approving grunt from Sergeant McCain. "Alright. Fill out these forms," he instructed, handing John the paperwork.

As John began filling out the forms, Sergeant McCain inquired, "Can you drive?"

"Ain't driven a car, but I can handle a mule team and some farm equipment."

"It's a start," McCain said, nodding. "We can train you further."

Paperwork completed; John exited the recruiting office. Spotting Timmy, he grinned, "Well, looks like we both gonna be part of the Armor Corp. Got myself signed up, too."

Timmy's eyes widened in surprise, then narrowed as a slow grin stretched across his face. They were stepping into a larger world, into a brotherhood bound by duty and honor. Together, they would face whatever came their way.

As they strolled along Main Street, Timmy's face radiated excitement. "Can you believe it, John? Fixin' to be tankers in the Army! I can feel it in my bones. Once this fightin' is over, we'll return as heroes, sure as sugar."

John laughed. "Fair piece of madness, ain't it? Never figured I'd be headin' on this path. After this ol' war, I'm aimin' to come on back home and makin' Sarah my bride."

Timmy gave him a playful punch on the shoulder. "I done knew it! You two been eyeing each other since we was jus' tadpoles. It's high time y'all be gettin' hitched!"

"True enough, she's my one and only."

"An' I'm right blessed to have Em in my life, I tell ya," he said, a hint of longing in his voice. John looked at him, sensing his friend's worries.

"Yer frettin' 'bout leavin' her behind, ain't ya?"

"I am. But she tough; she'll hold her own."

As they walked, John turned the conversation. "You done gave thought 'bout what kind of work you plan to pick up when you get back?"

Timmy's face lit up as he pictured the future. "I want to expand the family ranch. Been raisin' cattle since I can remember, but I got a mind to add horses, maybe even race 'em."

"Ain't that a heck of a plan! You'd be the finest cattle and horse rancher in Georgia, mark my words!"

"I sho' appreciate them kind words. How 'bout you?"

"I got my sights set on becomin' the biggest cotton grower in all of Georgia. Aim to stretch out pa's farm and growin' the finest quality cotton. And bless her heart, Sarah's forever had a hankerin' to live on a farm, so it's perfect."

"Her folks might have a word or two 'bout it? Heard they hopin' she set her sights on one with deeper pockets." Timmy said.

"Let 'em talk. Sarah and I know what we got. And once I've built up the farm, they'll see."

Timmy chuckled, "Can imagine y'all with young'uns running 'round. And who knows, we might find ourselves hitchin' our wagons together. You tend the cotton, and I look after the critters."

"Well, I reckon' it's a deal. We'd be a force like a hurricane through Savannah!"

WITH ONLY TWO DAYS left before John's departure for the army, he and Sarah resorted to deceiving their parents. He had told his parents he was camping out and going night fishing with Timmy, while she had told hers she was spending the night with Emily since Timmy was off on what could be his last fishing trip for a while.

They spent the entire day exploring the woods together, wandering along the winding streams and hidden paths they had known since childhood and spending time under their special tree. They had shared countless adventures in these woods over the years, but this one felt different.

There was an unspoken understanding between them, an urgency to make the most of their time together. As the sun dipped below the tree line, they sought refuge in the shelter of the old wooden structure-the barn which had been the setting for so many of their childhood games and secrets.

John took off his jacket, laying it on the hay. As they lay there, enveloped in the comforting warmth of each other's presence, he could feel his heart swell with affection for her. Their laughter mingled with the gentle rustle of the hay beneath them, while whispered sweet nothings echoed through the barn, heightening their intimacy.

"You sure 'bout this, darlin'?" John asked, his voice gentle, searching her eyes for any sign of reluctance.

With a nod and an encouraging smile, she replied, "Yes, there's no one else I'd rather be with."

Their initial hesitations evaporated in the face of their shared yearning. As their lips met, their bodies began to move in a rhythm as ancient as the stars above them. As the faint moonlight spilled through the cracks of the barn, they began to explore each other.

Her blouse, fastened with tiny pearl buttons, was first. His fingers gently undid each one, revealing the soft, cotton camisole she wore underneath. As the fabric slipped off her shoulders and onto the hay below, she grabbed the hem of his shirt, her fingers trembling as she lifted the rough cotton material over his head.

Her skirt was next, the worn fabric falling to her feet to reveal layers of petticoats. His trousers followed, the buckle of his belt clinking lightly against the quiet rustle of their clothes landing on the barn floor. With each garment shed, they left behind the constraints of their world, becoming more present in their shared yearning and passion.

The slivers of moonlight streaming through the slats danced over her skin, illuminating her collarbone and shoulders. It painted her bare form in hues of silvery-blue, a sight which made him catch his breath. The pureness of the moment, her trusting eyes and their shared desire, was more breathtaking than anything he'd ever seen.

Her voice was a whisper against the backdrop of the silent barn, the calling of his name stirring the still air around them. "John...," she said, the simple utterance loaded with the promise of shared desire.

He responded to her plea, his deep voice sending a shiver of anticipation down her spine. "Sarah..." The way he said her name, a growl mixed with a tenderness only heightening her longing.

His lips traced a tantalizing path along her neck, each kiss igniting sparks under her skin. His breath, hot against her sensitive flesh, sent delightful tremors through her body, setting her senses aflame.

Their movements started like a gentle spring drizzle, cautious yet full of anticipation. But as they became more familiar with each other, their actions turned into a tempest, bodies intertwined in a fervent dance mirroring the thunderous passion building between them.

Their shared desire transformed the barn into a secluded refuge. Whispered words and gasps of affection echoed through throughout, the air itself seemed to pulse with their shared passion.

As her fingers threaded through his hair, she pleaded softly, "Don't ever let me go."

His response was a murmur against her skin, a breathless affirmation, "Darlin', you're all I've ever yearned for," his words were a sacred vow, an anchor in the tumultuous sea of their shared ecstasy. This stolen moment of paradise was theirs and theirs alone.

Afterward, they found comfort within each other's arms. Their bodies were aglow in the aftermath, fingers tracing lazy paths over skin still warm and tingling from their shared experience. Their eyes would occasionally stray upwards, meeting the twinkling stars which seemed to wink back in silent approval. Their slumber was one of tranquility and satisfaction, their bodies remaining intertwined, expressions of contentment gracing their faces.

As dawn approached, the loud crowing of the rooster nudged Sarah from her peaceful slumber. The golden rays of the morning sun streamed through the wooden gaps, washing over her and the man whose arms she remained cradled in. Stretching, she realized their bodies fit perfectly against each other.

John awoke to her gentle movements, a sleepy smile spreading across his face. Their eyes met, sparkling in the morning light, a silent acknowledgment of the profound experience they had shared. The silent secret of their newfound intimacy lingered, further cementing their relationship.

After they dressed, he walked her home, holding her hand as they walked along the path. The morning was quiet, with only the sound of the birds singing and the leaves rustling in the breeze. As they walked, she felt a lump forming in her throat, knowing he would soon leave for war. She tried to push those thoughts aside, instead focusing on the present moment with him by her side.

As they stood on her front porch, the morning air was crisp and the distant chirping of birds heralding the dawn. Sarah's heart was heavy, she couldn't wrap her head around the idea of days and months without him. But she knew she needed to stay strong. Looking up at him, she tried to memorize every feature of his face. She wanted to remember everything. His words, his mannerisms, his smile - as something to hold onto in the lonely days to come.

"I reckon' this ain't gonna be a breeze, but it's a path I'm compelled to tread," John said.

She responded, "I wish we could stay here, the two of us, forever."

He took her hand, squeezing it. "Well, me too, darlin', but it's somethin' I gotta do," he replied.

She nodded, tears streaming down her face. "I understand, it's...hard," she managed to utter.

John pulled her close as she cried. They embraced for a few minutes, drawing comfort from each other's presence. As they pulled away, her gaze met his, weariness and sorrow etched in her features.

"Promise me you'll come back," she said in a voice barely more than a whisper.

Looking at her with eyes filled with determination, he said, "I give you my word, sweetheart. No matter what." Then, he pulled out a small silver pocket watch, placed it in her hand, and closed her fingers around it, holding them there for a moment. "Here, take this. It was my grand pappy's. I want you to hold on to it, as a token to remember me by," he added.

She opened it, admiring the elaborate design and the small ticking mechanism inside. She knew it was a precious item, one he must cherish deeply, and the fact he was giving it to her filled her with deep love and appreciation.

A fresh wave of emotion washed over her, once again as he pulled her close, and she cherished the warmth of his embrace. She buried her face in his chest, inhaling his scent and enjoying the feel of his arms around her. In the moment, nothing else mattered but their love for each other, and she clung to him, not wanting to ever let go. But she knew she had to, and with great reluctance, she pulled away.

"Wait. I have something for you too," she said.

With her hands trembling with excitement, she ran inside the house, her mind racing with thoughts of him and their uncertain future. She retrieved the small, intricately crafted locket she had made as a surprise for him before he left to fight. As she clutched it in her hand, she felt comforted knowing he would carry a piece of her with him wherever he may be.

When she emerged from the house, he turned back to her, his eyes filled with curiosity. Her heart swelled with love and emotion as she opened the locket to reveal a small portrait of herself inside.

"Take this with you," she said as she placed the locket in his hand. "It will remind you of me when you're far away and keep me close to your heart."

John pulled her close once again, she whispered words of love into his ear, "I'll be here waiting for you," she said.

The kiss following was passionate, filled with all her love and longing. She poured her heart into it, wanting it to linger in his memory forever. As he pulled away, she watched him go, her heart heavy with a mix of worry, fear, and hope.

Amidst her fears and doubts, she made a solemn vow to wait for him, no matter the length of time. She pledged to write him, providing updates of life in Warrenton and expressing her boundless love. Each night, she would pray for his safety, holding onto the hope he would return unharmed to be with her once again.

Chapter 7

The Journey Begins

In the cozy room of their home, dimmed by the night's advance, Timmy and Emily found their sanctuary. The glow of a single bedside lamp held the shadows at bay. Set to leave at dawn's break, Timmy sat at the edge of the bed. Beside him, Emily, radiating a soft glow, showed the telltale signs of impending motherhood.

He rested his hand on her round belly, laughing, "Ya' feel that? Our lil' one's got some strength. Might be a boxer... our tiny Jacob, perhaps?"

Her eyes bright yet teary, retorted with an endearing grin, "Or a dancer, our graceful Anne?"

Their laughter, light and heartfelt, filled the room, echoing their shared joy and expectations. "Jacob or Anne... no matter which, they be jus' right," he replied, "long as they favor they pretty mama."

Her smile dimmed, as her eyes reflected a deep-seated fear. Her grip on his hand tightened. "Timmy, give me your word... swear to me you'll return. Losin' my brother nearly broke me... I can't bear losing you too. I... we need you, darlin.'"

In response, memories of her devastation upon learning of her brother's demise on the U.S.S. Arizona at Pearl Harbor flashed in his mind. He lifted her hand, pressing a gentle kiss onto her skin.

"Em... I give ya my word, I be comin' back to you. To our little one, be it Jacob or Anne. It's a promise from my heart." His promise filled the quiet room, a commitment made in the quiet night.

After sharing a quiet moment, he helped her lower herself into a more comfortable position on the bed, careful not to jostle her too much. Once she was settled, he climbed in beside her. They eased under the quilt's warm embrace. His arm found its familiar place around her, pulling her close. Her head rested on his chest, the rhythm of his heartbeat a comforting presence in the quiet room.

"Nite, Em…" he whispered, pressing a tender kiss to her forehead.

She snuggled in closer, whispering back, "Goodnight, Timmy… you best stay safe."

As the gentle glow from the lamp began to fade, it was replaced by the soft silver light of the moon peering through the window. Exhausted by the emotions of the day, they fell asleep, their bodies pressed close, wrapped in the shared joy of their life together and his unwavering promise.

A few miles away, John was also deep in slumber. But his rest was short-lived. His father roused him early on a chilly December morning in 1943, long before the sun had risen. Despite the early hour, he was wide awake, eager to commence his military journey. He donned his warmest clothes, pulling on a thick woolen sweater and his worn leather boots.

From the foot of his bed, he grabbed his bag and began packing. He stowed the new journal atop his belongings - a gift from his mother and a secret habit since he was eight, known only to his parents. As he leafed through his old journal, past memories and reflections stirred deep nostalgia within him. Yet, he was aware of the need to leave the past behind and focus on what lay ahead.

In the drawer of his nightstand, where he intended to keep the old journal, his eyes caught the glint of the locket next to his bible. It was the one Sarah had given him. Relieved he remembered its location, he felt a surge of emotion holding it, and slipped the locket in his pocket.

As he made his way to the kitchen, the intoxicating aroma of fresh coffee and sizzling bacon wafted through the air. "Mornin', young'un. We got a hearty breakfast all set for you." His father said as he entered the room. Over breakfast, his father began to share a story from his own experiences serving in World War I, his voice seasoned with years and memories.

"Ya know, when I was a sprightly lad, 'bout your age, I was over in France," he began while cutting into his eggs. "I recall it was around this season, the breeze was beginning to nip with winter's chill. We were hunkered down in them trenches, and I gotta tell ya, it was no picnic. Cold, drenched, and the rats... But it's a tale for another day."

He paused for a moment, sipping his coffee, and then continued, "We had this fresh-faced boy in our unit, Robert. He was a good sprout, but had a habit of diving headlong into things without a thought. One day, orders came to scout a potential enemy spot. Rob, itching to make his mark, raised his hand to go." He paused, taking a bite before continuing, "Things seemed to be on track until a lone gunshot echoed in the distance. We all felt a cold dread, and sure enough, it was Rob. He'd pushed too close, too quickly. Miraculously, he lived, but he toted a bullet in his leg for the rest of his living days."

He leaned back in his chair, studying John for a moment before offering his advice. "The moral of this here story, boy, is patience. Don't be in such a hurry. In the throes of war, it ain't 'bout being the quickest or the mightiest. It's 'bout being sharp, taking stock of your surroundings, and never belittlin' the predicament you're in. Keep it in your thoughts, and you'll return safe and sound to us."

His mother, who had been quiet throughout breakfast, finally spoke as they finished their meal, her voice shaking. "John, my dear boy, I need ya to know we're brimmin' with pride for ya, and we'll be sittin' tight, awaitin' for ya to get back home. It ain't gonna be no cake walk, but we're stickin' by ya every inch of your journey."

He looked at his mother, tears welling up in her eyes. He realized this was as tough for her as it was for him. She had been his rock, his source of strength and comfort. He couldn't imagine leaving her behind. "I'll be missing ya, Ma," he said.

"I'll be a missin' you too, my love," she replied with tears streaming down her face. "I know you'll do us proud. Jus' make darn sure you return to us, you hear?"

Shortly after, they loaded the truck and headed out to pick up Timmy. As he and his father approached his house, they could see him waiting outside with Emily at his side, his bag packed and ready. His parents were also there, standing proudly but with a hint of apprehension.

John's father pulled next to them and greeted Timmy's father. "Mornin', Jerimiah. Nice seeing ya again," he said, extending a hand.

"Likewise," he replied, his grip firm and steady. A shared understanding passed between them, a silent acknowledgment of the journey their sons were embarking on.

"Morning, Timmy!" John called out, a smile on his face.

"Hey John!" he replied, a mix of excitement and nervousness clear in his voice.

Before leaving, Timmy turned towards his parents. Embracing each in turn, he murmured his goodbyes, the words carried away in the crisp morning air. His mother held onto him, a few tears escaping despite her best efforts to remain stoic. His father, a pillar of strength, slapped him on his back, his pride evident in his gaze.

Then came Emily's turn. He approached her, placing a hand on her belly. "Look after our lil' one," he said, his voice choked with emotion.

She placed her hand atop his, meeting his gaze. "And you mind your well-being, ya hear?" she responded, trying to inject some levity into the tense moment.

He pulled her into an embrace, holding her close. "I be back 'fore you can blink, darlin'" he whispered into her ear.

She nodded, pulling back to look into his eyes. "We'll be here waitin'. Both of us," she said, placing his hand on her belly again. She held his gaze, her eyes glistening with unshed tears but also filled with love and pride. With a lingering kiss and one last look, he turned and joined John and his father.

Together, they loaded his bag into the truck, then climbed in. Timmy settled into the passenger seat with John in the middle. As they headed towards town, the countryside rushed by in a blur of muted colors, the trees and fields stripped bare by winter. The sense of excitement and trepidation hung thick in the air, leaving them to speculate on the future awaiting them.

As they drove through town towards the train depot, his father handed him a small package wrapped in brown paper. "I had a mind to give you somethin' 'fore you go."

Curious, He opened it and saw his father's favorite pocketknife, with a bone handle and a sharp blade, gleaming in the early morning light. He felt a lump rise in his throat as he realized how much the knife meant to him. "Thanks pa," he said.

His father smiled. "Mind it gently. It's been a trusty companion to me, and I reckon' it'll be the same for you. Don't forget 'bout them words I laid on ya. Stay sturdy, keep your wits 'bout ya, and don't lose sight of who or what you're scrappin' for."

John nodded, his heart heavy. His father's words of encouragement helped ease the burden, though, and he felt a surge of pride and determination.

As they pulled into to the small train depot, his father brought the truck to a gentle stop. The depot, composed of rich, brown wood, seemed to resonate with the echoes of numerous farewells and reunions it had overseen. It bore a roof of weathered grey, offering shelter to the building and its visitors from the harsh weather.

Several windows adorned its sides, their frames trimmed in pristine white, allowing slivers of light to pierce the internal darkness. The entrance, a fusion of white and brown, opened up to a wood stove, the buildings sole source of warmth against the biting cold.

The small platform outside was abuzz with groups of young men, all gathered from surrounding areas, their faces painted with a blend of seriousness and contemplation. Many wore pins or emblems from their hometowns, and some clutched letters or mementos, perhaps from loved ones. Soft murmurs of conversation, punctuated by occasional laughter or a nervous joke, filled the air.

John absorbed his surroundings with a mixture of apprehension, feeling the energy and tension emanating from the crowd. Each man seemed to carry his own weight of anticipation and worry, a unique story behind his decision to serve. It was evident they all were united by a shared purpose, yet each with personal reasons which brought them to this moment.

Leaving his family and Sarah weighed heavily on his heart, but he knew it was necessary. He took a deep breath, bracing himself for the journey ahead, and stepped out of the truck. A tight hug was exchanged with his father, a silent goodbye mingled with words of encouragement and hope.

"This is the crossroads. You're holdin' your own reins now, but we've got faith in you," his father said, confidence brimming in his voice. He nodded, meeting his father's gaze, absorbing each word. This was the turning point he had been preparing for, a transition from his past life to the beginning of a new adventure.

"Steer clear of harm's way, boys, and remember, we love you," his father said. John's father then turned to Timmy, placing a sturdy hand on his shoulder and giving it a reassuring squeeze. "Look out for each other," he told them both, his gaze alternating between the two young men. John embraced his father once more, a lump forming in his throat. He waved a final goodbye, acutely aware this might be the last time he saw his father for a considerable length of time, or possibly ever again.

As the train chugged into the station, its engine roared with power and the screech of metal against metal filled the air, mingling with the sharp tang of diesel fuel. As they stepped onto the platform, a pungent, acrid scent of the train's exhaust wafted towards them, assaulting their nostrils.

When they approached the train, Sergeant McCain was there, clipboard in hand, checking off names to ensure everyone was accounted for. As they neared him, he looked up.

"Anderson... Griffin...," he called out, his eyes scanning over them. "You boys ready for this?"

"Yes, Sergeant," John replied, his voice firm despite the whirlwind of emotions he was feeling.

"We ready, Sergeant," Timmy chimed in, standing tall and meeting the Sergeant's gaze.

He nodded approvingly, marking something on his clipboard before waving them through. "Good to hear. Griffin see the second car back? It's the colored car. Anderson yours is the first car. Go on now, get on board and find yourselves a seat. We're in for a long haul."

The train, aged by years and countless journeys, bore chipped paint and creaking floorboards. A musty odor permeating the carriage spoke of its long years of service. The wooden benches, hard and unyielding, offered little comfort, but the discomfort was scarcely noticed. Their minds were buzzing with anticipation, the stark reality of their situation pushing any trivial discomforts to the background.

Timmy was separated from John for the drawn-out ride. He found himself in the colored car, mingling with other black enlistees, while John occupied a seat in the car ahead of him. They located a couple of vacant spots near the back of their respective cars and got comfortable, steeling themselves for the extended trek which lay ahead. As the train shuddered into motion, the rhythmic clatter of wheels on tracks began to echo through the carriage, providing a soothing, if monotonous, backdrop to their thoughts.

Warrenton slowly receded from view, the familiar sights giving way to an endless expanse of barren countryside. Leafless trees and frost-coated fields passed by their window in a blur of muted colors. The cold winter air crept in through the cracks in the windows, prompting them to huddle closer for warmth.

As the train pulled out of the station, Billy watched from a distance, feeling relieved. The rumors of John and Timmy leaving for the war had circulated for days, but seeing them board the train made it all too real.

John's absence presented him with the unimpeded opportunity he had been waiting for: the chance to pursue Sarah without a rival. As the train faded into the distance, he found himself already envisioning his forthcoming visit to her.

Sarah, the only girl who had ever had the audacity to refuse him, was now within his grasp. To him, she was the forbidden fruit, a challenge he was keen to overcome. No one turns down Billy Harrington, he reminded himself with a newfound sense of determination. He was convinced. Soon enough, he would change her 'no' into an enthusiastic 'yes'.

Chapter 8

Standing Tall

As they drew closer to their destination, John felt his excitement turning into nerves. He tugged at the hem of his sweater, trying to distract himself from his racing thoughts. *What awaits us at Camp Wheeler? Am I truly prepared for what's to come?*

The rhythmic clattering of the tracks combined with the engine's hum formed a soundtrack to their journey. John's grip on his bag tightened until his knuckles paled, the weight of anticipation heavy in the air.

The train began to decelerate, its brakes hissing and screeching in protest until the metal wheels came to a halt. A loudspeaker sputtered to life. The roar of the engine muffled the announcement, but John caught the phrase, "Welcome to Macon," amidst the static.

As the train doors slid open, a biting cold greeted them, infused with the sharp scent of diesel and metal. Disembarking, they were swept into a whirlwind of activity on the platform: soldiers in crisp uniforms and civilians bundled up, all moving purposefully.

With their boots hitting the hard pavement, a surge of nerves and excitement coursed through both Timmy and John. Amidst the bustling crowd, they searched for each other. When their eyes met, the unfamiliar sights and sounds around them seemed to pause for a moment. This new place hinted at the challenges awaiting them, but seeing a familiar face gave them both strength and determination.

The station buzzed with young men, diverse in backgrounds but unified in their mission. All were drawn to the service of their country.

Guided by signs reading 'Destination: Camp Wheeler', John and Timmy approached a soldier with a clipboard, his stern gaze scanning the new arrivals.

"Names?" he asked, glancing at them.

"Timmy Griffin," Timmy replied first.

"John Anderson," John followed, meeting the soldier's gaze.

The soldier scanned his list before checking off their names. "Alright, y'all are set. Board the bus," he instructed, then added as he pointed towards a line of olive-drab military buses, "Remember Griffin, colored folks in the back."

"Yes Suh!" Timmy replied.

The standard-issue buses rumbled with powerful engines, their matte green paint worn from ferrying countless recruits. Inside, the hard benches spoke to the utilitarian nature of the vehicle, built to withstand the heaviest military gear. John and Timmy exchanged a glance, their minds racing with the impending reality.

They approached the buses and noticed compartments underneath for luggage. where a soldier was already loading other recruits' bags. Following suit, they tossed their bags into the designated area, watching as the soldier secured them underneath.

Once their bags were loaded, they headed to the bus entrance. The stern-looking driver, dressed in uniform, nodded at them. Their boots echoed on the metal steps as they boarded.

Inside, the bus was filled with young men. A mix of excitement and apprehension hung in the air. John located an open spot upfront. Timmy, reminded of their earlier train ride, found a seat in the back.

They settled in, backs straight, eyes forward, lost in thought. As the engine's vibrations rumbled beneath them, the scent of exhaust wafted in briefly before the doors sealed shut. Gripping the cool metal of their seats, they braced for the journey.

John felt the excitement building inside of him, a restless energy waiting to be unleashed. As the bus approached the camp, the sprawling base loomed in the distance, reminiscent of a fortress rising from the earth. Tall trees framed the barracks and training grounds, their branches swaying in the wind. The base was alive with activity, as soldiers and recruits moved with purpose, engrossed in their duties.

As John and Timmy stepped off the bus and began orienting themselves to their new surroundings, a stern-looking Sergeant with a clipboard in hand approached them.

"Anderson... Griffin...," he called out, his eyes scanning the two from top to bottom. "Anderson, you're assigned to Barrack 7. Griffin, you'll be in the negro barracks, Barrack 12. Report there immediately. Afterwards, head to the Quartermaster for your issue - linens, toiletries, the works. Any questions?"

"No, Sergeant," both young men replied in unison.

"Good," he replied curtly, marking something on his clipboard before moving to the next group of fresh arrivals.

John was assigned to Barrack 7 and Timmy to Barrack 12, each designated as their homes for the duration of their training. Along the way, Timmy walked past signs boldly declaring 'Colored Troops'. It was a glaring reminder of the racial barriers they confronted, even in service to their nation.

Inside, both barracks bore the same scent of worn leather, weapon oil, and the mustiness of old canvas. They each staked out an available bunk; the meager mattress and skeletal frame a poignant reminder of the comforts they'd left behind.

With their new living arrangements settled, they independently made their way to the Quartermaster's, where they were each issued their linens and toiletries. A soldier behind a counter was efficiently handing out the essentials, a steady stream of recruits passing before him.

"Next!" he called out as they approached, a bored expression on his face. "Names?"

After providing their names, the soldier handed over bundles containing their issued items, nodding to each as he spoke. "Make sure you keep track of these. Lost items come out of your pay. Dismissed." Arms laden with their new military possessions, they returned to their barracks, signaling the official beginning of their new lives.

The first week tested John and Timmy in ways they hadn't imagined. Burdened with heavy packs and boots which still felt awkwardly new, they found their uniforms stiffened by the freezing temperatures chafing with each movement.

As they ran through the icy obstacle courses and dropped for push-ups, the physical demands began to take their toll. Each breath materialized as white vapor, underscoring the frosty air biting their exposed skin. Pushed to their limits and beyond, their bodies rebelled against the relentless demands of the training, with every muscle aching in protest.

The second week marked a shift from pure physical training to lessons in weapons handling, navigation, and tactical communication which filled their days. The evenings saw them bonding with their peers, sharing stories, experiences, and forging friendships.

With each new day, the camaraderie between the men grew stronger. They were a group of individuals who, through shared experiences and common challenges, were rapidly transforming into a united team - more akin to brothers than mere acquaintances. The break of dawn not only signaled a new day filled with intense training; it marked a step closer to the war they would soon be facing.

They were miles away from home, each grappling with the rigors of their training, shouldering the weight of responsibility, fear, hope, and dreams. Yet, they didn't bear these burdens in isolation; they shared their experiences, leaning on each other's strength. It was this brotherhood which brought them together, making them resilient.

Timmy's days mirrored John's, blurring into a monotonous cycle of predawn wake-up calls, grueling drills, lessons in tactics, and the ever-watchful scrutiny of their instructors.

Yet, amidst this regimen, an unanticipated bond grew between him and his fellow black enlistees. Men from diverse backgrounds found unity in shared challenges and the dream of fighting for a brighter, more equitable future. Their camaraderie was forged in adversity, and every trial only reinforced their collective determination to stand up for their rights and the hope of a better tomorrow.

As the grueling weeks of basic training drew closer to a close, a wave of pride and accomplishment washed over both of them. They had not only survived the intense physical and mental demands of training but emerged stronger and more disciplined. Yet, they knew their journey was far from over.

One night, while swapping stories and sharing cigarettes at the smoke pit with Timmy, John took a moment to reflect on his personal growth since arriving at the camp. Beyond the rigors of combat and strategy, he recognized the true lessons ran deeper. He was gradually discovering the strength to stand up, not only for his comrades, but also for himself.

"You know, I didn't think I'd be able to do half of what I've done," John admitted, taking a drag from his cigarette. He paused, letting the smoke curl into the night air. "And it's not only 'bout defending others," he continued. "I'm beginning to see I need to stand up more for myself too."

Timmy nodded in agreement, exhaling a puff of smoke. "Sho' 'nuff. Ain't only 'bout learnin' to throw a punch. It's 'bout findin' our own worth and protectin' it, while banding together no matter how hard the wind blows 'gainst us." As they parted ways to settle in for the night, both felt a growing sense of purpose, drawing them ever closer to their shared goal.

With only days left until graduation, John sat around the barracks one evening, playing cards with the others. A grizzled veteran named Staff Sergeant Reynolds, their supply Sergeant, joined them. He had been training soldiers at Camp Wheeler since the beginning of the war and had seen the horrors of combat firsthand during his service in the Great War.

"Quiet down, boys," he said, his voice gravelly but strong, commanding instant attention. He shuffled the deck of cards between his gnarled hands, a legacy of many years in service. "Let me tell you a story."

He paused, ensuring he had their full attention before he began. "It was the winter of 1917, during the Great War. I was a fresh-faced lad, much like yourselves, stationed in the trenches on the Western Front."

"The temperature had dropped well below freezing, turning the muddy terrain into a cruel, icy wasteland. We were on guard duty, huddled in our trench, trying to keep warm. We'd been quiet for days, expecting an attack any moment. The air was tense, weighed heavy with anticipation."

"Suddenly, in the dead of night, the enemy attacked. Gunfire erupted, whizzing overhead. The world descended into chaos. Men were shouting, scrambling to their stations, the air filled with the acrid stench of gunpowder and fear."

His voice became softer, more introspective. "You know, it's funny how you learn to tell the sound of bullets apart. I remember one, in particular, it was a tracer round, whizzed right past my ear, I could hear it sing."

He shook his head, his gaze distant for a moment, before refocusing on the young men around him. "It was a bloody night; one I won't forget. We lost many good men, friends, brothers...But we held our ground. We were scared, but we did not falter. We stood fast because we understood what was at stake."

The lines on Sergeant Reynolds' face seemed to deepen, and his voice took on an edge which made everyone sit a bit straighter. "That is the kind of discipline and courage you boys will need to show when you go to war. War is brutal, it's unyielding, but we must be stronger. Remember, your actions will determine the course of this war, the lives of your brothers in arms, and the future of our nation. But if you stick together and keep your wits, you can survive."

Not a soldier stirred. The only sound heard was the soft, uneven breathing of young men deep in thought. Meanwhile, in his hands, the deck of cards danced rhythmically, the shuffle providing a soft, soothing soundtrack to their introspective silence. Glancing at the deck, he let out a light chuckle.

"Alright, boys," he began, his tone firm yet lighthearted. "Enough of the heavy stuff for one night. How about we shift gears and enjoy a good old round of five card draw?"

Upon saying this, he began dealing the cards around the circle. The subtle sound of the cards landing on the wooden table served as a comforting rhythm, a brief moment of respite from the looming significance of the days ahead.

The day they had all been anticipating, and for some dreading, had finally arrived: Graduation Day. With the first light of dawn, Camp Wheeler came alive with an unusual buzz of activity. Soldiers were whispering among themselves, their faces eager with anticipation and evident nervousness.

The parade ground, which mostly served as their drill field, had been transformed overnight. Rows of chairs lined the open space for special guests who had come to see their transition from trainees to soldiers. A large stage had been erected at one end, where the Camp Commanding Officer would address the gathering and conduct the graduation ceremony.

As they assembled on the parade ground, they stood not as recruits, but as proud soldiers. Their crisp, newly issued uniforms, boots polished to a high shine, and expressions of resolve reflected their transformation. It was a scene from a postcard: rows of soldiers at attention, the American flag fluttering behind them in the morning breeze.

The ceremony started with the playing of the national anthem, a moment filling each heart present with patriotism and pride. It was followed by the Commanding Officer's address, his words of praise for their hard work, commitment, and the importance of their role in the ongoing conflict reverberating through the crowd.

After the speech, the pinnacle of the ceremony arrived with the issuing of orders. Each name called out marked the end of basic training and the beginning of a new chapter. It was a bittersweet moment, filled with pride over their achievement and a sobering realization of moving closer to the front lines. Having conquered this first hurdle, John and Timmy now faced rigorous tank training at The Armored Force School in Fort Knox, Kentucky - a promise fulfilled from when they first joined.

The next morning, as John packed his bag, he gathered all the letters Sarah had written to him over the past weeks. He smiled as he read her familiar handwriting, finding comfort in the words she had penned to him. He tucked them into his bag, knowing they would be a source of inspiration and support during the challenges to come.

Next, he grasped the cherished locket from Sarah, staring at her photo inside, which sparked vivid memories. The cool metal of the locket evoked her laughter and warm embraces. To him, it wasn't just jewelry; it symbolized their love and shared dreams.

His bunkmate catching a glimpse of the photograph as John closed the locket, watched as he placed the keepsake in his pocket. "Looks like you've got yourself a good one," he commented as he gave John a friendly slap on the back. "Hold on to her tight."

John nodded as he said, "I intend to." He zipped his bag, ready to face whatever challenges lay ahead.

While John and Timmy were excited to embark on their new journey, they also felt a touch of sadness on saying goodbye to their comrades, their new brothers. They'd gone through so much together, pushing each other, laughing and sharing stories, strengthening each other's spirits when times got tough.

John and Timmy both boarded the bus taking them to the Macon depot, the same one where they had first arrived as simple country boys. Now, as they prepared to depart, they did so as soldiers. Following the signs for the train bound for Fort Knox, they boarded, filled with anticipation and a sense of adventure.

As the train departed the depot, the rhythmic clatter of its wheels on the tracks echoed like a heartbeat, guiding them towards their destiny. They cracked open the window, feeling the cool breeze on their faces and the warmth of the sun on their skin.

As the train rumbled on, they pressed their faces to the window, looking out at the world unfolding before them. While John's thoughts were filled with the adventures ahead, he remained unaware of the challenges and struggles Sarah had been facing in his absence.

Chapter 9

The Encounter

Meanwhile back in Warrenton, Sarah had been feeling unwell for days. Her stomach churned persistently, and she felt her energy waning with each passing hour. The once-inviting aroma of pine logs burning in the fireplace, typically a comforting winter scent, now turned her stomach.

The distant sound of wind rustling the bare branches, normally a soothing reminder of the season, felt piercing to her ears, making her temples throb.

At first, she dismissed it as the stress of John being away, but the symptoms persisted and worsened. One morning, after struggling to drag herself out of bed, she began to suspect she might be pregnant. She knew it was a possibility, given her recent lack of energy and frequent nausea.

The uncertainty of the timing of the potential pregnancy while John was still in basic training, and the fear of the unknown left her feeling overwhelmed with a mix of emotions, including excitement at the prospect of starting a family with him.

She nervously approached her parents, holding her breath as she prepared to share her news. Her father was sitting in his armchair, reading his newspaper, while her mother stood at the sink, washing dishes and staring out the window at the garden. The tension in the room was intense.

"Mom, Dad, I have something important to tell you." She said, her voice shaking slightly.

Her father shifted his gaze from his newspaper. "What is it?"

"I'm pregnant," she said, bracing herself for their reaction. There was a moment of stunned silence before her mother spoke. She could see her mother's face harden, and her shoulders slump with disappointment.

"What do you mean you're pregnant? How could you be so careless?" her mother scolded, tossing the dish rag into the sink.

"I didn't plan it, it just happened." She explained, tears starting to form in her eyes.

Her father cleared his throat uncomfortably. "Who is the father?" he asked.

She took a deep breath and answered, "It's John's."

After a prolonged silence, during which only the bubbling of the stovetop percolator and the ticking of the nearby clock could be heard, her father spoke. "This is unacceptable. You should have known better," he said sternly.

"I know, I'm sorry," she replied, feeling ashamed.

"You're going to have to figure out how to take care of this on your own. We won't be able to help you," her mother said firmly.

Her heart sank as her mother's words registered. *I had hoped for understanding, maybe even support. But expecting joy from them was unrealistic*, she thought to herself. After the conversation, feeling a mix of disappointment and sadness, she returned to her room to gather her thoughts. As she contemplated telling John, her mind was filled with concern. *How will news of my pregnancy weigh on him while he's away?* With his well-being in mind, she decided, *It's best to omit this from my letters, at least for now.*

MEANWHILE, BILLY HAD been observing Sarah's daily routine with keen interest, biding his time to make his move. He knew she worked at the general store until noon, and if she turned left after leaving the store, she was either heading home or taking a leisurely stroll around town.

On the other hand, if she turned right, she would typically head to the post office and then take a shortcut through one of the deserted alleyways on her way home. He had studied her pattern, and he was ready to pounce when the perfect opportunity presented itself.

He had his eye on the secluded alley, which was shrouded in shadows and offered a prime location to corner her alone. With each passing day, he grew more and more determined to make his move and take her for himself, no matter the cost.

As he stood in front of his mirror, he couldn't help but feel excitement coursing through his veins. For weeks, he had been planning his move on her, and today felt like the day everything would fall into place.

He meticulously adjusted his hair and straightened his shirt, ensuring he looked his best for her. The anticipation of their encounter brought a smile to his face. Nonetheless, he knew he had to be cautious. He didn't want anyone to suspect his intentions. He was determined to make sure she would come to him, willingly or not, without arousing any suspicion.

Taking one last look in the mirror, he hoped today was the day she would go right. With his mind focused on his plan, he made his way out of his home, ready to make his move on her.

Hurrying through the alleyway towards her house after mailing a letter to John, Sarah was unaware of the impending encounter. As she turned a corner, Billy stepped out from the shadows and blocked her path. She froze, her heart pounding as she recognized him.

When he approached her, a crooked grin spread across his face. His eyes roamed over her body, making her feel exposed, a piece of meat to the butcher. She took a step back, feeling a cold shiver run down her spine.

"Where do you think you're going, sweetheart?" he said.

She swallowed hard, words sticking in her throat. She tried to sidestep him, her heart pounding against her chest like a drum. "Let me pass," she managed, her voice shaky yet defiant.

He anticipated her moves, agile as a fox, blocking her at every turn. His laughter echoed off the cold, brick walls, a chilling reminder of the danger she found herself in.

"Didn't your mother tell you not to wander into dark alleys?" He taunted, his grin growing.

Summoning her courage, she clenched her teeth, eyes flashing with defiance. "What do you want?" she demanded, her voice barely above a whisper yet firm.

"Now, isn't that a question?" he mused, stepping closer.

A tight knot of fear settled in her stomach as the grim reality of her situation set in. She regretted ever venturing into the forsaken alleyway.

With both hands, he seized the fabric of her dress at her shoulders, pushing her harshly against the weathered brick wall. With such force, the back of her head collided sharply with it.

She was dazed as he pressed his body against hers and she could feel his breath on her neck. He could smell the light perfume on her and her breasts against his chest. 'Why should John be the only lucky one', he thought to himself.

He whispered in her ear, "Time for you to see what you been missing."

As she regained her senses, she realized what he meant by those words. As he was pressed against him, she could tell he was aroused. She wanted to resist but he was too strong for her to push him away, and her telling him to stop didn't help as he was persistent.

He backed off her and took one hand off her shoulder to slide under her dress. She realized this was her chance and brought her right knee into his groin.

He yelled and began to double over in pain, his grip tightened on her shoulder, flinging her to the ground as he collapsed to his knees screaming, "You bitch! You'll pay for this!"

After she crashed onto the pavement, a searing pain exploded in her abdomen. Writhing on the cold concrete, she clutched her stomach, her body curling inward to ease the agony. His gaze fell on her and the way she was holding herself. It was then, he realized with a sickening jolt... something was terribly wrong.

She struggled to rise off the ground. The pain was overwhelming, radiating through her body with each labored breath. Despite the discomfort, she managed to drag herself out of the alley, her heart racing with fear and adrenaline as she stumbled towards the safety of her home.

Each movement was a struggle, her head swimming with dizziness and nausea. Her heart raced with fear and her mind was in a haze as she stumbled through the front door. She could still feel his hot breath on her neck and his rough hands on her body, and the memory made her want to vomit. As she collapsed on her bed in a heap, tears streamed down her face, and the pain consumed her. She felt violated, ashamed, and utterly alone.

Billy watched as she stumbled away, her grip on her stomach puzzling him. Was she sick, injured, or dealing with something he couldn't comprehend? The aggressive lust which had consumed him mere moments before turned into slight unease. He knew he had crossed a line, venturing into dangerous territory, and the ramifications of his choices loomed large.

While Billy was still on his knees, he heard a voice asking if he was okay. Looking up, he recognized Chadwick Bronson, known as 'Chad,' a foreman at his father's mill, who was now standing before him. Chad, recognizing Billy as well, asked nervously, "Mr. Harrington, are you okay?"

Panic set in as Billy thought, *What did he see? How long had he been in the alley? If he saw anything, who would he tell?*

With a shaky hand, he reached out to Chad, who helped him to his feet. "Tripped is all," he stammered, trying to suppress his nerves. He glanced at Chad again, forcing a grateful smile onto his face. "Thanks, Chad." Without waiting for a response, he turned and hurried out of the alley, leaving the scene behind.

As Chad turned to leave, he scratched his head in confusion. He had not seen him trip and wondered what could have caused him to clutch his groin. He couldn't shake off the feeling something was not right, but he decided to let it go for now. He had other issues to worry about, like the looming deadline at the mill. Nonetheless, as he walked away, he made a mental note to keep an eye on him and the alleyway.

Sarah's encounter with Billy had left her struggling to sleep at night, her mind replaying the horrific incident over and over again. Even the simplest tasks, like walking along the street or checking the mail, filled her with anxiety and fear.

She knew she needed to tell John what had happened, but the thought of burdening him with her troubles while he was in training weighed heavily on her. She also began to feel guilty for not telling him of the pregnancy sooner, worried he would be upset she had kept such an important secret from him.

DAYS AFTER HIS ENCOUNTER with Sarah, Billy was caught in a whirlwind of emotions. On one hand, he felt angry and resentful towards her for thwarting his advances. On the other, he was gripped by the fear Chad might have witnessed the event and would share it with others.

Each time he heard a knock on the door, or the phone rang, a jolt of anxiety passed through him. He wondered if someone had reported what had happened to his father. Despite his internal turmoil, he made an effort to maintain an outward appearance of normality. Yet, beneath the surface, a challenging mix of emotions towards Sarah continued to trouble him.

One day, as he was lost in thought, he heard a knock on the door making him jump. He opened the door and recognized the man in front of him as one of his father's most trusted employees, who looked grave as he delivered the news for him to report to the mill's office at once.

He was surprised and anxious, as his father rarely summoned him unless it was important. His heart sank as he imagined all sorts of worst-case scenarios. The employee's grave expression confirmed this wasn't any routine matter.

His heart pounded with a mix of fear and anticipation as he made his way to the mill. *Had Chad seen what happened in the alley and informed my father? What will the consequences be if he did?* His hands trembled as he entered the mill, and he found himself repeatedly glancing over his shoulder, half-expecting to encounter Chad or anyone else who knew his secret. By the time he arrived at the office, he was sweating profusely, his nerves frayed to the edge.

As he pushed open the heavy wooden door to the office, he was hit with an overwhelming sense of tension. The atmosphere was thick and suffocating, like a heavy fog had settled over the room, and the blinds were open, allowing a pleasant warmth to filter through and bathe the room in a soft glow of sunlight. The silence was so absolute, he could hear the ticking of the clock on the wall with painful clarity.

His father sat behind his massive oak desk, his face completely unreadable, like a stone statue. The hairs on the back of his neck stood as he made his way toward the desk, his legs feeling like they were made of jelly. He tried to force himself to walk with confidence, but his steps were unsteady, like he was walking on a tightrope.

As he approached the desk, he couldn't help but feel foreboding settling in his stomach, his heart racing with fear and uncertainty. He tried to maintain his composure as he stood in front of his father, "You wanted to see me?" He managed to force out, trying to keep his voice steady.

His father stared at him with a stone-cold expression. "Sit," he said, gesturing to a chair in front of him. As he took a seat, his anxiety intensified, wondering what news could possibly be worse than the scenarios already playing in his mind.

"Billy," his father's voice was cold and calculated, "I've made arrangements with someone at the War Department. Thanks to my political connections, I've secured a spot for you in the United States Army Air Forces. Specifically, a waist gunner role on the B-17 bomber. It requires minimal training, but you'll still have to go through basic training in Biloxi, Mississippi, which lasts 8 weeks. From there you will go to Harlingen Army Airfield in Texas for your gunner training."

The news caused his jaw to drop, and he felt as if the ground was shaking beneath his feet. The thought of joining the military and going to war wasn't something he had entertained before, and the reality of it all hit him like a ton of bricks. His mind raced with anxiety as he wondered if his father had found out what had happened with Sarah, and he was using this as an excuse to punish him.

Before he could speak, his father continued, "I know you may be hesitant to join, but it's important you do. Most of the young men in this town have already joined or been drafted, and we can't have our own family not serving if we want to win the government contract for providing the cotton to make uniforms. Plus, the Army Air Force is safer than being on the ground."

He was still in shock, trying to process the news. "But, Father," he stammered, "I don't know anything about serving in the military. How am I supposed to do this?"

His father's expression turned to anger, and he leaned forward, his hand gripping the edge of his desk. "You will do this!" he said. "If you don't, you'll be cut off financially, disowned, and thrown out of my house to live on the streets. This is not a request!"

He felt like he had been punched in the gut. Never had he seen his father so angry, and he knew there was no way out of this. Nodding in defeat, a mix of fear and uncertainty swirling inside him, he asked quietly, "When do I leave?"

His father leaned back in his chair, taking a moment to consider before responding. "You'll leave in two weeks," he said. "That should give you enough time to say goodbye to your friends and get your affairs in order." Billy sat there for a moment longer, feeling numb. He knew his life was about to change in ways he couldn't even imagine and couldn't help but wonder what the future held for him.

As he left his father's office, he couldn't shake off the feeling of dread settling in his chest. The thought of going to war terrified him. He had so many questions and fears, but he didn't know who to turn to for answers as he had few friends.

Over the next few days, he tried to adjust to the idea of going to war. He couldn't bring himself to tell his few friends of his impending departure, fearing their reactions. He spent more time alone, lost in thought regarding what was to come.

At night, he would lie in bed, his eyes fixed on the dim shadows dancing across the ceiling, plagued by the unknown. During those long, restless nights, he couldn't shake off the nagging thought: was this God's way of punishing him for what had transpired with Sarah in the alleyway? Perhaps this relentless torment was his fate, his penance for the mistakes he had made.

He couldn't shake off the feeling he was being sent to war by his father as a form of punishment, and the guilt of what he had done weighed heavily on him. Despite his fears and doubts, he knew he had to face his new reality and had no choice but to do this. He only hoped he could make it back home alive. With these thoughts swirling in his mind, the day of his departure crept up all too quickly.

As he stood under the dull overhang of the depot, his heart was heavy with uncertainty and sadness. The wail of the train, now drawing near, seemed to echo his internal turmoil.

He hugged his mother, feeling the damp heat of her tears soaking his shirt. "Take care, Billy," she murmured into his shoulder, her voice thick with emotion.

His only response was a nod, the knot in his throat making words impossible. As he let go of his mother, his father, standing at a respectable distance, extended a hand.

He hesitated, then took it. The handshake was brief, formal - as cold as the man who offered it. "Do well," his father said, his voice as impassive as his steel-grey eyes.

He let his father's hand slip away. "Sure."

Afterwards, his father turned on his heel and walked away, leaving him alone on the platform. The rumble of the train mingled with the heavy thud of his own heartbeat, each pulse resonating with the tumultuous mix of emotions stirring within him.

As he boarded the train which would take him away from everything he knew, he felt a mix of emotions. Fear, sadness, and uncertainty all fought for dominance.

He took a deep breath and tried to steady himself as the train pulled out of the station, leaving his old life behind and taking him towards an uncertain future.

Chapter 10

Steel Beasts

John and Timmy approached the Armor School at Fort Knox, Kentucky, their eyes sweeping over the sprawling complex of barracks, training facilities, and tanks stretched out before them. The maze of steel and concrete promised to be both exhilarating and daunting.

As they passed through the gates, John's heart raced with excitement. All around, the air was thick with the smell of diesel fuel and the metallic tang of steel, while the distant echoes of engines and gunfire hinted at the rigorous training ahead.

In the initial days, they underwent rigorous exams and orientations, trading worn uniforms for new gear which came with strict maintenance instructions. The training curriculum, updated from experiences in the Pacific Islands, combined physical exercises, lectures, and hands-on sessions, pushing each recruit to their limits.

With the war intensifying, the U.S. Army was in a rush to train and deploy new soldiers. The Armor School played a pivotal role, equipping them with the vital skills for the battlefield. Proud to be part of this mission, John, Timmy, and their peers embraced their training wholeheartedly.

Early morning calls began grueling days of mastering the intricacies of various tanks, from their mechanical systems to their armaments. Even amidst exhaustion, they persisted, studying tank tactics, refining combat techniques, and fostering teamwork and communication, constantly eager to learn more.

Finally, the day they had eagerly anticipated arrived: tank assignments. As instructors called out names, the recruits stood at attention, waiting to hear their respective tank assignments.

"Baker, you're with the M3 Lee!" barked one of the instructors. "Smith, you're on the M10 Wolverine! Johnson, you're with the M18 Hellcat!"

John and Timmy's hearts raced as they waited for their names to be called. Finally, they heard the instructor call out,

"Anderson, you're with the M4 Sherman."

"Griffin, you're with the M4 Sherman."

They exchanged glances, sharing their enthusiasm with the other trainees who were also assigned to the Sherman. The next day, they were introduced to their designated tank. Approaching it, John was struck by its sheer size.

The Sherman stood like a steel titan, its olive paint proudly bearing the white star emblem on its turret. The 75mm cannon hinted at its might, complemented by its armor. But what caught John and Timmy's attention was the hum of its engine-a beastly Continental R975-C1. "400 horsepower," Timmy whistled, impressed.

The instructor pointed at the Sherman. "Impressive, isn't it? But its strength lies in its crew. Understand this machine, but more importantly, understand each other."

They listened closely as the instructor continued his lecture. "Now, let's talk about the different types of ammunition you'll be using. This is the 75mm Armor-Piercing Round commonly called an AP round, which is effective against most enemy tanks. And here we have the High Explosive round known as an HE round, which is ideal for destroying buildings and fortifications. You'll need to know when to use each type of round, so pay attention."

As the lecture unfolded, they absorbed every detail - the mechanics of loading ammunition, the nuances of the tank's controls, the crucial methods of communicating under duress. They took mental notes, their minds keenly focused on the task at hand. Their future success in combat would hinge on their ability to work together and effectively utilize the tank's weapons and ammunition.

As they moved from the lecture hall to practical exercises, the importance of teamwork and communication was hammered home. Instructors punctuated their lessons with constant reminders. "Remember, your crewmates are your lifeline in combat," one veteran instructor said, his voice resonating with hard-earned experience.

"You need to trust each other and work together as a well-oiled machine. It's the only way you'll make it out alive," said another.

Finally, the words they had been waiting for left the Lead Instructors mouth, "Go ahead and hop in and check her out."

John was thrilled as he lowered himself into the driver's seat. He marveled at the tight space and took in every detail of the compartment. He noticed the numerous gauges and dials on the dashboard, each displaying crucial information regarding the Sherman's performance.

He saw the handbrake to his left, which would be used to lock the tracks in place when the tank was stationary. He also noticed the numerous levers and switches controlling the tank's lights, and other accessories.

He took a closer look at the gearshift and was surprised by the unique design. The Sherman tank had a synchromesh transmission, which was relatively new technology. He could feel the weight of the gears as he shifted them, and he knew he would have to be careful to avoid stripping them during combat.

As he continued to explore the driver's compartment, he noticed the escape hatch located directly below the seat. The hatch was designed to provide a quick exit in the event the tank was hit and began to burn.

The driver's compartment was one of the most dangerous places in the tank during combat, and he felt a weight of responsibility as he sat in the seat, knowing the lives of his crewmates depended on his skill and expertise in driving the tank through rough terrain and dodging enemy fire.

The ensuing weeks were a relentless whirlwind of learning. As John settled into his role as the driver, exhilaration began to stir within him. The first time he gripped the steering levers of the Sherman, he was overtaken by a rush of adrenaline. The tank, a hulking mass of metal, lurched into motion at his command.

The roar of the engine reverberated in his chest, drowning out all other sounds. He tightened his grip on the controls, his heart thumping with a potent blend of excitement and apprehension. He glanced at his instructor, a triumphant grin spreading across his face.

Over the engine's roar, the instructor yelled, "Feels like a beast under your control, right?"

John grinned. "It's like harnessing an entire army's might."

He focused on the terrain ahead, scanning for any obstacles or hazards which could impede their progress. As the tank gained speed, he felt the wind rushing past him, buffeting his hair and clothes as he sat in the open hatch.

He could feel each bump and jolt of the tank's tracks as they crossed over rough terrain, and he instinctively compensated for any shifts in the vehicle's balance.

With each passing day, he grew more confident in his abilities. He navigated the tank through winding courses, over hills and around tight corners, learning how to adjust the vehicle's speed and direction to match the terrain. His body reacted instinctively to the movement of the steering levers, and he felt exhilarated realizing the control he had mastered over the Sherman.

Sergeant Wilson, his primary instructor, was a gruff but knowledgeable man. Seated in the Assistant Driver's seat, he was a combat veteran of the Pacific and understood the importance of thorough training firsthand. "Good job, Anderson," he barked as John expertly maneuvered the Sherman around a tight corner. "But remember, smooth turns are crucial. Any jerky movements could throw the crew off balance, impairing their firing accuracy."

John nodded, digesting the advice, and pledged inwardly to fine-tune his movements. Sergeant Wilson was a demanding but fair instructor. He relentlessly pushed the recruits to strive for excellence, never allowing them to forget the stakes they were training for.

"You're doing great!" Sergeant Wilson's tone softened a touch. "You show a natural talent for this, but remember, complacency is the enemy. We're molding you into the best of the best, which means relentless pursuit of perfection." A swell of pride surged within John as he took in his words.

As the days passed, the scenarios became more complex and challenging. They were put through intense simulations of armored assaults and ambushes, learning to react to changing conditions and communicate effectively with one another under fire, as well as evacuation drills to quickly exit the tank if need be.

In one training scenario, they had to navigate through a dense forest while facing simulated attacks from enemy tanks and infantry. Using the tank's weapons and armor, they simulated defending against the enemy and practiced their maneuvers in a simulated combat environment.

The roar of the tank's engines echoed through the forest as they raced through narrow paths, narrowly avoiding obstacles and simulated enemy fire. The sound of explosions filled the air as they fired simulated rounds at enemy positions, using their training and tactics to coordinate their movements and effectively neutralize the threat.

Even without live ammunition, the training drills' intensity felt akin to a real battle-high stakes, extreme pressure, and a mandate to perform at their best. They relied on their rigorous training and the Sherman's state-of-the-art communication system to navigate the challenging terrain and fulfill their mission objectives.

However, their training was about to take an unexpected turn. Anticipating the diverse challenges these soldiers might face in the theater of war, the War Department had devised a fresh obstacle for them. Nestled within the confines of the vast military base was a unique urban training ground, a mock cityscape painstakingly designed to mirror European urban environments.

This synthetic city, complete with narrow alleyways, tall buildings, and hidden corners, was a departure from the forest and open fields they had grown accustomed to. Now, they had to adapt their skills to the urban jungle - a glimpse of the unpredictable challenges waiting across both the Pacific and Atlantic.

In this rigorous training scenario, John's tank crew grappled with navigating through the simulated cityscape. The mock environment, complete with narrow cobblestone streets and looming multistory buildings, emulated historic European cities. The tight corners and confined spaces pushed the Sherman's maneuverability to its limits, contrasting starkly with the open terrains and woodlands they were accustomed to.

The realism of the training scenario was striking. Machine-made smoke billowed from designated areas to replicate the haze of battle; simulated artillery strikes caused pre-constructed rubble to emulate combat-damaged buildings. Amidst this chaos, the crew had to maneuver their tank, all the while staying alert for potential enemy positions. The objective of this intense practice was to prepare them for potential urban warfare, ensuring they were as equipped as possible for the challenges ahead.

Even in the face of the training's intensity, John found his confidence and competence growing with each passing day. He understood the skills he was acquiring could mean the difference between life and death on the battlefield, fueling his determination to master them.

Though the hours were long and the training grueling, pride and camaraderie blossomed among the crew members. They realized they were part of something much larger than themselves.

The training's taxing nature demanded much from them, but evenings brought a comforting routine: writing letters to their loved ones back home. Before lights out, John penned his to Sarah, sharing his experiences at the Armor School and his progression towards becoming a skilled tank driver.

In addition to the letters, he continued to document his experiences at the Armor School in his journal, detailing all aspects of the training and challenges they faced. In her response, Sarah shared details of her life back home and expressed how deeply she missed him.

As the days and weeks passed, he eagerly looked forward to receiving her letters, each one bringing comfort and a feeling of connection to his life back home. In one of them, she wrote on how the war effort was affecting their town, saying how supplies were becoming scarce and prices were rising.

She told him of the struggles her father's general store was facing due to the shortage of goods. "I'm proud of what I'm doing at the store, but it's not easy," she wrote. "We're doing our best to keep the shelves stocked, but with so many products being rationed, it's getting harder and harder to get what people need." He could feel the weight of the war effort even more with her letters, knowing the sacrifices they were making at the Armor School were only a small part of the greater whole.

He smiled as he read her words, feeling grateful for her support and encouragement. "Don't worry." He wrote back. "I'm learning from the best and I'll do everything I can to keep myself safe. I love you and miss you and can't wait to hold you close once again."

Yet, as John found comfort in his correspondences, only a short distance away within the same sprawling expanse, Timmy was grappling with a cocktail of emotions - excitement mingled with apprehension.

ALTHOUGH PARTED FROM John, the thought of his best friend somewhere within the same vast training compound - each confronting his own set of hurdles - fueled Timmy's resolve to make the most of the circumstances enveloping him. The heartache from the separation lingered, but determination and a silent hope for reunion anchored his spirit.

As Timmy climbed into the commander's hatch, he paused to take in his new environment. The loader's station felt daunting with its tight confines. The walls seemed to close in on him, making every inch of space precious. On both sides, ammo racks were filled to capacity with rounds. He took a moment to survey the tools around him, from cleaning supplies to a crucial tool kit, ensuring he recognized everything he'd need in the thick of action.

The loader had one of the most physically demanding jobs in the crew. The average Sherman shell weighed 40 pounds and had to be loaded rapidly and without error. To prepare for this, Timmy's days were filled with strenuous exercises to build his strength and endurance. He spent hours loading dummy shells into practice cannons, working on his speed and technique until his muscles screamed for relief.

As he acclimated to his role as the loader, he began to master the various tasks associated with his position. Timmy mastered loading various ammunition and clearing any jams, ensuring the gun was continuously ready for action.

During one relentless training session, Timmy's arms quivered under the weight of each shell. His movements became an agonizing dance, his once nimble fingers struggling to grasp and load. Sweat streamed down his face, stinging his eyes, as hours stretched into what felt like eons. Training to be a loader-a role demanding speed, strength, and precision - felt overpowering that day.

As Timmy climbed out of the tank, he was met by the sharp blue eyes of his instructor, Sergeant McAnnalley. The lean, stern-faced white man from Texas watched Timmy closely beneath the rim of his cap. Noticing Timmy's struggle, he approached.

"You alright, Griffin?" He asked.

Leaning against the Sherman tank, Timmy wiped the sweat from his forehead and glanced at McAnnalley. "Jus' strugglin' a bit to keep pace, Sarge. Feels like I'm tryin' to catch a greased pig, can't get a hold of it all."

Sergeant McAnnalley, a veteran of the first war who'd seen many young men grapple with doubts and fears, nodded. "Break down the loading process, Griffin. Focus on each step. It's not about speed now, but precision. You have potential. Keep practicing."

This simple advice was a lifeline for Timmy. With renewed determination, he nodded at the Sergeant, grateful for the guidance. Despite the prejudices of the time and the color of his skin, he knew his purpose: to serve his country. And he was ready to put in the work, however tough it might be.

Back in the barracks, they often shared stories and deep conversations regarding their shared experiences as black soldiers preparing for war and the state of their country. Thoughts of John often crossed Timmy's mind. He wondered about his friend's experiences in training, aware of the distinct worlds they each inhabited on the same base.

Over the weeks, Timmy's once-awkward movements became fluid. His strength and resilience grew profoundly. The Sherman tank, once daunting, had become familiar.

Each letter from Emily, in her familiar handwriting, brought news from home and insights into his life at camp, from the drills to the friendships he was forging.

He shared with her the intricate details of his role as the loader, his pride evident in his words. The awe-inspiring power of the war machine was balanced by the immense responsibility it bore. Despite the harsh realities of his training, he found purpose and dedication which spurred him on.

One day, one arrived different from the rest. The moment he saw it, his heart leaped with anticipation. As he unfolded the letter and began to read, his eyes widened. "It's a boy?" he thought he whispered to himself, the words barely escaping his lips. The surge of joy and excitement washed over him like a tidal wave, leaving him momentarily breathless.

However, his whisper turned out to be louder than he realized. His fellow crew members, who had been observing him with curious eyes from across the room, instantly reacted.

"Did he say 'boy'?" one of them asked, his eyes sparkling with excitement. Without waiting for an answer, another sprang to his feet, shouting, "Well, ain't no point in dilly - dallyin', Timmy! Spill it!"

With a grin, he read out loud, "We got us a little boy, Jacob, jus' like we settled on if it was a boy!"

A chorus of whoops and cheers erupted around him. It was a moment of pure joy amidst the relentless intensity of their training. It was a reminder of the life awaiting him beyond the confines of the camp, a life growing, even as he was away.

The thought of his newborn son back home fueled his determination. He felt a newfound sense of responsibility, not only as a soldier but as a father. Knowing Emily was there, standing strong and taking care of their child, gave him an immeasurable sense of warmth and comfort.

Each letter from her, each word of encouragement, and each update on Jacob became his beacon of hope and motivation, reminding him of what he would be fighting for and the future ahead of building a family.

In the face of adversity, Timmy held onto his pride. As a young black man in uniform, he was making a statement-both to himself and to the world. His thoughts often wandered to the day he'd soon reunite with John, sharing tales and hopefully fighting side by side.

Segregation and physical distance had separated them in training, but their shared purpose - to challenge oppression and safeguard their loved ones - kept their spirits intertwined. Their journey had many miles yet, but both Timmy and John were poised, ready to face whatever came next.

A COUPLE OF DAYS BEFORE graduating Armor School, they were finally given the opportunity to call home for the first time since they left. The anticipation was high among the troops, as everyone awaited their turn to speak with their loved ones.

They were put into two single file lanes, and each soldier was given two minutes to make their call before the next person took their turn. John stood in his queue, the white soldiers lining up separately from their black counterparts. His palms were slick with sweat as he counted the remaining men in front of him. The ring of the old rotary phone echoed throughout the room, followed by hushed conversations punctuated by the Drill Sergeant's stern, "Time's up!"

John stepped forward as his turn finally arrived, his pulse quickening as he dialed Sarah's number. The sound of ringing filled his ears, intensifying his nerves as he awaited a response.

Sarah's father had already left for the store, and she, along with her mother, was eating breakfast when the phone rang. The unexpected call so early in the morning sent a ripple of curiosity through the room. Sarah, after a brief pause to glance at the clock, walked over and answered the receiver with a cautious yet pleasant, "Hello?"

When John finally heard her voice, a wave of relief washed over him. "Hey beautiful," he greeted, a hint of excitement in his voice.

"John! Oh, I'm so glad you called."

"I miss you so much."

"I miss you too! How are you doing?"

"I'm doing alright. We're 'bout done with training, then I'll be coming home."

"When will that be?" she asked, her curiosity piqued.

"We'll be coming home on Wednesday 'bout 9:00 am according to the train schedule. We'll have a two-week furlough before having to report back for our next assignment."

"Oh, wonderful! I can't wait to see you!"

"I can't wait to see you too darlin'!" They chatted for a few moments more, but their time was limited, and a Sergeant soon yelled out one minute had passed.

He told her he loved her as the Sergeant yelled "Time!" in which he promptly hung up the phone and stepped away, feeling grateful to hear her voice even if for a couple of minutes. The next soldier then stepped forward and the process began all over again, each soldier eager to hear the voice of their loved ones again.

Across the room, Timmy stood in line as well. The process was the same, the wait equally agonizing. When it was finally his turn, he took a deep breath and dialed Emily's number. As he heard her voice on the other end, he felt a wave of nostalgia, a feeling of home that took his breath away. They reminisced about the simple joys of life - their hometown, family, and, of course, their newborn son, Jacob.

"Em, my time's 'bout up," he said, glancing at the Sergeant who was keeping an eye on the time.

"I know, sure wish you didn't have to go."

"I be home soon, promise, darlin' can't hardly wait to meet our boy, cradle him in these arms."

"Jacob misses you. He's snoozin' away right now, but I swear on my life he's your spittin' image."

"Tell him daddy loves him somethin' fierce, and I'm jus' countin' the days 'til I get to see him for the first time."

"I promise... we'll be right here waitin' for you. We sure do love you."

As their conversation drew to a close, their words - steeped in longing and promises of reunion - carried a weight beyond their spoken sound. Timmy found himself hanging onto each syllable, each shared laughter resonating deeply within him.

His heart throbbed painfully as he heard the Sergeant bellow, "Time!" he said his goodbyes, the dial tone ringing hollow in his ears as he placed the receiver back.

He turned around then, and his gaze found John. Despite the distance between them, they had been through the same grueling weeks of training, shared similar experiences, fears, and dreams. Their eyes met and held. A slow smile crept onto John's face, mirroring the one spreading across Timmy's own.

In the moment, the room seemed to shrink, the divide between them becoming less significant as they communicated their shared camaraderie, longing, and understanding in a silent exchange. Their nod was a mutual acknowledgment of the hardships they'd endured and the battle they still had to fight.

The sight of his friend - his brother in arms - filled Timmy with resolve. They might be separated by a man-made divide, but the friendship they had was stronger than any line on the ground.

Later the same day, their paths crossed again, this time near the mess hall. In that fleeting moment, their exchange evolved beyond mere glances; they shared hurried words, whispering promises of reunion once they were free from the rigors of training.

"Can't wait to swap tales with ya, Timmy," John said.

"Me neither, John," Timmy replied. "We gonna have ourselves a whole mess o' things to jaw 'bout.

Their promise, full of anticipation for shared stories and laughter, hung in the air as they parted ways, each returning to their respective side of the divide.

Yet, this brief moment was sufficient. It served as a potent reminder of the deep connection they shared, fortifying them with the strength needed to endure the remainder of their training.

MEANWHILE, THEIR LOVED ones - Sarah and Emily - shared in this anticipation, eagerly waiting for the day they could embrace their men once more.

The long-awaited day had finally dawned. In the early hours of a late April Wednesday, under a sky still dark yet hinting at the approaching dawn, Sarah and Emily were roused from their shared anticipation. Sarah had opted to spend the night at Emily's house, so they could journey to the depot together. Aunt Jean, ever kind-hearted, had also decided to stay over, offering to watch over sleeping Jacob until their return.

The house was alive with activity, buzzing from the underlying current of excitement and anticipation shared by them all. To Emily, this buzz was overwhelming, hard to fully absorb. The air was thick with emotions - joy at the prospect of reunion, tinged with the nervousness of venturing into uncharted parenthood. Emily felt as if she was observing everything through a foggy window, connected yet strangely detached.

Repeatedly, she found herself drawn to Jacob's crib, guided more by instinct than affection. Her fingers lightly traced the softness of his cheek, a mechanical gesture yet laden with an unspoken promise of protection. However, with each repetition of this gesture, she felt increasingly hollow rather than filled with maternal warmth.

As dawn began to seep through the windows, painting the bustling household in a rosy hue, a peculiar sense of wakefulness enveloped

Emily. The reality of her newfound role as a mother was asserting itself, growing louder with each moment that passed.

Seeing her standing by the crib, Sarah lightly touched Emily's arm, a concerned expression on her face. "Em, are you okay? You seem a bit distant," she said.

Emily gave her a small, tired smile. "I'm fine. Jus' adjusting, I guess." Her voice was a whisper, her eyes fixed on the crib, revealing more than her words could conceal. Sarah gave Emily's hand a reassuring squeeze, her eyes mirroring the worry Emily was struggling to conceal.

Emily then stepped back and twirled around, her floral skirt flaring out around her. "Do I look alright?" she asked, her eyes sparkling with excitement.

"You look beautiful," responded Sarah. "The skirt's colors suit you, and the blouse... it's stunning."

Emily laughed, her face flushing at the compliment. She ran a hand through the loose bun of her hair. "Much obliged. You ain't too shabby yourself!"

Turning her attention to the crib where her baby lay, Emily's tone softened. "Well, my little prince, it's 'bout time for Momma to step out for a spell." Her fingers tracing over Jacob's chubby cheeks, eliciting a gurgling response. His tiny hand reached for her fingers. With a final smile, she added, "Aunt Jean's gonna look after ya."

Aunt Jean entered the room, her warm smile radiating reassurance. "Don't you worry," she said, her voice soothing. "Jacob and I, we're gonna have ourselves a heap of fun right here. Now, you two go and fetch your men."

They thanked Jean, their hearts full of gratitude. As they made their way toward the depot, the excitement was palpable. Their heels clicked on the pavement, punctuating the quiet streets with their presence. Passersby turned their heads, admiring the two women who looked like they had stepped straight out of a fashion magazine.

The sun had barely risen, casting a warm golden light on their styled hair and glowing skin. Sarah's deep blue dress beautifully complemented her fair skin, while the soft cream color of Emily's blouse highlighted her rosy cheeks, and the bright floral pattern of the skirt drew attention to her slender frame.

As they entered the depot, all eyes turned to them, and they couldn't help but feel a surge of pride and anticipation at the thought of being reunited with their men. The station was already bustling with activity, with passengers rushing about, some boarding trains, while others disembarked.

They made their way to the platform, and their excitement and anticipation rose as they found a spot to wait for the train's arrival. They settled in, chatting about what it would be like to finally be reunited with their loved ones.

Finally, the train pulled into the station, and a throng of people began to stream out of the carriages. They eagerly scanned the faces in the crowd, their eyes straining to catch a glimpse of John and Timmy.

But as the crowd began to thin, it became apparent their loved ones weren't among the disembarking passengers. Sarah's heart sank as she began to fear the worst. *What if something's happened to them?* she thought, her mind racing with worry.

Emily sensed her friend's distress and put a comforting hand on her shoulder, trying to offer reassurance. "Reckon' they might be runnin' a bit late," she said, trying to stay positive despite her own growing concern. But as time passed and there was no sign of them, their worry only increased.

With desperation, they approached the conductor, hoping for some answers. They asked if anyone else was supposed to get off at this stop, but the conductor shook his head. "No, ma'am," he said.

The reality of the situation began to sink in, and they were left feeling confused, anxious and scared. *Why weren't their loved ones on the train? Where could they be?* As the train pulled away from the station, they were left with only questions and no answers.

Chapter 11

Skyward Bound

While John and Timmy faced their challenges, Billy grappled with his own during basic training in Biloxi, Mississippi. The experience nearly pushed him to his breaking point.

He struggled with the intense physical demands, his lack of athleticism often leaving him lagging behind his peers. Moreover, the strict military discipline weighed heavily on him. The myriad of rules made him feel confined and powerless.

Compounding his difficulties was his simmering anger over Sarah's rejection. Deeply in love with her, he was constantly reminded of what he couldn't have. His bitterness towards John grew, as he was convinced that he deserved Sarah's love more than John ever could. Despite his efforts to focus on training, the sting of unrequited love persisted, refusing to leave him.

After the conclusion of basic training, the daunting prospect of becoming a waist gunner loomed over him. There was no escaping it. Soon, he was on a train to Texas, heading to Harlingen Army Airfield.

The journey, marked by cramped seats and constant delays, added to his trials. As the landscape rolled by, he dwelled on his father's insistence on his enlistment and the advanced training awaiting him.

As the train pulled into the Airfield depot, his heart sank. It was nothing like he had imagined it would be. Instead of pristine hangars and runways, he saw a chaotic jumble of tents, temporary buildings, and rough dirt roads.

When he stepped off the train the heat was oppressive and planes of all sizes and shapes dotted the runway, their engines roaring as they took off and landed. Soldiers bustled about, loading and unloading supplies, directing traffic, and performing maintenance on the aircraft. He felt a knot form in his stomach as he realized this was to be his new home for the foreseeable future, as he and the others from the train were led toward the reception area tent.

As he arrived at the reception area, he was greeted by a stern-looking officer who directed him to a table where a group of soldiers was filling out paperwork. "Name, rank, service number, and date of birth," the officer barked at him. He rattled off his information, a nervous feeling stirring in his gut. "Medical records?" the officer asked, and he handed over a file containing his medical history. He was then led to a small room for a thorough flight physical examination.

During this examination, he tried to push the thoughts of Sarah out of his mind and focus on the task at hand. The doctor's probing and prodding left him feeling exposed and vulnerable, but he gritted his teeth and endured the discomfort, determined to pass the exam and move on to the next phase of his training.

The doctor, an older man with a grizzled beard and wire-rimmed glasses, had kind eyes that observed his unease. "You've never been through this before, haven't you?" he inquired, his voice a mix of professional distance and gentle warmth.

"No, sir," he responded, trying to project a calm facade. Yet beneath it, his heart raced, burdened by a looming sense of judgment.

The doctor continued his examination, pushing and pulling at joints. "Your vitals seem strong," he noted. "But I can tell you're a bit on edge. Anything on your mind?"

"Just...someone. A woman."

"Ah, the heart, the most unpredictable muscle."

"That's one way to put it," Billy chuckled, finding a small relief in the admission.

"I'll tell you what," the doctor said, writing on his clipboard. "Take care of your heart, both physically and emotionally. Resilience and balance are as crucial as strength."

After completing the examination, Billy's thoughts naturally turned to Sarah. He was filled with confidence that his military service would not only refine his skills and resilience but also prove his worth to her, solidifying his belief that he could win her heart upon his return.

Stepping out of the examination room, he felt his ego bolstered, viewing the impending challenges at Harlingen Army Airfield as vital steps towards achieving this goal.

The moment he received his military flight uniform marked a significant milestone. As he donned the uniform, a mix of fear and pride swirled within him. The weight of the fabric seemed to embody the gravity of his commitment and the challenges ahead. Hearing others discuss the rigors of gunner training sparked some worry.

Despite being daunted by the strict rules and the prospect of an extended stay at the airfield, he headed toward the cacophony of roaring engines and oppressive heat with a determined resolve to prove himself the best.

As Billy navigated through the bustling airfield, he took in the sights and sounds that would soon become his daily reality. The area was a flurry of activity, with soldiers hustling about and aircraft constantly taking off and landing.

Eventually, he reached the living quarters assigned to him - a row of tents set up for the trainees. Stepping inside his assigned tent, he was immediately struck by the stark difference from what he had known back home.

Inside the tent, it was cramped and smelly. "Where do I put my stuff?" he complained.

When another trainee tried to help, Billy gave him a dismissive glance. In his mind, his family's name should have entitled him to better accommodations.

Unbeknownst to Billy, his arrival had not gone unnoticed by the staff. What he didn't know was that Sergeant Thompson, a strict and no-nonsense instructor, had already heard of his impending arrival and was prepared to challenge any notions of entitlement.

Among the staff, it was widely known that Billy's father's wealth and connections at the War Department had secured him a spot in the coveted aviation program. Aware of the recruit's privileged background, Sergeant Thompson steeled himself for their first encounter, ready to address any misconceptions head-on.

As Billy swaggered into the facility, his face wore a hint of entitlement, which didn't escape Sergeant Thompson's notice. With years of experience molding disciplined soldiers, Sergeant Thompson immediately saw through Billy's façade.

As Billy approached, the Sergeant crossed his arms, his expression stern. He was familiar with recruits who leaned on their family's influence, but here, where sweat, determination, and merit were paramount, he was intent on setting Billy straight.

"Listen up, recruit," his voice snapped like a whip. "Your family name doesn't mean a damn thing here. You have to earn your place, just like everyone else."

Billy's initial reaction was one of suppressed irritation. Deep down, he felt Sergeant Thompson didn't understand his caliber. Nevertheless, he managed to nod in acknowledgment, though a trace of his cocky demeanor lingered.

"In ground training, you'll see the challenge of being a B-17 gunner," Sergeant Thompson continued. "It's demanding, both mentally and physically. No special treatment, no shortcuts. Got it?"

Swallowing a retort, Billy straightened up. While part of him resented the implication that he hadn't earned his place, another part acknowledged the need to prove himself.

Sergeant Thompson, noticing the slight shift in Billy's attitude, softened his tone slightly. "Success or failure here depends solely on your efforts. Remember that."

Billy's journey took a real turn at that moment. He was still confident in his abilities and quick learning skills, but he began to understand that real respect and recognition would come from hard work and dedication, not just from his family's name.

Under Sergeant Thompson's strict guidance, Billy faced challenges he hadn't anticipated. His initial arrogance clashed with the reality of the rigorous training. "Focus, recruit! You won't succeed if you continue like this," Sergeant Thompson reprimanded during a particularly tough session.

"I will give it my all," Billy responded with a mix of defiance and determination. Over time, his confidence shifted from being centered on his ego to reflecting the skills he was developing. Slowly, he started to earn the respect he had once assumed was his by right.

As his training progressed, Billy was introduced to various types of equipment and weaponry crucial to his role as a gunner. Each new piece of machinery presented its own set of challenges, demanding both physical and mental agility.

It was during one of these training sessions that he first encountered the M2 Browning .50 caliber machine gun, a hefty 84-pound weapon that would test his skills and resolve in ways he had not yet experienced.

The M2 Browning's weight and size were challenging, but continuous practice acquainted him with its intricacies. From stationary to moving targets, his expertise grew. The deafening gunfire, intense recoil, and vibration of the aircraft with each shot tested him. Yet, the excitement of mastering the weapon was undeniable. While Billy's arrogance had waned since his arrival, a hint of his old self-confidence was evident in his posture and actions.

Still observing Billy's inflated self-assurance, a trace of annoyance flickered across Sergeant Thompson's face. He approached, his tone laced with a mix of exasperation and authority. "You think you've got it all figured out, don't you? Well, let me make one thing crystal clear. Arrogance won't get you far in this training. You need discipline and respect for the process."

Billy's eyes narrowed, a subtle challenge flickering in his gaze. "I know what I'm doing, Sergeant. I've got this under control."

Sergeant Thompson's stern expression hardened. "Is that so? We'll see. The range doesn't care about your swagger. It cares about precision, focus, and the willingness to learn."

Their dialogue remained tense, a constant battle of wills, as Sergeant Thompson pushed Billy to recognize the importance of humility and respect.

During a particularly challenging simulation, Billy's overconfidence led to a moment of carelessness. While he generally hit his targets, a critical lapse due to his attitude caused him to miss an important one.

Sergeant Thompson didn't miss a beat. "You've got the skills, Billy, but your attitude stinks," he remarked, frustration evident in his voice. "Hitting the target isn't enough; you need consistency, humility, and teamwork to truly excel."

For a brief moment, Billy's confident facade faltered, revealing a hint of understanding. He masked it with his usual smirk, but the Sergeant had already seen the crack in his armor.

"I get it, Sergeant," Billy retorted, trying to maintain his composure. "Just a slip-up."

Sergeant Thompson's expression remained stern. "A slip-up that could cost lives. Remember, it's not only about your skills. True success here is how you grow and work within a team."

Billy managed a nod, a subtle shift in his demeanor suggesting he was beginning to take the lesson to heart. His journey in the training program continued to be marked by a mix of his innate talent and the ongoing struggle to temper his ego.

For a split second, as Thompson's words cut through, Billy's confident facade wavered. He masked it with a smirk, but the brief vulnerability was not lost on the observant Sergeant.

Billy scoffed dismissively. "I get the point, Sergeant, but I'll handle it."

Sergeant Thompson's gaze hardened. "You may be talented, but true success isn't just individual skills. Remember that."

A smug smile curled on Billy's lips, refusing to back down. "I'll prove you wrong, Sergeant. You watch."

Billy's undeniable talent was clear, but so was the friction his arrogance caused with others. Sergeant Thompson constantly reminded him of the importance of humility and teamwork. Billy often smirked, believing his individual skills made him superior.

This ongoing conflict between Billy's self-assuredness and the need for teamwork was highlighted during his waist gunner training. He showed exceptional proficiency in navigation and operating the B-17's communication systems, but his attitude often reflected superiority. His disdain for certain instructions was evident, often rolling his eyes or responding with a smugness that irked both his instructors and peers.

It was during one particular training session, after Billy had successfully completed a challenging exercise, that the tension between his ego and the necessity for teamwork came to a head.

Sergeant Thompson, observing his performance, commented, "Impressive, but remember, it's teamwork that makes us succeed."

Billy, with his characteristic cocky grin, retorted, "I think I'm managing pretty well on my own."

Thompson, steadfast in his efforts to instill unity, firmly replied, "This isn't a solo show. We succeed or fail together."

During his high-altitude training, Billy mastered the use of oxygen equipment and learned to recognize signs of hypoxia.

However, it was the thrill of flying in the B-17 that captivated him. On one flight, Sergeant Thompson's voice came through the radio, breaking into his thoughts. "Enjoying the view?" he asked.

With a confident smirk, Billy responded, "Of course. But I could do this with my eyes closed."

Thompson came back over the radio, a hint of exasperation in his voice. "Always the show-off, Billy. Remember, we all play a part here."

Despite Thompson's persistent efforts to ground him, Billy's ego remained inflated. He believed his burgeoning skills alone set him apart, yet the importance of teamwork was starting to resonate with him, albeit slowly.

Each day, as the sun set, Billy returned to his tent, wearied by the day's rigorous demands. The constant drone of planes taking off and landing became the backdrop to his evenings. Despite the noise and the physical and mental toll of the training, he stayed laser-focused on his goal.

As the weeks passed, Billy's prowess as a gunner developed significantly. He became adept at operating the gun, communicating effectively with his crew, and understanding the aircraft's systems and navigation procedures.

However, amidst his professional growth, Billy felt a deep sense of loneliness. Unlike his fellow trainees who received letters and care packages, he felt cut off from his family and friends. The lack of personal correspondence underscored feelings of abandonment, adding to the isolation he felt in this demanding environment.

He tried to shove these feelings aside, concentrating on his training. But in quieter moments, especially at night, the sense of disconnect from the outside world was evident and sometimes overwhelming.

Despite his overconfidence and arrogance, his time at Harlingen Army Airfield had taught him a great deal on perseverance. He had come to admire the hard work and dedication required of those serving in the military, and he was beginning to see the value in the skills he had acquired during his training.

On his last day of training, Billy stood on the tarmac, taking a moment to admire the B-17 bomber he had grown intimately familiar with. The thunderous roar of its four Wright R-1820 Cyclone engines filled the air, a powerful symphony that overshadowed the runway's clamor.

He marveled at its sleek yet formidable design-the massive wings, sturdy construction, and an impressive wingspan of 103 feet. The propellers roared to life, and the nose's array of machine guns, flanked by top and bottom turret firepower, spoke of its deadly capabilities.

Despite its impressive size and armaments, Billy was acutely aware of the bomber's vulnerabilities. The reality of flying in combat loomed large in his mind, a stark contrast to the controlled environment of training.

Lost in thought, he was brought back to the present by the familiar voice of Sergeant Thompson. "A beauty, isn't she, Harrington?"

Billy turned, surprised to hear Thompson address him by his surname for the first time. It marked a shift, a recognition of his transition from trainee to airman. A small smile played on his lips. "Yes, she is, Sergeant," he replied, his respect for the aircraft mirrored in his tone.

Thompson placed a hand on Billy's shoulder, his voice taking on a serious note. "You've come a long way, Harrington. But remember, flying in combat is a different beast from training. We rely on each other up there."

A silent nod from Billy acknowledged the weight of Thompson's words. The journey ahead would be perilous, and his training had only been the beginning.

Thompson gave him a brief, approving nod. "Take care, Harrington," he said, removing his hand from Billy's shoulder. With that, he turned and walked away, blending into the airbase's activity.

Billy watched him leave, feeling a mix of gratitude and determination settling within him. His gaze lingered on the B-17 for a moment longer, etching the image of the mighty aircraft in his memory. Turning away, he knew the next time he saw it, he'd be heading into the very heart of the war.

As Billy walked away from the plane, a surge of anticipation marked the onset of his deployment. The path ahead, fraught with uncertainties, was tempered by the confidence he had honed through rigorous training. His heart beat in tandem with his steps on the tarmac, a blend of fear and excitement stirring inside him.

The morning sun rose higher, casting long, golden streaks across the horizon and bathing the airfield in a warm, radiant glow. Billy's stride was firm and purposeful as he moved toward the briefing tent, ready for his first assignment. The sunlight seemed to symbolize his journey-a transition from the structured world of training to the unpredictable realities of war.

Chapter 12

Into the Fray

John leaned against the railing of the SS George Washington, staring out at the vast expanse of the Atlantic. The rhythmic rocking of the ship and the hum of the engines seemed to lull his thoughts, taking him back to the unexpected day in the Auditorium.

They had been seated, eagerly awaiting the graduation ceremony and the much-anticipated start of their furlough. Then the sharp command of "Attention!" had resonated through the room, jolting everyone into an instant state of alertness.

To their astonishment, it was Major General Nathanial Collins, the commander of the US Army Armor School, who stepped onto the stage. His appearances at graduation ceremonies were rare, and John couldn't help but wonder why this particular occasion merited his presence.

Collins' voice, authoritative yet filled with pride, echoed in his memory. "Men, congratulations on completing your training. Late last night, I received an urgent telegram from the War Department concerning you troops."

"I am saddened to inform you, effective immediately all furloughs are cancelled, and the phones have been cut off. There will be no more outside communication for the near future. Your loved ones will be notified by telegram informing them you have been deployed to a location which cannot be disclosed at this time. I felt it only right I should be the one to tell you."

The General's announcement of Operation Bolero, as they now understood it, had taken everyone by surprise. But what felt like a gut punch was the subsequent cancellation of furloughs. John vividly remembered exchanging bewildered glances with Timmy, both reeling from the rapid succession of changes.

He remembered how the Battalion Commander had instructed them to use the latrines, marking the imminent nature of their departure. And before they knew it, they had found themselves at the Hampton Roads Port of Embarkation in Virginia, surrounded by throngs of soldiers and equipment.

As they boarded the once grand ocean liner, converted for war, the crew moved efficiently around them. John recalled the sight of the protective convoy escorting the George Washington, including the imposing USS Texas and the swift USS Satterlee. Each ship, with its own story and reputation, was now part of their journey.

As the vast sea stretched out before him, John's thoughts inevitably gravitated toward Sarah. He wished he could've sent her a message, some sign to let her know what had transpired. The hope was she would understand, and their relationship could weather the trials of war and time.

Amidst the two-week voyage, the ceaseless chatter and routines of the ship barely pierced his daydreams. The mystery of their destination gnawed at him, deepening his anxiety. Still, his heart consistently found its way back home, lingering on the precious moments with Sarah, and the comforting shade of the old oak tree where they'd shared many a quiet moment.

The letters he wrote to Sarah sat in his pack, along with his journal he had spent days writing in. He knew he wouldn't be able to mail them anytime soon, but writing helped him feel closer to the love he left behind.

Occasionally, he struck up conversations with other soldiers, sharing stories and jokes to pass the time. One of the soldiers, a tall guy from Texas named Jake, regaled them with tales of horse wrangling and rodeos, while another, Pete, a New Yorker, had the crew laughing with anecdotes from his time as a cab driver in the bustling city streets.

"Did you ever meet anyone famous driving your cab, Pete?" John asked one day, trying to stave off the boredom.

"You wouldn't believe half the people I've met," he responded, a wry grin on his face. "I had a fare once, all the way from Times Square to the upper east side. The lady in the back, all dolled up and smelling like roses. Turns out she was a famous actress. Can't recall her name now, but boy, did she tip well."

The stories brought camaraderie and moments of laughter among the men, helping them momentarily forget the danger they were heading into. Despite the uncertainty of the future, these shared moments helped lighten their burdens, if only for a moment.

The journey seemed to stretch on indefinitely, the vast expanse of the Atlantic proving both awe-inspiring and unsettling. The ship, a hulking mass of steel and strength, swayed and groaned in rhythm with the unyielding waves.

Each roll of the ship sent a shiver down its spine, mirroring the shivers running down the spines of the men within. This relentless motion of the sea made it clear why they had been issued sea sickness pills before leaving Fort Knox.

At first, John and Timmy had scoffed at the provision of these pills, but now, amidst the rough sea journey, they considered it a blessing. Many of their comrades from other locations weren't as fortunate.

The uncomfortable sounds of sickness filled the ship, creating a symphony of discomfort. Men clung to their bunks, pale and sweaty, their eyes betraying a weary discomfort from the ship's relentless motion.

One evening, Timmy found himself on the upper deck, wrestling with his own wave of nausea. He muttered to himself, "I ain't signed up for this," as the relentless rocking of the ship took its toll.

Across from him, John looked equally green but managed a wan smile in an attempt to offer some semblance of comfort. "Ain't one of us did, Timmy. But we're in it now, gotta bear with it. Jus' some mean ol' waves is all."

The drone of the ship's engines filled the air, a persistent hum broken only by the occasional creak of the ship as it navigated the stormy sea. The noises did little to soothe the discomfort most of the men were feeling.

In the midst of discomfort and the cacophony of illness, the men clung to whatever respite they could find, their thoughts of someday returning home serving as their sole beacon of comfort in the tumultuous sea.

Sometime later resting on his bunk, John's pen stilled mid-sentence in his journal as a burst of laughter echoed outside his bunk. Curiosity piqued, he tucked his journal away and ventured out to investigate. A huddle of soldiers, faces illuminated by a single dim bulb, were gathered around a makeshift poker game, their raucous energy cutting through the ship's usual nocturnal solemnity.

A lanky Sergeant with a thick Southern drawl, his uniform accentuating his slim frame, noticed John and beckoned him over. "Hey there. Ya lookin' a mite bored. How 'bout you join us?"

John hesitated, his gaze darting towards the closed door leading to the officer's quarters. The risk of getting caught gambling wasn't one he'd typically take. But the prospect of camaraderie, a welcome departure from the relentless monotony, was too enticing to resist.

"Sure," he replied, a hint of reluctance still in his voice. He shuffled over and sat cross-legged on the cold steel floor next to the Sergeant.

A deck of worn-out cards was thrust into his hands, and he cast a sidelong glance at the stakes-a small mountain of cigarettes at the center of their circle. "Well, I ain't got much to wager," John admitted.

The Sergeant chuckled, giving him a friendly slap on the back. "Ain't no need to fret. We ain't gamblin' for cash here. Cigarettes? Now they're worth their weight in gold on this here tub."

As the night wore on, punctuated by rounds of laughter and light-hearted banter. John found himself getting drawn into the game, caught up in the fun helped soften the harsh reality of their journey. Despite the sea sickness, the biting cold, and the underlying fear of what lay ahead, for a few precious hours, they were simply a bunch of guys playing poker, bound by shared circumstances and the simple desire for a fleeting moment of normality.

As the night gave way to dawn, the atmosphere shifted. The card game ended, and the men gradually dispersed, each lost in their own thoughts about the day ahead.

As the convoy of ships finally approached the shore, John and Timmy, along with their comrades, stood on the deck, straining to catch a glimpse of the unknown land before them. The sea breeze ruffled their hair, and the salty mist tickled their noses, but they paid it no mind.

Their eyes were fixed on the distant shore as it gradually came into focus. The sea's blur of blues and greens gradually gave way to the distinct colors of the landscape-a mosaic of browns, greens, and grays. Outlines of buildings, trees, and people began to emerge. Amidst their uncertainty regarding their exact location or the specifics of their mission, a blend of nerves, excitement, and anticipation coursed through them.

Breaking the silence, a navy hand nearby spoke up, "Welcome to Portsmouth!"

John turned towards him, his expression a mix of confusion and curiosity. "Portsmouth?" he asked.

The sailor, his face weathered from years at sea and a salt-and-pepper beard framing his smile, chuckled at John's expression. "Aye, lad. Portsmouth's a city on the southern coast of England. It's one of the major naval ports in all of Europe," he explained, his voice carrying a hint of pride.

John exchanged a glance with Timmy, the same question mirrored in both their eyes. "But why England?" he asked.

The sailor shrugged. "Can't tell you. Orders come from above, and we follow 'em. But don't you worry, all will be clear soon enough."

His reassurance did little to quell John's puzzlement, but he nodded, keeping his speculations to himself. Whether they were in England for a layover, tactical strategy, or training exercise, John knew the purpose would become clear eventually. For now, he had orders to follow, just like the sailor.

Upon arrival, the bustle of the docks enveloped them. The soldiers were ushered off the ship onto the waiting docks. John and Timmy paused for a moment, taking in the unfamiliar sights and sounds of Portsmouth. The air carried the tang of salt and the distant cries of seagulls, while the horizon was dotted with silhouettes of ships and cranes.

"Never thought I find myself in England." Timmy muttered, his eyes scanning the horizon.

"Yeah," John replied, "jus' another one of them surprises in a long string of 'em."

Their musings were cut short as they were herded onto waiting trucks. The journey through the town offered fleeting glimpses of cobbled streets and historic buildings, contrasting sharply with the stark reality of military life.

Arriving at a makeshift camp, they found rows of tents set up in an orderly fashion. The tents were basic, a far cry from the comforts of home, but a welcome change from the cramped confines of the ship. The soft earth underfoot and the spaciousness of the tented area were small comforts they didn't take for granted.

As they arranged their gear inside their assigned tent, Timmy commented, "Least we got some room to breathe here."

"Yep, and no rolling waves to deal with," John added, stretching his legs.

Their moment of relief was brief. The chatter of the camp abruptly ceased as a stern voice pierced the air. "Private Anderson! Private Griffin!" yelled Corporal Mathers.

He stood at the entrance of the tent, his crisp uniform starkly contrasting with their worn fatigues. A serious expression etched his face, his eyes shadowed beneath the brim of his cap. John and Timmy shared a brief, glance before stepping out of the tent, bracing themselves for whatever was to come.

"Here, Corporal Mathers," John replied.

"I need you to two to follow me. You're wanted in the command tent," Mathers said.

John and Timmy quickly gathered their bearings and followed Corporal Mathers. As they trailed behind, the camp's usual hustle and bustle gradually receded, replaced by an undercurrent of tension that seemed to thicken the air around them. Their boots crunched on the gravel as they made their way to the command tent.

Upon stepping inside the command tent, they were immediately struck by the drastic change in atmosphere. It was as if they had entered a different world, one defined by urgency and authority. The space was dominated by an intimidating map sprawled across the center table, while the constant hum of radio equipment and the low murmur of voices formed a backdrop. Officers with serious expressions, deeply engrossed in their tasks, paused briefly to glance at the newcomers, acknowledging their arrival with measured looks.

At the far end of the tent, a Major, deeply engrossed in conversation with another officer, noticed John and Timmy as they entered. He wrapped up his discussion abruptly and walked towards them, his sharp gaze indicating the importance of what was to come.

"Good afternoon," Major Reynolds began, his voice resonating with authority. "I'll be assigning your new roles. We're gearing up for a significant operation, one we believe could shift the war's momentum." After a brief pause, he continued. "Both of you will play critical roles. Anderson, you're assigned to Company B of the 67th Armored Regiment, a unit of the 2nd Armored Division, 'Hell on Wheels,' commanded by General Patton."

Turning to Timmy, Major Reynolds added, "Griffin, you're headed to Company C of the 761st Tank Battalion, known as the 'Black Panthers.' This colored battalion is currently under General Patton's command and has been attached to our division for the operation."

John and Timmy felt a surge of excitement at the mention of General Patton, known for his pioneering role as a tank officer in World War I.

After the briefing, Major Reynolds concluded, "You'll join your units in the morning. For now, get some rest and have your meal. Dismissed." As the Major turned away, John and Timmy exchanged a glance of anticipation and pride, then quietly exited the tent.

Once outside, John turned to Timmy. "What you reckon' the Major meant by 'somethin' big?'" His question hung in the air, reflecting their shared curiosity regarding the impending operation. Despite their excitement on joining the Division, the reality of being assigned to separate units cast a shadow of disappointment.

Timmy shook his head, a slight shrug rolling off his shoulders. "Ain't rightly sure. Tall tales tend to swirl 'round parts like this, y'know."

John nodded, "Reckon' you're right. But can't help to chew on it a bit."

Timmy, attempting to remain grounded in the present, responded with a forced smile, "We'll jus' have to sit tight, see what they got for us," His tone carried a hint of optimism, yet it couldn't fully mask the underlying uncertainty that they both felt. "Remember," he added, his voice gaining a bit of strength, "no matter which iron horse we ridin' in, we lookin' out for one another." John managed a small smile in response, but his gaze soon drifted away, lost in thought on the challenges ahead.

As they walked toward the mess tent, snippets of conversation from other soldiers floated around them, each speculating on the Major's cryptic words. It was clear that uncertainty was a common thread among them all, adding to the weight of the unknown that lay ahead.

As they stepped into the mess tent, John and Timmy split up as protocol dictated. They picked up their trays and moved through the line, attempting to engage in small talk with the soldiers around them. Yet, the air was thick with tension, making the conversations brief and somewhat strained. Each person was deeply absorbed in their own thoughts and concerns regarding the impending challenges.

After finishing their meal, they reconvened outside, deciding to explore the camp a bit. The area was a hive of activity, buzzing with soldiers bustling about, each one playing their part in the preparations for the unknown mission ahead.

Their stroll led them past the motor pool, where John caught sight of a line of tanks and armored vehicles. These robust machines, he realized, would be their home and fortress for the days to come. A mixed feeling of pride and solemnity washed over him as he observed the formidable array of military might.

As they continued their walk, they passed a group of soldiers gathered around a map, discussing possible scenarios for their upcoming mission. They stopped to listen in, hoping to glean some information.

One soldier pointed to a spot on the map, saying, "I heard this is where the Germans are massing their forces. We'll need to be prepared for a fierce battle."

John and Timmy exchanged a glance. "Sounds intense," John murmured, his voice barely above a whisper.

Timmy nodded, his face solemn. "We knew what we was signin' up for."

As they made their way back to their barracks, John and Timmy walked in silence, each lost in thought. The conversations they had overheard in the mess tent and the scenes they had witnessed around the camp had left a lasting impression, stirring unease in John that lingered as they settled in for the night.

The break of dawn came quickly. Barely had the first light crept across the sky when they were roused for an early start. As they were escorted to meet their new units, the reality of their situation hit them afresh.

Arriving at their destination, they were immediately struck by the sight of a row of M4A3 Sherman tanks. Each tank stood as a symbol of formidable power and purpose. John and Timmy paused for a moment, their eyes wide with a mix of awe and apprehension, as they took in the magnitude of what lay ahead.

"Heck of a sight, isn't it?" John said.

Timmy nodded, his gaze locked on the tanks. "A bunch of beauty's ain't they," he replied smiling.

Their conversation was interrupted as they reached the Regimental command post. Corporal Mathers, who had led them, halted and turned to face them. "Wait here," he ordered crisply. His face was stern as he disappeared into the tent. They stood in silence, their anticipation building as the minutes ticked by.

"Feeling nervous?" John finally broke the silence, his voice barely above a whisper.

Timmy shrugged, "A bit, you?"

"Same." John admitted with a slight chuckle.

Before they could continue their conversation, the flap of the tent opened and Corporal Mathers reappeared. His expression was unreadable. "Sergeant Major Matthews will see you now," he said, his voice firm.

They exchanged a quick glance before stepping forward. "Alright, here we go," John muttered under his breath.

As they entered, they were greeted by the sight of Regimental Commander, Lieutenant Colonel Brown, studying a map spread across his field table.

Upon noticing them, he looked up and turned to his Sergeant Major. "Replacements? For who?" Lieutenant Colonel Brown asked, his brows furrowing in confusion.

"Remember the Driver for Sergeant O'Brien in Bravo Company, he tried to show out, doing a front flip like an idiot off the front of their tank, breaking his ankle in the process? And then there was the loader for Sergeant Williams in the colored unit who came down with a stomach virus and is in the infirmary," Sergeant Major Matthews replied.

The Lieutenant Colonel, looking tired and worn, responded, "That's right. Sorry, it's been hard to keep up with all these planning briefs I've been having to attend lately. Go ahead and assign one to 2nd Platoon in Bravo Company and the other one to Charlie Company in the colored unit. They will both be under command of Captain Evans in Bravo Company." Afterwards he returned to studying his map.

"Understood, Sir," Sergeant Major Matthews replied, then turned to address John and Timmy. "Griffin, you will be assigned to Sergeant Williams, and Anderson, you will be with Sergeant O'Brien," he stated firmly.

John and Timmy acknowledged in unison, "Yes, Sergeant Major!"

Sergeant Major Matthews then directed his attention to Corporal Mathers. "Corporal, you heard the Old Man. Take them to their respective units," he instructed.

Corporal Mathers responded promptly, "Yes, Sergeant Major!"

With a final nod, Sergeant Major Matthews turned and walked back toward the Colonel. Corporal Mathers gestured to John and Timmy to follow him. "Alright, let's move out. Your new units are waiting," he said, leading the way out of the tent. John and Timmy followed closely, ready to meet their new units.

As they approached the line of Sherman tanks, John's eyes were drawn to one with the name 'Barracuda' boldly painted on its main gun barrel. Corporal Mathers stopped in front of the tank, where a stocky man with a stern face stood waiting.

"Sergeant O'Brien, this here's Private Anderson," Corporal Mathers introduced. "He's been assigned as your new driver."

Sergeant O'Brien, with a nod, extended a firm hand to John. "Welcome to Barracuda," he said gruffly. "We don't have much time for pleasantries. You'll learn on the go."

"Thank you, Sergeant. I'm ready for whatever comes," John replied with a respectful nod.

O'Brien gestured to 2nd Lieutenant Jacobs, standing by another tank. "That's Lieutenant Jacobs. He's your platoon leader under Captain Evans. He's tough and knows his stuff. Follow his orders, and you'll be alright."

John turned his attention to Lieutenant Jacobs, immediately struck by the officer's tall and authoritative presence. He nodded in acknowledgement, taking in the new information. His gaze then shifted back to the formidable Sherman tank, 'Barracuda.' A mix of awe and determination filled him. This was where he would play his part in the war - a reality which was both daunting and invigorating.

Near the 'Barracuda,' another young man stood. "Who might you be?" John inquired.

The man extended his hand. "Private Todd Davis, assistant driver."

John shook his hand, but their handshake was interrupted by Sergeant O'Brien.

"Glad to see you're getting acquainted with your crew, Anderson," O'Brien said. "We've got work to do. Prep our tanks for the upcoming mission. Help load the ammo, get your rations sorted, and ensure we're fueled up. We need to be ready when the time comes."

His words spurred them into action. John, along with the rest of the crew, understood the importance of their task. The road ahead would be challenging, and they needed to be fully prepared.

Nearby, Timmy was led to his assigned tank, named 'Crazy Horse,' a proud part of the groundbreaking 761st 'Black Panthers' Tank Battalion. The unit was a significant symbol of progress as the first African American armored unit in U.S. military history.

Timmy found some comfort in learning that 'Crazy Horse' was tasked to support John's company. Despite being in separate tanks, he felt reassured that their brotherhood would be maintained as they faced the same battles side by side.

Corporal Mathers led Timmy to Sergeant Williams, a newly promoted young leader, and introduced them. "Sergeant Williams, this is Private Griffin. He's your new loader."

Sergeant Williams extended his hand. "Griffin, good to have you," he said, his grip firm and reassuring.

After ensuring that Timmy was in good hands, Corporal Mathers gave a brief nod. "I'll leave you to it then. Take care, Private." With that, he turned and departed, leaving Timmy with his new crew.

Timmy was greeted by the rest of the crew: Corporal Turner, the humorous gunner, gave a lighthearted grin; Private Harris, the eager driver, nodded enthusiastically; and Private Sampson, the steadfast and reliable assistant driver, offered a friendly smile.

Each member of the crew welcomed Timmy enthusiastically. Sergeant Williams, observing the interactions, spoke up. "Alright, let's get to it. We have a lot to prepare and not much time. Every check, every drill we do will make a difference out there."

Motivated by Sergeant Williams words, they dove into meticulous preparations. Each movement was a silent pledge to uphold the honor and integrity of their groundbreaking unit.

The checks were rigorous, spirits were high, and determination was unwavering. Every crew member felt the weight of expectations, representing not only their battalion but paving the way for those who would follow in their footsteps.

As the days merged into nights and preparations reached their peak, dawn broke on the 9th of June - three days after the historic D-Day landings. John and Timmy, in their tanks with engines roaring to life, ascended the metal ramp of a Landing Craft Tank ship.

Bound for the shores of Omaha Beach, they braced themselves for the journey across the choppy waters. The salty sea spray lashed their faces as they anticipated the landing, and the relentless crash of waves against the ship's hull was overpowered by the steady hum of their tank engines.

As John sat in the driver's seat, he couldn't help but think of Sarah. He hoped she would receive his letter soon. Back in England, their commander had set up a makeshift mailbox in the HQ tent, a rare bridge to home in these times of war. John had dropped in his letter to Sarah, hoping it would find its way across the Atlantic amidst the stream of military dispatches and personal messages.

Approaching the now partially secured Omaha Beach, John, Timmy, and their crews scanned the horizon from their hatches. The once chaotic landing site seemed deceptively calm. Over the now humming engines of the tanks, readied as they approached the landing zone, John's voice cut through, "Looks quiet, doesn't it?"

"Too quiet," Todd responded from his assistant driver's seat.

When they reached the beach, the ship ground to a halt and the metal ramp clanged down onto the sand. With a jolt, John's tank rolled out onto the beach first, kicking up clouds of dust and sand. Timmy's tank followed shortly after, maintaining a safe distance.

"We're on the ground now, boys," Sergeant O'Brien's voice crackled over the radio. "Stay sharp."

Although quieter than during the initial landings, Omaha Beach bore the somber remnants of recent battle. Wreckage and debris lay scattered, a vivid reminder of the war's fierce reality. The men remained silent; their eyes focused on the land ahead as they cautiously moved forward with the other troops.

Timmy surveyed their surroundings. "Any sign of Germans?" he asked.

"Nothing yet," Sergeant Williams responded. "Stay ready."

The absence of immediate enemy contact didn't ease their tension. They knew all too well that danger could be lurking in any unturned corner of this war-torn landscape.

Relief washed over them as they ventured further inland without incident. In the lead tank, John couldn't help but voice his relief. "Still nothing," he muttered. "Guess we might get through this after all." But even as he spoke, he knew they were far from safe. This was only the beginning of their journey.

All the secrecy, urgency, and meticulous preparation they had experienced back in Fort Knox and England suddenly fell into place. They were now active participants in Operation Overlord, known among the officers as D-Day - the military shorthand for a day destined to change history.

But the reality of the situation set in as they moved closer to the village of Rubercy, France. The roads were littered with destroyed vehicles and buildings, and the sound of gunfire could be heard in the distance. As they moved forward, a swarm of American bombers escorted by fighters passed overhead, heading deeper into enemy territory and disappearing from view.

They eventually arrived at the outskirts of the village and set up camp for the night. The crew members of their tanks and the rest of the platoon worked together to ensure their vehicles were maintained and ready for imminent confrontation with the enemy.

John had trouble sleeping during his first night in the tank, which was parked in the tree line alongside the rest of his platoon. The driver's compartment was cramped, and each tiny movement felt restricted.

The ambient sounds of crickets filled the air, providing a stark contrast to the silence of the armored vehicle. Above, the moon cast an eerie glow over the landscape, its light filtering through the trees, creating shifting patterns on the ground.

He tried to shift his focus to the mission which lay ahead; however, memories of Sarah kept intruding upon his thoughts. Retrieving the locket from his pocket, he opened it to gaze at her picture. The sharp twinge of guilt he felt for not being able to keep his promise to visit her was overwhelming. He could vision her standing alone at the depot, waiting, hopeful.

The cool metal of the locket pressed against his fingers as he traced the contours of her cherished face. Tucking it back into his pocket, he leaned back, his mind drifting over the whirlwind of training and preparation from the past few weeks.

As he tried to find comfort in the quiet of the night, an underlying anxiety tugged at him, making him ponder the trials and confrontations that lay ahead.

BACK HOME, DAY AFTER day, Sarah and Emily returned to the depot, their hopes for news of Timmy and John dwindling with each visit. It had been weeks since Sarah last heard his voice on the phone.

On this particular day, they arrived back at Emily's house, their spirits low, when an unexpected knock at the door broke the somber mood. Emily, a look of surprise and curiosity crossing her face, asked Sarah, "I wonder who it could be?" Together, they approached the door, a wave of apprehension washing over them.

As Emily opened the door, both women stood frozen, speechless at the sight of the man on their doorstep. Dressed in a navy-blue uniform adorned with gold buttons and trim, a gold badge shining on his lapel, he was a harbinger of news they had dreaded.

His blue cap, emblazoned with a gold badge, bore the word 'Western Union,' a detail that struck Sarah profoundly. A sinking feeling enveloped her heart, and a lump formed in her throat, the implications of his presence cutting through the silence of the room.

Accustomed to such reactions after a year of delivering news of this nature, the man's voice carried a practiced, yet detached tone. "Mrs. Griffin?" he inquired, breaking the silence.

Emily answered with a barely audible, "Yes."

The man reached his hand. "Telegram for you ma'am." Her hand was shaking as she took it from him. The man turned and promptly returned to his car to resume his deliveries.

As Emily stood in the doorway, she stared at the telegram, unable to open it. Tears welled in her eyes. Sarah watched her, her own heart filled with concern. "Would you like me to open it and read it to you?" she asked, reaching out and taking the telegram from Emily's trembling hand. With a sense of foreboding, she unfolded the paper.

"Dear Mrs. Griffin," she started, her voice wavering, "I regret to inform you that your loved one, Private Timmy Griffin, has been sent to serve overseas. Due to security measures, we are unable to disclose his exact location, but please know he is serving our country with honor and dedication." Emily's hand flew to her mouth, her eyes brimming with tears. Sarah squeezed her friend's hand, offering a silent comfort as she continued to read the words aloud.

"Please do not attempt to contact Private Timmy Griffin or anyone involved in his deployment. It is imperative no sensitive information is leaked. We understand this may cause anxiety and uncertainty, but the safety and success of our mission depend on our collective adherence to operational security protocols," Sarah paused, looking up at Emily. She saw the fear and worry etched on her face and took a deep breath before continuing.

"We will inform you of any updates as they become available. Until then, please keep Private Timmy Griffin in your thoughts and prayers.

He is well-trained and well-equipped to carry out his duties with excellence. Signed, Commanding Officer William Andrews, Colonel, United States Army." Sarah finished reading, her own voice choked with emotion.

She looked at Emily, her eyes filled with sympathy and concern for her friend. Her hand trembled as she set the telegram on the table, overwhelmed with a feeling of helplessness. She knew John must be with him wherever they were, and his family would most likely be receiving the same type of message.

She couldn't help but wonder if he was safe wherever he was. The reality of the war had finally hit her, and she realized how little control she had over their fate.

Chapter 13

Sacrifices Made

Sarah sat under the old oak, the soft rustle of leaves above her providing a soothing background. In her hands, she held John's letter, her fingers tracing its edges almost obsessively. Weeks had passed since she last heard from him, the weight of worry and uncertainty gnawing at her like a persistent hunger. Now, at last, she could reconnect with him.

With trembling hands, she unfolded the crisp paper. As she began to read, the world around her faded away, her focus solely on the words before her. The emotions she had been holding back finally broke free, and tears streamed down her face, each one a small release of the pent-up worry and uncertainty.

She felt transported as she read on, immersed in his experiences. She could almost smell the musty barracks and feel the scorching sun on her skin. His letter was bittersweet: he provided an address to write to, but still, he couldn't reveal his exact location. He reassured her of his safety and his dedication to returning. Finishing, she clutched it tightly, comforted by his thoughts of her.

As the initial rush of emotions from subsided, Sarah felt a heavier burden weighing on her. *I can't keep this from John any longer.* The time had come to share her secret, even at the risk of causing him distress. *Will he ever forgive Billy? Can he avoid the path of revenge?* She hoped that with time, he would come to understand. In her next letter, she resolved to reveal the truth on Billy's departure and their encounter in the alleyway. John deserves to know. Yet, for now, she sat in contemplative silence, her thoughts wandering. *What might John be doing at this very moment?*

AS DAWN BROKE, JOHN'S anxiety from the night before confronted him directly. The calm of the previous evening was disturbed by quick skirmishes, signaling the confrontations they had anticipated were beginning. John and Timmy were drawn into these clashes, defending themselves against sporadic attacks as they pressed forward.

As they approached the town of Saint-Lô, the atmosphere was tense, with the sharp scent of gunpowder still drifting in the air. Capturing the town was more than a strategic move; it was the linchpin of their entire operation. The Germans had turned it into a fortress, with deep trenches, cunningly hidden bunkers, and other fortifications.

Sounds of gunfire and explosions filled the air, painting a picture of the intense conflict ahead. John looked skyward, watching a group of B-17s bombing the area and could hear the ominous whistle of the falling bombs followed shortly after with a thunderous boom. The American forces were trying to weaken the German defenses from the air before their ground troops moved in.

The orders for Bravo Company were clear. Captain Evans had explicitly ordered Lieutenant Jacobs to lead the 2nd Platoon in clearing the hill, emphasizing its strategic importance.

John's mind kept returning to the specifics of their mission. *Protect the right side, push through, gain the high ground.* The repetition became a mantra. They were to break through the tough German defenses around Saint-Lô and then move to take control of a crucial piece of higher ground. This would give them a vantage point to protect the infantry soldiers as they advanced.

As they commenced their advance, the sun bore down on them, casting long shadows of the tanks on the green fields of Normandy.

Birds, which would normally be chirping during this time of year, were silent, perhaps sensing the impending violence. The fields, lush and verdant from recent spring rains, seemed to stretch endlessly.

Captain Evans was not lured into complacency by the serene landscape; unease gnawed at the pit of his stomach. The light resistance along his path felt wrong. *Where are the enemy tanks and motorized infantry?*

He had been briefed to expect enemy armored support in their area yet had seen none. A metallic glint to the right caught his eye: a moving shadow, an ominous steel beast heading towards a nearby hill. The realization struck him like a thunderbolt.

"Shit, a Tiger!" Captain Evans muttered. Through his binoculars, he saw the German Tiger tank - a formidable enemy with heavy armor reflecting the sun's harsh glare - advancing towards 2nd Platoon.

He felt a surge of adrenaline as he assessed the imminent danger. Isolated on the hill, his men were vulnerable, and the rest of the company, dispersed in the field, were not in a position to offer immediate support.

"Corporal Davis! Get all units to the hill, now! 2nd Platoon's about to face a beast," he yelled into the radio.

Corporal Davis responded with swift efficiency, relaying the orders to the company. Captain Evans, eyes fixed on the Tiger, felt a torrent of thoughts rush through his mind. The tank's menacing silhouette stood in stark contrast to the tranquil Normandy fields. *This is what we trained for, but nothing can truly prepare you for the reality.* Visions of potential destruction - burning tanks, shattered lives - were vivid in his mind, all too real in this brutal theater of war. *Stay calm, stay focused*, he silently urged himself, deeply feeling the weight of command and the responsibility for his men's lives.

"Driver, hard right! We need to reach that hill - now!" Captain Evans commanded.

The tank lurched into motion, its sudden movement jostling him against the hatch's side. Grasping the hatch's edge for stability, his eyes remained intently fixed on the hill. His men were there, unaware of the oncoming assault. A heavy responsibility weighed on him. They were in grave danger, and every second counted.

As 2nd Platoon steadily ascended the hill, the Sherman tank's engine growled beneath them, its tracks gripping the uneven terrain. Inside, Sergeant O'Brien's voice was calm but alert, "Eyes sharp, boys. We're heading into unknown territory."

The crew, tense and focused, scanned the surroundings. The anticipation of conflict hung heavily in the air, but nothing specific had been sighted yet.

Reaching the crest of the hill, they were met with an unnerving sight. Before them lay an open field, and unbeknownst to them, lurking within the distant tree line was a formidable line of German Tiger tanks, their barrels ominously pointed in their direction. Accompanying the tanks, a scattering of infantry soldiers crouched in strategic positions, ready to spring into action.

On the other side of the field, Hauptmann Klaus Schmidt, commander of the lead Tiger tank, watched with calculating eyes as the American armor crested the hill. The sound of their engines amplifying the tension across the field.

Schmidt smiled with satisfaction; he'd correctly predicted the Americans approach. He'd sent two of his tanks to flank them, aiming to cut off their retreat. He turned to his gunner, "Get ready, Hans," he said, his voice cold and confident.

Hans nodded as he kept his eyes fixed on the approaching tanks. He already had the first shell loaded into the gun and took aim. As the American tanks crested the hill, Schmidt gave the order to fire.

John's gaze was drawn to the tank advancing on their left. Suddenly, a fiery blast engulfed it. The shockwave reverberated through John's tank, a stark reminder of the tank's vulnerability. "Cherry's hit!" He shouted over his mic.

"Keep pushing!" replied O'Brien. He had seen the German Tiger in front of them spot the Cherry, its gun tracking the unsuspecting tank.

O'Brien had swung his turret as fast as he could onto the Tiger, and shouted fire as the Cherry was hit. Only a moment too late, he had killed the Tiger but not before it had claimed a victim of its own.

Schmidt's first shot had hit one of the American tanks, setting it ablaze. Schmidt's moment of triumph was short-lived. But before he could fire again, an explosion rocked his Tiger. An incoming shell had struck them with lethal precision. In a blinding flash and deafening roar, both Schmidt and Hans met their instantaneous end.

"We're in trouble!" Todd shouted; his voice filled with urgency as he exchanged a quick glance with John.

From his hatch, O'Brien spotted German Tigers and infantry in the tree line, while other Tigers tried to flank and encircle them.

"Damn it!" O'Brien muttered to himself as he scanned the battlefield for any sign of an escape. "We need to break through their lines." He said, his voice steady despite the chaos around them. "Get ready to make a hard push."

"Fire at will!" He called out, his voice firm and commanding.

Their tank thundered as it fired, the shot streaking through the air with deadly precision and slamming into a German tank. The explosive impact echoed across the battlefield, drowning out all other sounds for a moment. However, the enemy tanks kept firing as well with near misses.

The battlefield transformed into a frenzied dance of death and survival. Engines roared like beasts, shells shrieked through the air, and the relentless rhythm of gunfire underscored the mayhem. Each move was a gamble between life and death, each decision a desperate bid for survival.

The battle raged on as John and his Platoon engaged fiercely with the Germans. For a moment, time seemed to slow. John's eyes locked onto a Tiger tank aiming directly at them. But before his heart could sink in dread, there was a blinding flash followed by a deafening explosion.

One by one, he watched as the German tanks in front of him were consumed by flames and smoke. The earth beneath them trembled with the force of each blast. The German infantry, overwhelmed and disoriented, began to retreat, making their way back towards Saint-Lô.

"What the hell!" John yelled.

Without warning, a thunderous roar of engines from the left overpowered the sounds of battle. John squinted against the sunlight, trying to make out the shapes of approaching tanks. It was then he saw the familiar insignia of Bravo Company.

"Calvary's arrived boys!" O'Brien's voice, filled with relief and triumph, came over the comms.

Leading the charge was Captain Evans, his tank surging forward like an avenging titan. The Germans, caught off-guard by this new threat, were thrown into chaos.

Bravo Company, with their superior numbers and the element of surprise, tore through the German lines. The Tigers, once a symbol of German might, were now burning wrecks on the field. The tables had turned dramatically. Captain Evans's timely arrival was not only a relief; it proved to be the decisive factor which shifted the tide of the battle in their favor.

As the dust settled, and they secured the top of the hill, John was overwhelmed with a mix of exhaustion and gratitude. Next to them, Timmy's tank rolled into position. They exchanged a nod of mutual respect and relief. This had been their baptism by fire, a battle they'd certainly not forget. But thanks to their skills and the timely intervention of Bravo Company, they emerged victorious.

After the Company set a perimeter and settled in for the night. John, Timmy, and Todd sat together behind John's tank, recounting the events of the battle in hushed tones. Sergeant O'Brien and Sgt. Williams were nearby, reviewing the tasks they had been given for the following day.

"Cherry took a direct hit," John said solemnly. "Didn't even see it coming."

"Damn shame. They was a good crew," Timmy added.

Sergeant O'Brien, overhearing the conversation, walked over and joined the group. "They did their duty and fought valiantly," he said solemnly. "We'll make sure they're not forgotten." His words cast a somber silence over the group.

John sat there, lost in his thoughts. *They're gone, just like that. Sacrifices made, and so many more to come. How many of us will be left to remember?* The weight of his own mortality and uncertainties of the future hung heavily on him in that quiet moment.

Later that night, as the tanks once again became their temporary refuge, John sought comfort in the pages of his journal. The scratching of his pen was a stark contrast to the distant, muffled sounds of gunfire and explosions.

In ink, he etched the bravery of his fallen comrades from the Cherry and its profound impact on the Platoon. Writing, in these moments, provided him comfort, bringing a semblance of order amidst the surrounding chaos.

Exhaustion swept over the tank crew, their soft snores filling the interior of the Sherman. John, too, felt the heavy pull of fatigue, but his mind replayed the day's events, keeping sleep at bay.

He tucked his journal into the front of his shirt, his thoughts drifting to Sarah. *Has she received my letters?* he wondered. *I hope she knows I'm safe, at least for now.*

Despite the cramped confines of the tank, his mind wandered freely, conjuring up images of Sarah beside him - her familiar scent, her soothing voice. It was a comforting thought from the harsh reality surrounding him. But as the fatigue deepened, his resistance waned. Slowly, the weight of his eyelids triumphed over his efforts to stay awake, and he drifted into a fitful sleep.

The next morning dawned gray and quiet, a stark contrast to the previous day's turmoil. John awoke to a newfound calm that hadn't been there before. Pushing thoughts of Sarah aside, he refocused. Their tanks held their position on the hill, aiding the infantry in their mission to secure Saint-Lô.

As the days passed, the sound of gunfire in the distance grew more sporadic, and they began to feel relief, knowing the town was slowly but surely being secured by the infantry.

During this time, the different tanks of his Platoon took turns on watch duty, scanning the surrounding areas for any signs of German activity. They also took the opportunity to perform routine maintenance on their tank and equipment to ensure they were in top condition for any future engagements and tried to get some much-needed rest.

In the midst of their daily activities, the monotony was abruptly interrupted by a crackling voice over the radio. "All units, this is Command. Saint-Lô has been secured. I repeat, Saint-Lô has been secured. The Germans are in full retreat," the voice of the operations officer relayed over the radio, a note of reserved relief in his tone.

Inside John's tank, the news was received in quiet acknowledgment. There was no cheers or loud celebration. They were all too weary, too acutely aware of the harsh realities they faced. With every victory, they knew, came a significant cost.

"Well, we've made it through this one, boys," Sergeant O'Brien said, his voice steady and unflappable. "Good work. We held the line."

The crew absorbed his words, with only the hum of the tank engine filling the quiet. Then, the young assistant driver, Todd, spoke up, "What's our next move, Sarge?"

"We push forward. We've secured Saint-Lô, but there are more cities to liberate, more battles to fight," O'Brien replied.

A heavy weight settled within the tank as the gravity of their situation became clear. They had survived their first major engagement, but the reality was stark - the war was far from over.

In the days following, their progress was punctuated by more skirmishes and close calls with the retreating Germans. As John's tank traversed the narrow streets of Coutances, its imposing silhouette cast shadows over quaint French homes.

They narrowly avoided disaster when a Panzerfaust rocket, launched from a hidden soldier atop a rooftop, narrowly missed their tank, exploding into the building beside them. John's crew retaliated swiftly, obliterating the source of the attack.

Meanwhile, Timmy's crew navigated the dense hedgerows of the infamous 'Bocage' country, vigilant for concealed enemy units. Near Lessay, an ambush by a concealed German anti-tank gun resulted in a close call: the shell it launched was a dud and merely bounced off their tank's armor.

Both survived these and other harrowing encounters. Their battle-worn tanks marked by close encounters showed the extent of their struggles but once in Avranches, they were hailed as heroes. The jubilant cheers of the liberated French stood in contrast to the grim realities of war they had faced. Still, the weight of their experiences remained.

In the countryside, signs of the German's rushed retreat were clear: deserted encampments, smoldering enemy vehicles. Amidst this quiet backdrop, new orders came in: their next objective was Mortain, a strategically crucial German-held town. As the impending battle neared, the brief calm was replaced with a thick air of tension.

Chapter 14

Into the Darkness

In their relentless push through German lines, John and his Platoon faced peril at every turn. Their tanks, navigating the hedgerows of the French countryside, became more than instruments of war; they were their sanctuaries.

After a particularly fierce encounter at Mortain, which left scars both on the land and their spirits, John found a moment of rest with Timmy. Under the shade of a tree, Timmy looked at John, worry evident in his eyes. "I ain't too certain I'm gonna see the end of this here war."

John looked squarely at Timmy. "Now don't you start thinkin' like that, Timmy. We're both gettin' out of this together."

Timmy shifted uncomfortably, visibly wrestling with something deep inside. "John," he began, "there's somethin' been weighin' on me. Somethin' I oughta tell you 'fore... well, jus' in case."

John leaned in closer. "What's troublin' you"

"I been carrying a secret for a long time" Timmy admitted, his voice barely more than a whisper. "It's 'bout Em's daddy. Folks 'round our parts say he drowned, but..."

John interrupted with a frown. "Timmy, everyone knows 'bout it. Poor soul drowned in the river."

Timmy looked away. "That ain't the whole truth. I was there. Went to surprise Em, and I saw... I saw somethin'. Somethin' that got me all riled up... He was tryin' to..."

Before Timmy could finish, the voices of Sergeants O'Brien and Williams echoed nearby, having wrapped up their talk with Lieutenant Jacobs. Their stern faces spoke more than words ever could: the next battle was looming large.

"We talk on this later," Timmy whispered, rising quickly. John stood too, his mind churning with all the unknowns.

"Listen up, folks," O'Brien called out, gathering everyone around. "We've got new marching orders. We're teaming up with the Canadians and Poles to shut the Falaise Pocket tight."

"The Falaise Pocket?" Todd asked, looking confused.

"It's a narrow gap between the German armies in Normandy and Brittany," Williams explained. "It's become a killing ground for Allied forces, and we've been tasked with helping to close it." John nodded grimly. He had heard others talking on the fierce fighting taking place in the area and knew this would be a difficult mission.

"We'll be joining the Canadians of the 4th Armored Division and the Poles of the 1st Armored Division," O'Brien continued. "Our objective is to link up with them in the town of Chambois and close the pocket." John and Timmy exchanged a worried glance. They knew the Germans would not give up the pocket easily.

The Platoon, now refueled and resupplied, prepared for their next move. They set out, heading southeast towards Chambois, their engines rumbling a steady rhythm against the backdrop of war-torn landscapes.

Along the route, John observed a stream of Canadian and Polish tanks and vehicles also making their way to the front lines. Evidence of the operation's scale and international effort. The sight of these allied forces, each unit playing its part in the larger strategy, instilled in John a feeling of unity and purpose amidst the chaos of war.

Sergeant Williams' voice came through, seeking guidance from their leadership. "What's the plan, sir? Where do we go from here?" he asked, directing his question to Lieutenant Jacobs.

Jacobs took a moment to consult his map and then pointed towards a hill in the distance. "We need to head towards Hill 262," he responded.

"And what's the situation on the ground?" Sergeant O'Brien asked, joining in on the conversation.

"The Canadians and Poles have been pushing hard," Jacobs replied. "But the Germans are putting up a fierce resistance. We need to join with them and provide support."

John listened and could feel the tension in the air as they continued towards Hill 262. He saw smoke rising in the distance and could hear the sounds of gunfire getting closer. It was clear they were heading into a hot zone.

It was late evening as they approached the hill, where they saw Canadian and Polish tanks taking their positions on the high ground. John could see the Canadian tanks had already taken a beating, with several of them sporting damage from enemy fire. But despite the odds, they looked determined and ready to fight. They stopped when a Canadian officer approached them.

"Welcome to the fight, lads," the Canadian officer greeted them, his tone grim yet cordial. "We've been bearing the brunt on the right flank. Your support there is much needed."

"Understood, sir," Sergeant O'Brien replied with a nod.

Lieutenant Jacobs nodded in acknowledgment. "Yes sir. We'll take our positions and prepare to support."

As the Canadian officer departed, Jacobs reached for the radio to relay the situation. "O'Brien, the Canadians have been holding the line. They need our support on the right flank. We're to take position and stand ready."

Switching on the intercom, O'Brien's voice echoed through the confined space of the tank. "Alright, men. We're supporting the Canadians on the right flank. Let's get into formation and be ready to give these Germans hell tomorrow."

After O'Brien's brief instructions, John guided the tank toward their position on the line for the night. The rest of the Platoon followed suit, each tank looming ominously as they faced the German lines across the open terrain.

Inside each tank, the crews worked in silence, each man lost in his own thoughts, the weight of the upcoming clash heavy in the confined space.

As the sun began to rise the following morning, the order to advance was given, and their platoon moved out alongside their Canadian and Polish allies.

The battle was fierce and brutal, with tanks and infantry from both sides engaged in a deadly dance of death. The Germans fought fiercely to prevent the pocket from being closed.

Their Platoon's tanks were pushed to their limits, firing relentlessly at the enemy positions while maneuvering through the treacherous terrain. Despite their best efforts, they were unable to break the German defenses, and the fighting only grew more intense.

Sergeant O'Brien was constantly scanning the battlefield for enemy targets. Unexpectedly, he spotted a German gun emplacement nestled in the trees. "Anti-tank gun! Left!" He shouted over the radio.

"On it!" Johnson replied, as he aimed the main gun at the target. The tank roared as the main gun fired, the explosion tearing through the trees and destroying the enemy position in a shower of debris and smoke.

John's tank continued rumbling forward, its guns firing relentlessly as they advanced. The ground shook beneath them as they approached more entrenched German positions. "Target destroyed!" he shouted, as he watched a plume of smoke rise from the enemy bunker.

Despite the victory, he couldn't help but think of the bravery of the infantry advancing on foot, exposed to the withering fire of the enemy. "They're taking a beating out there." He muttered to himself, his heart heavy with the weight of the ongoing battle.

The victory felt short-lived as the German artillery intensified. John's tank shook violently with each explosion, and he could hear the sharp ringing of metal against metal as the shells impacted near them. Each blast sent shudders through his frame, every instinct urging him to retreat. He tightened his grip on the controls and focused on keeping moving, dodging debris and trying to avoid the incoming fire.

"Sarge, we're taking some heavy fire!" John's voice wavered, a hint of panic seeping through the radio. His usually steady tone betrayed the rising fear within him, causing a brief moment of concern among the crew.

"Hang in there!" O'Brien replied.

Then it happened. The tank unmistakably marked with the name 'Crazy Horse' -Timmy's tank, a symbol of their shared determination-was hit by a barrage of German fire and engulfed in flames.

"Timmy!" He shouted aloud, his voice filled with fear and desperation. But there was no response, only the roar of the battle around them. He felt paralyzed for what seemed an eternity until Sergeant O'Brien's voice over the comms snapped him back to reality.

"Snap out of it! Move! Dammit, move!" O'Brien's voice quaked with a mix of fear and rage.

Paralyzed by the haunting memory, John fought with the overwhelming urge to give up. The image of Timmy's burning tank seemed to sear itself into his mind's eye.

With a shaky breath and dwindling confidence, he tried to force himself to focus on the mission ahead, knowing he had to move if he wanted to survive.

The sun's rays struggled to pierce through the thick smoke rising from the burning tanks and destroyed vehicles, casting a dim haze over the landscape, making it difficult to see ahead.

He could hear Sergeant O'Brien yelling over the comms, urging him to continue. "I can't see a damn thing!" John shouted back; his voice strained.

After advancing barely 10 yards, a deafening explosion rocked their tank. John was slammed forward into the tank's controls, his world turning momentarily black. Amidst rising smoke, coughing and gasping for air, he realized they had lost power and were hit.

Turning to his right, he called out for Todd. The sight that met him was chilling - Todd slumped forward, his lifeless eyes staring back in a haunting gaze.

With a heavy heart, knowing there was nothing he could do for Todd, John quickly made his escape. He struggled through the escape hatch, the acrid smoke searing his lungs as he crawled from under the tank's wreckage. Flames and thick black smoke billowed from the turret. It was a grim sign of the fate that had befallen his crew.

As he stumbled away from the inferno, he collapsed on the ground, his ears ringing. The battlefield around him was a maelstrom of gunfire and explosions. Despite his tattered uniform and minor injuries, he knew he had to move. Pushing himself to his feet, he took one last, heart-wrenching look at his destroyed tank.

Through the smoke, he spotted a figure near a burning Sherman. *Friend or foe?* He squinted, trying to discern details through the haze. The uniform seemed American. But just as he was about to confirm his suspicions, the figure crumpled to the ground. Ignoring the bullets whizzing past, he rushed forward.

Upon reaching the fallen man, he recognized the American uniform but not the face beneath. Severe burns had distorted it, making the man look inhuman. His hair was singed, and blood poured from a wound on his left side. The man was alive but barely.

John's heart raced as he knelt beside him, torn between the urgency to help and the chaos enveloping them. "We gotta get out of here." He said.

With a surge of adrenaline, he hoisted the wounded man over his shoulder in a fireman's carry, grateful he remembered how to do it. He scanned the surroundings and saw a tree line 30 yards away and dashed towards it.

As the dust and smoke momentarily parted, Private Müller caught sight of the American moving swiftly - one who appeared to be carrying the other. He readied his Karabiner 98k rifle, inhaling deeply as he took aim. But just as he prepared to pull the trigger, the two disappeared into the tree line. Cursing under his breath, Müller pursued.

Within the trees, John laid the wounded soldier on the ground. His heart sank as he assessed the grave injuries. Desperate, he searched his pockets for anything to stop the bleeding but found nothing. He resorted to using his hand to apply pressure, aware it might not be enough. Feeling the man's hand grow colder, John knew time was running out. The man whispered something, drawing John close.

Unbeknownst to John, hidden in the foliage Müller approached, a predatory grin on his face. Quiet as a shadow, he closed in, reveling in his prey's ignorance. He imagined the accolades awaiting him for another kill. Taking careful aim at the back of John's head, Müller steadied his breathing.

Oblivious to the imminent danger and consumed by grief, John was barely aware of the battle's closeness or the approaching threat. The wounded man's breaths grew fainter, his grip on John's hand easing in a final, silent goodbye.

As John watched the life fade from the man's eyes, he was engulfed in a deep sorrow - for this man, for himself, for all the losses wrought by war. Then, as if the forest itself was reaching out to him, seconds later, he too was enveloped in darkness, his body collapsing onto the forest floor.

Chapter 15

Shared Sorrow

The aftermath of the battle was a somber panorama. The sky was obscured by smoke, and the air held the acrid scent of burnt rubber, metal, and the ever-present reminder of death. Distant echoes of explosions and gunfire punctuated the eerie silence.

Captain Evans, along with the surviving members of his tank Platoons, navigated the devastation. The landscape was scarred with shattered trees and strewn with debris. Burnt-out husks of tanks stood as grim monuments to the confrontation, their charred remains a stark reminder of the crew's sacrifices.

Only one tank from 2nd Platoon remained untouched, a solitary survivor amidst the losses suffered by other Platoons. The stark reality of their heavy toll against the Germans was undeniable.

During the search for survivors, Evans gestured towards the tree line. "Sergeant, check over there too."

The Sergeant nodded and made his way to the tree line. After a few moments, he called out, "Sir, over here!"

Rushing over, Evans and a few men found a severely burnt, unrecognizable soldier. Dead, the grim reality was clear at first sight. Evans knelt, removed the soldier's dog tag, and placed it in his pocket, feeling the weight of another loss. *At least he made it out without burning alive, even if only making it briefly.* "Ensure he's taken to the rear for proper send-off," he ordered. "Then, prepare to move out."

"Yes, sir," the Sergeant responded, directing a Private to retrieve a body bag.

As they made their way back to their tanks, Evans addressed his First Sergeant. "Unfortunately, it's time to send the casualty report," he said. "We also need to restructure to try and make full platoons."

The First Sergeant nodded. "Yes sir. I'll get on it right away."

Walking back, Evans felt the loss acutely. Yet, amidst the sorrow, he knew they had achieved a crucial victory at the Falaise Pocket. Pride in his men's bravery mingled with his grief.

Climbing into his tank, Evans surveyed his men. Exhausted and worn, the toll of war was evident on each face. Having witnessed the horrors of war firsthand, it had taken its toll on them. He knew the road ahead would be difficult, but he also understood they had to keep pushing forward. Winning one battle didn't mean they had won the war.

He looked straight ahead and sternly ordered, "Move out!" All the tanks lurched forward once again, following the direction of the German retreat.

EACH DAY AROUND NOON, after leaving the general store, Sarah would stop by the small-town post office, a habit she had formed since John's departure. The modest red brick building welcomed visitors with its large wooden door, opening into an interior that felt like stepping back in time. Inside was a blend of the functional and the historical.

A worn counter, polished by years of use, stood under the watchful gaze of World War II propaganda posters. These posters, with their bold colors and stirring slogans, spoke of duty and resilience in the face of adversity. The air held a faint scent of dust and ink, echoing the passage of time and countless messages of hope and sorrow that had passed through this very place.

Sarah approached the counter, where Mr. William Brown, the postmaster, stood waiting. He was an older man, his kind smile and warm eyes belying his years. His silver hair was neatly combed, and he wore a crisply pressed white shirt. A fixture in the town, his presence at the post office was as constant as the building itself.

"Good afternoon, Sarah," he greeted her, his eyes twinkling behind wire-rimmed spectacles.

"Anything for me today?"

He shook his head sympathetically. "I'm sorry, nothing today." He could see the disappointment on her face. Smiling, he continued, "I know how hard it must be for you, waiting for news. But don't give up hope. I'm sure he'll write soon."

Sarah forced a smile and thanked him, feeling a familiar twinge of discouragement as she turned to leave. Despite Mr. Brown's reassuring words, the silence from John was becoming increasingly hard to bear.

Each day without news was a struggle against the growing fear that something might have happened to him. As she walked away, her steps were heavy with worry. The thought that something might have happened to John lingered persistently, casting an unwelcome shadow over her mind. She reminded herself to stay strong in her faith, clinging to the belief that he was safe.

The day was still young, the sun shining brightly overhead, prompting her to visit Emily. It had been a few days since they last saw each other. Maybe Emily has heard something from Timmy, or even John? She thought.

As she approached Emily's quaint white cottage, she noticed the colorful flower beds in full bloom and the white picket fence surrounding it. Emily was sitting on the front steps, her head in her hands.

"Hey, Em!" she hollered with a smile. But Emily didn't respond; she only sat there as if frozen, seemingly unaware of her presence. *That's strange*, she thought.

Drawing closer, she lowered her voice, concerned. "Em, Emily?" she called out softly. Then she noticed a piece of paper on the step below Emily's feet.

With a growing sense of unease, she picked it up and unfolded it, her eyes scanning the words: *The Secretary of War desires me to express his deep regret your husband, Private Timothy Griffin, has been killed in action in defense of his country...*

She didn't need to read any further; the words on the page were enough to make her slump beside Emily, overwhelmed. Tears welled up in her eyes as she placed her arm around her and pulled her close, feeling the warmth of their shared grief. She whispered, "I'm sorry. I'm so, so sorry, Em."

Emily finally broke down, and tears streamed down her cheeks as she repeatedly asked, "Why? Why him?" through her sobs.

The sound of their cries filled the air, their sorrow mingling together. Sarah sat on the porch with her for as long as it took her to let it all out, offering comfort in the shared grief.

A short time later the quiet was broken by the creak of the front door. Aunt Jean staggered in, balancing baby Jacob in one arm and a bag of groceries in the other. Her hair was disheveled, and fatigue was evident on her face.

Sarah took a deep breath and walked toward them, preparing to offer whatever support she could.

"Sarah!" she said when spotting her, looking around the living room, "Where's Emily?"

"Aunt Jean, I need to tell you something."

"What is it, dear?" She asked as she set the groceries on the counter, then moved to take a seat with Jacob cooing in her arms.

"It's Timmy," she managed to say, "He... he didn't make it." Taking a deep, steadying breath, she extended the telegram towards Jean, her hand trembling slightly.

As she read, her hand instinctively flew to her mouth, reflecting the shock that rippled through her. Her eyes brimmed with tears, the words of the telegram sinking in. "Oh, sweet heavens," she whispered.

"I put Emily to bed. She didn't take it well" Sarah hesitated before continuing. "It's more than grief though Aunt Jean. She's feeling... overwhelmed. As if she's failing Jacob. She can't seem to find the joy in motherhood she used to talk about, it's like she's stuck in this... perpetual cloud of self-doubt and despair."

Jean nodded, fighting back tears. "I'll take care of her. You've done enough today sweetheart. Thank you."

Sarah caressed Jean's hand, giving it a reassuring squeeze, "I'll check back in a day or so, make sure you're all okay."

Jean nodded, wiping away her tears. "Thank you, Sarah. I don't know what we'd do without you."

"You take care of yourself too, Aunt Jean," she said before turning toward the door.

As she stepped outside, the reality of their shared loss hung heavily in the air. Leaving Aunt Jean, baby Jacob, and Emily behind, she was painfully aware that life here would never be the same.

Halfway to her intended destination, she abruptly stopped, a chilling realization gripping her: Timmy and John were together, and she hadn't heard from John either. *What if something has happened to John too?* The thought sent a shiver down her spine. Compelled by this sudden worry, she quickly changed her direction, heading towards John's house with a growing sense of urgency.

Approaching John's home, she stopped when she saw his parents on the porch. His father held and comforted his crying mother. Out of the corner of her eye, the familiar dark green of a Ford sedan pulling down the drive caught her attention. The 'Western Union' printed in bold yellow letters on its side confirmed her worst fears.

As she watched the car pull away, a flood of emotions surged within her. The weight of what the telegram might contain pulled her towards a familiar refuge. Taking one last look at his parents, she turned, each step heavy, and made her way towards the woods.

The cool breeze kissed her tear-streaked cheeks, contrasting with the warmth of her tears. As she reached her destination, she collapsed against the rough bark of the old oak, sinking to the ground with a heavy heart. *How can I move forward alone?* The silence of the woods enveloped her, amplifying the deafening emptiness she felt inside. She bowed her head and wept, alone with her sorrow.

After what felt like hours in the woods, she eventually made her way back home. The comforting familiarity of her house greeted her, a stark contrast to the tumult she felt inside.

A FEW DAYS AFTER HER visit to Emily, whispers of the tragedy began to echo in the corners of the small town, casting a somber shadow over its tight-knit community. Sarah found herself sitting in her living room, her parent's usual criticisms regarding John replaced with softer tones.

We didn't much approve of John, which you know," her father began, looking uncomfortable. "But we also know how much he meant to you." Sarah bit her lip, trying to suppress her rising emotions.

Her mother, sensing her daughter's pain, added, "Your heart is allowed to grieve, darling. Whatever our feelings were, we're here to help you through this."

Sarah bowed her head, her gratitude mixed with doubt and sorrow. *It's not the time to question their intentions, but I do wonder,* she thought.

Days had passed since her talk with her parents and with each new sunrise, the weight of her loss grew heavier, and the need to connect with the Andersons became more pressing.

She and John had shared countless memories, many right on the very porch where she often saw his parents. Avoiding them had been her way of preserving those memories, keeping them from being overshadowed by their shared grief.

Yet, as another Saturday morning dawned, Sarah found the strength to confront what she had been avoiding. She mustered the courage and decided to approach the Andersons home.

The morning sun cast a warm glow as Sarah approached the Andersons doorstep, with the chirping of birds providing an incongruous backdrop to her mounting apprehension.

Pausing for a moment, she felt the weight of the situation pressing on her, each second stretching out before she finally took a deep breath to steady herself and knocked.

"Mr. and Mrs. Anderson?" she called out, "It's... it's Sarah. I thought I should come see you." She waited, each second stretching on, for their response. She knocked softly again, the silence on the other side amplifying her anxiety.

The door opened slowly, revealing Mrs. Anderson. Her expression softened at the sight of Sarah. "Sarah, dear, we're so glad you came by," she said, embracing Sarah in a tender, motherly hug. Gently releasing her, Mrs. Anderson gestured towards the interior. "Please, come in. We understand how hard this must be for you too."

As Sarah stepped inside, taking in the familiar surroundings of the Andersons home, Mr. Anderson nodded in acknowledgment. "We want you to know we're here for you," he said with a sincerity that touched her deeply.

As she stood there, surrounded by their love and compassion, fresh tears came to her eyes. "I'm sorry it took so long for me to come visit," Sarah said, her voice trembling with emotion. "I know this has to be hard on you as well."

Mrs. Anderson squeezed her hand, "It's alright, dear. We understand how difficult it has been for everyone. We're all simply trying to find our way through this together."

"We can't give up hope Sarah." Mr. Anderson added.

Sarah's expression clouded with confusion and uncertainty. "What do you mean by hope?" she asked. "He's gone. I saw the Western Union car," she paused, her gaze moving between Mr. and Mrs. Anderson. And you were both on the porch, in tears, after receiving the telegram." Her eyes searched theirs, desperate for clarity in the swirl of emotions and uncertain hopes.

Mr. Anderson walked over to the counter, grabbed an envelope, and handed it to Sarah. "Here, read this for yourself."

She hesitantly took the envelope, her fingers trembling slightly. Carefully, she unfolded the paper inside. Her eyes rapidly scanned the words, her mind racing to decipher their meaning amidst a whirlwind of emotions. The lines of text blurred together, the words swimming before her eyes, refusing to settle into coherent sentences.

Finally, she looked up, her eyes clouded with confusion and a hint of fear. "What does this mean?" she whispered.

Chapter 16

Into the Unknown

Müller aimed his rifle at the unsuspecting American soldier when a memory surfaced in his mind, a reminder from his Captain. He had emphasized the importance of gathering intelligence from the enemy, and capturing a prisoner alive would be invaluable. Müller hesitated for a moment, considering his options.

Knowing the risk of disobeying orders, Müller slowly and silently flipped his rifle around and struck the soldier with one swift blow to the back of the head with the butt of his weapon. The soldier crumpled to the ground.

Müller bound the man's hands and checked for a pulse. He was relieved to find the man was still breathing. He checked the other soldier as well, but he was dead. He grinned to himself, knowing his Captain would be pleased with his valuable captive.

John at last opened his eyes and felt a throbbing pain at the back of his head. As he tried to come to his senses, the distant echoes of artillery fire were a grim reminder of the ever-present battlefront.

Dust particles danced in the slivers of light penetrating the truck's canopy, and the rough fabric of his uniform clung to his damp skin. As his vision cleared, he realized he was in the back of a truck, and he was not alone. Two other soldiers were beside him, their hands bound as well.

He tried to move, but the ropes binding him were tight, digging into his wrists. The memories of the past few hours rushed back to him.

He strained to hear any sounds outside of the truck, but all he could hear was the rumble of the vehicle's engine.

As he looked around, he noticed the other soldiers were also in a state of confusion and pain. One of them groaned, his face contorted in discomfort. John watched as this soldier, almost involuntarily, licked his parched lips, a grimace indicating the metallic taste of blood.

An oppressive stillness had settled, broken only by the intermittent shuffle of restrained movement and the muffled sobs of fellow captives. He then noticed the two-armed German guards riding in the back with them, their gazes cold and expressionless.

As the truck finally came to a stop, he was jostled around as he was herded out of the truck and pushed along with the other prisoners towards a large, fenced-off area. Soldiers, both American and British, were being brought in from various areas, each looking as confused and disoriented as he was.

It was a depot, a holding area for captured soldiers. The worn wooden planks, bleached by the sun and rain, were harsh against his boots. Each step raised a small cloud of dust, making the dry air even harder to breathe. He could hear the murmurs of men speaking in German, their voices carrying the unmistakable tone of authority, but the words were indistinct.

They were lined in front of several tables for processing. A German soldier sat at each table, flanked by a guard, while a watchful Lieutenant strolled behind them.

As John approached the table, the guard swiftly cut the ropes binding his hands. The soldier at the table inquired about his details in heavily accented English, his tone cold and detached.

He provided the information, which the soldier meticulously recorded in a worn logbook and on two separate cards. He then instructed him to remove any items he might have on him.

He emptied his pockets, revealing his father's knife, the locket Sarah had given him, and his dog tag, and placed them on the table.

He then hesitantly removed his small journal from the front of his shirt and placed it next to his other items.

The table before him, scarred and worn from heavy use, felt cold to the touch. His belongings, now laid out in front of him, held the distant echoes of home. The leather of the journal's cover, the locket, and the metal knife each stirred memories he could no longer physically touch.

The German soldier tossed the knife into a box beside the table with a metallic clang, saying, "No weapons."

The loss of the knife, the precious heirloom once belonging to his father, filled him with sadness. Next, the soldier flipped through the journal. Its pages were filled with scribbled sentences he couldn't decipher. Carefully, he placed it in a small canvas bag.

He then turned his attention to John's dog tag, cross-referencing the name with the information John had provided. After a moment, he handed it back to John with a nod, indicating he could keep it for the time being.

His gaze then fell upon the locket. He paused, inspecting it closely. It was made of gleaming silver, featuring delicate engraving on its surface. This showcased its fine craftsmanship.

A nearby Lieutenant, alert for any signs of theft, noticed the soldier examining the locket closely. The Germans sought intelligence on the Americans and British, and these valuables could serve as leverage during future interrogations.

With measured steps echoing in the room, the Lieutenant approached the soldier. "Is everything in order, Private?" he asked in a stern tone, his eyes scrutinizing the soldier's actions.

The soldier, visibly startled, straightened. "Yes, Lieutenant," he replied.

Nodding, the Lieutenant watched as the soldier carefully placed the locket into a bag along with one of the cards, tying it shut with a tight knot. The bag was then added to a separate large box, joining other similar bags, all marked for further scrutiny.

The soldier then handed John the other card, instructing him to keep it on him as his new identification. The soldier then called out, "Next," his voice firm and authoritative, as the guard directed him away to a large row of benches where he would wait to board the train.

As John settled on the bench, his gaze was drawn to a line of civilian men, women, and children standing a few cars down the track. They were being loaded into boxcars.

The cries of the women and children reached his ears, and he couldn't help but wonder why they were being taken away. Then, the strange cloth bands with star-like symbols on the men's arms caught his attention, leaving him perplexed. With more guards overseeing them than soldiers, it became clear to him, this was no ordinary transport.

Before he could ponder further, he was abruptly ordered to stand and was directed into a separate dim, cramped boxcar. The air inside was heavy, a mix of fear and the pervasive scent of sweat. Struggling to adjust to the dim light, John could hear the labored breathing of fellow captives, combined with occasional whimpers of pain.

Seeking some respite, he nestled into a corner of the crowded car and sat against the cold wall. Closing his eyes, his mind drifted back to the haunting scene from the last battle when he had encountered the severely burned man. His inability to recognize him due to the extensive burns on his face added a layer of regret which was difficult to shake off.

In his mind, he replayed the dying soldier's last words: *Tell Em I love her, and I'm sorry. Promise me you look after her and Jacob.* In that heart-wrenching moment, he recognized the voice as Timmy's. He had whispered back, *I promise. I'll tell her, and take care of them,* as Timmy had drawn his last breath. The memory sent a shiver down his spine, and he could feel the sting of tears in his eyes.

In the suffocating darkness, he struggled to grapple with the weight of his guilt and the tragic loss of his best friend. *The promise I made to Timmy... it now fuels my will to survive. I have to stay alive, not only for Sarah but to honor Timmy's final wish as well.* Wrapped in these heavy thoughts, sleep eventually claimed him, though it was far from restful. His dreams were filled with images of war and whispered promises.

The jolt of the train coming to a sudden halt shook him from his troubled slumber. He blinked, trying to adjust his eyes to the dim light seeping through the cracks in the boxcar.

The heavy, wooden door creaked open, and the light from outside momentarily blinded him. A rush of cold air greeted them as they were herded out of the boxcar and onto the platform.

Anxiety surged through him as he caught his first glimpse of the sign reading, "Stalag VII-A." The compound, enormous and surrounded by barbed wire fences and ominous watchtowers, loomed before him.

As they were led into the camp, the murmurs of other prisoners, distant shouts of guards, and clang of metal gates filled the air. The odor of unwashed bodies and the stench of waste assaulted his senses, along with the acrid smell of smoke from somewhere nearby.

This is it... this is where I might end up dying, John thought, his heart sinking as he took in the sight of the overcrowded and dilapidated barracks.

A profound sense of dread and anxiety settled in his chest. *How can anyone survive in a place like this?* He braced himself mentally, realizing that survival here wouldn't be only based on physical strength; it would be about holding on to who you are inside.

John's resolve deepened as he faced the grim reality of Stalag VII-A. He knew the days ahead would require not just strength but also inner fortitude and grit.

He and the other prisoners were then directed towards a processing area. They shuffled forward in line, the exhaustion and despair apparent on their faces. When it was his turn, he was confronted by Sergeant Schultz, a German guard with a weathered face and piercing blue eyes. His field-grey tunic, adorned with silver tress signifying his rank, and his peaked cap, bearing national emblems, spoke of authority.

Schultz checked the identification card John had received earlier and inspected the canvas bag containing his possessions. His curiosity piqued when he found a locket.

Flipping it open, he saw Sarah's picture inside. With a sly grin, he looked at John and remarked, "She's quite beautiful, isn't she? I think I'll keep this for myself. It'll make for a nice view on those lonely nights," he added with sarcasm. He then punctuated his statement with a cruel chuckle.

John felt his face flush with anger, a burning hatred towards the German soldier growing inside him. He clenched his fists, fighting the urge to lash out, aware of the risks in doing so. Schultz, still smirking, pocketed the locket and casually waved John towards the next station.

As John was led away, a deep ache settled in his heart for the lost picture of the woman he loved. The knife, now the locket - all his cherished possessions were gone. His thoughts also lingered on his journal, last seen as Sergeant Schultz carelessly tossed it into the canvas bag among other confiscated items. Its fate, like that of his other belongings, was a troubling uncertainty that weighed on him.

Time in the camp dragged on, each day bleeding into the next. Several weeks later, as John stumbled out of his wooden bunk, his body ached from the discomfort and the toll of restless nights.

He joined the other prisoners outside for the daily roll call. The morning air was cold and damp, sending shivers down his spine. Rubbing his arms for warmth, his hand drifted to the back of his head, touching the scar from the wound he had received upon capture. The scar stood as a silent reminder of the price of war and the memories of his lost friend.

A German soldier called out the names on the list, and the prisoners responded in a monotone voice, confirming their presence. He tried to stay alert despite the fatigue weighing heavy on him. The constant routine of accountability, followed by long hours of manual labor, left little time for rest or reflection.

As the morning roll call ended, Sergeant Schultz and another guard approached him with news of his new duty. "Ah, there you are," Schultz sneered. "You've been assigned to kitchen duty today. We wouldn't want you to get bored, would we?"

John nodded, keeping his face neutral despite the anger boiling inside him. Schultz, noticing his lack of reaction, decided to push him further. He pulled out the stolen locket with Sarah's picture in it and began to casually toy with it.

"You know, I've grown quite fond of this little trinket," he taunted, smirking as he glanced at the picture inside. "Such a pretty face, don't you think?" John's fists clenched, his jaw set, but he said nothing.

The other guard, sensing the tension, spoke up. "Alright, Schultz. Let him get on with his duties."

Schultz glared at the other guard, annoyed that his attempts to instigate him had failed once again. But he decided not to push his luck any further and pocketed the locket. "Very well," he said. "Get to work, then. And remember, I'm always watching."

John only nodded. He knew he had to bide his time and play it smartly; he couldn't let Schultz's provocations get the better of him. He took a deep breath and followed the other soldiers into the kitchen, where they were introduced to Sergio, the head cook.

Sergio, a stocky Italian with curly brown hair, a prominent mustache, a thick accent, and a no-nonsense attitude. The whispers around the camp indicated Sergio's reputation had preceded him.

Before the war, he had been a celebrated chef in Germany. Though he didn't support the Nazis, he found himself conscripted as a cook for the German high command when the war erupted.

One of those officers, now the commandant of Stalag VII-A, General Kurt Schneider, had fond memories of Sergio's culinary skills and personally requested him for the camp. The Führer himself had granted the request, and so Sergio found himself serving the camp occupants.

However, the rations for the prisoners and guards were often meager and of poor quality, making it challenging to prepare nutritious meals. Yet, despite these challenges, Sergio persevered and did his best to provide for them. He also had the daily task of cooking a separate meal for the commandant, a responsibility he took with great seriousness.

He made it clear from the outset he would accept nothing less than their best effort. "Listen up," Sergio said in heavily accented English, his eyes fixed on John and his companions.

"You three will be working in my kitchen the next couple of weeks. I won't tolerate any nonsense or slacking off. You will do exactly as I say. Understand?" They all nodded, intimidated by the intensity of his gaze.

John could feel the warmth radiating from the stove as he and the other soldiers undertook their kitchen duties. Tasks like slicing bread, peeling potatoes, and stirring large pots had his muscles aching from the effort. Yet, despite the physical toll, these tasks offered a reprieve from the daily grind of camp life.

Sergio, their overseer, monitored them with an unyielding stern gaze. John was intent on gaining this intimidating man's respect and proving to himself his capability in this new role.

Transitioning from grueling manual labor to kitchen work was a welcome change for John. Fueled by determination and a newfound sense of purpose, he tackled his tasks with vigor.

As Sergio surveyed the new workers, disappointment clouded his demeanor. He had seen many come and go, with only a few displaying the dedication and skill required to meet his high standards.

"More speed, you! This isn't a Sunday roast at your grandma's!" he barked at one, his voice reverberating in the expansive kitchen. Spotting another clumsily handling a ladle, he added, "And you! Hold the ladle properly; you're not stirring soup!"

His gruff voice continued to resonate through the kitchen as he paced, urging the soldiers to work harder and faster. "We have hungry mouths to feed, people!"

As the day wore on, John's capability and diligence shone through. Sergio, often a tough man to please, found himself nodding in approval at John's adept techniques, seeing a spark of potential in him.

As they wrapped up for the day, Sergio observed the kitchen staff tidying up. There was a subtle shift in his usually stern demeanor-a trace of begrudging respect.

"Alright, pack it up," Sergio's voice echoed in the now-quiet kitchen. He glanced around at the well-kept space and added, almost reluctantly, "It wasn't a complete disaster."

He noticed a few surprised faces turn his way. Grunting, he crossed his arms over his chest and warned, "Don't get used to the praise. You've got a long way to go, but... I suppose you all deserve a chance...for now."

A wave of relief washed over the tired workers as they completed their cleaning. As they began to file out of the kitchen, he added, "Rest up, tomorrow's another day. Let's hope it's a better one."

Near the end of the first week, the kitchen doors burst open as a couple of German soldiers struggled with a squealing pig they had confiscated from a nearby farm. Sergio's eyes lit up at the sight of fresh meat, a luxury they hadn't had in some time.

"A pig!" Sergio shouted, rubbing his hands together in anticipation.

The German soldiers struggled to keep hold of the squealing animal but managed to grin at Sergio's reaction. "Found it at a nearby farm," one of them explained.

"A local farm, you say. And they just let you walk away with their pig?"

The soldiers exchanged a glance. "Well, they didn't exactly have a say in the matter," the other soldier admitted with a shrug.

Chuckling, Sergio shook his head. "I can only imagine."

He then turned his attention to the three soldiers. As he spoke, his tone shifted to one of firm expectation. "Listen up, today we have a special treat for dinner, and I expect your best. Who among you will prepare this pig for me?" He punctuated his question by tossing aprons toward each of them.

With a sly smile, Sergio grabbed a large knife and held it out. "Come on, now. Don't be shy. This pig needs to be prepped for tonight. Or do you need your mothers to do it for you?"

John and the others hesitated, overwhelmed by the responsibility. While accustomed to following orders, leading such a critical task was unfamiliar territory. However, they knew Sergio was not one to be trifled with, and they could see the fear in each other's eyes.

"Hurry up!" He said, his voice growing impatient. "We don't have all day. The longer you wait, the hungrier I get."

"I'll do it," John said, stepping forward.

Sergio handed him the knife, and memories of his father teaching him how to butcher a pig flooded John's mind. He recalled the scent of warm blood and the pig's haunting squeals from days gone by on the family farm.

Slipping on the apron, he took a deep breath, and with steady hands, began to work. His hands moved with practiced ease, carving into the pig. Each slice was precise. It reflected the lessons he had learned from his father. The other soldiers paled at the sight, some even retreating to the corner, sickened by the scene. But John remained unwavering, his focus sharp.

From a distance, Sergio observed John's expertise, clearly impressed. The young man's adeptness and the fluidity with which he handled the knife spoke of experience and training. Witnessing his skill, Sergio couldn't help but nod in silent approval, recognizing the young man's competence.

When he finished, Sergio smiled. "Good work. Your father taught you well."

John smiled and replied, "Thank ya sir, we used to do it some back home to make us some BBQ."

"BBQ? I've heard of it, but I've not had the chance to try it."

"It ain't hard to make, only need a few ingredients. A little vinegar, sugar, spices, and a bit of tomato paste. I can make some for you to try if ya want."

Sergio considered the proposition, then nodded, a gruff affirmation escaping his lips. "Alright, let's do it. Let's see if it is as good as you claim."

Later in the evening as the day's dinner came to an end, he dismissed the other soldiers but held out a staying hand towards John. "You, stay back and prepare the BBQ you spoke of. I'll be watching." His tone was stern but there was an undercurrent of curiosity John noticed.

Under his watchful eye, John prepared the BBQ sauce, mixing the ingredients with care as the aroma of vinegar and spices filled the air. Some of the pork Sergio had saved sizzled on the grill, its juices mixing with the sweet and tangy sauce.

When it was ready, John served a portion to Sergio, who took a cautious bite, savoring the explosion of flavors in his mouth. His eyes widened with delight as he tasted the tender and succulent meat, complemented by the delicious sauce. "This is fantastico!" he said.

Sergio weighed the pros and cons in his mind, measuring the potential of the man before him. His years of experience had taught him the immeasurable value of having skilled workers, especially in a place as vital as the kitchen. It wasn't just the food - it was about morale, efficiency, and maintaining a semblance of normalcy in an otherwise tumultuous setting.

In the somber atmosphere of the prison camp, where suspicion and mistrust clouded each interaction, this man stood out. Amidst countless faces marked by despair, defiance, and resignation, he displayed a quiet distinction.

There was a humility in him, a consideration many had lost or had never possessed in the first place. It wasn't weakness, no, but rather a deep sense of respect - respect for the craft, respect for others, and, most importantly, respect for himself.

Given the daily turmoil, Sergio realized the strategic advantage of keeping him close. The kitchen could serve as an anchor, offering routine and structure. The meticulously prepared meals were more than sustenance; they were a source of comfort for both prisoners and guards.

This man's demeanor was notably different. His poised assurance was a rarity. He straddled a fine line: confident without arrogance, resilient without rigidity. He hadn't escaped the camp's oppressive atmosphere but had managed to retain his humanity and a core sense of worth.

Sergio believed in this man's inner courage and strength, seeing his indispensable role not only in the kitchen but perhaps even beyond.

Having made his decision, Sergio looked into John's eyes, seeing the hope and anticipation there. He finally spoke. "Would you like to remain working in the kitchen?" he asked, already hoping the answer would be yes.

Grateful for the opportunity, John replied, "Yes sir, I'd sure appreciate it."

Sergio smiled. "Good. From now on, you may call me Sergio instead of 'sir.' He paused, then added with a chuckle, "And what may I call you, instead of just 'hey you'?"

Smiling back, he replied, "Names John."

The atmosphere in the kitchen felt lighter, and he experienced an unexpected peace in the prison camp.

As they were sharing the moment, Sergeant Schultz burst into the kitchen, smirking. "Well, your little cooking escapade is over," he said, directing his gaze at John. "You have road detail tomorrow, so time to leave now."

Sergio, however, was quick to respond. "No, he doesn't. He is now permanently assigned to the kitchen, and he will be reassigned to the barracks next to the kitchen in the morning."

Schultz's face turned red with anger. "You don't have the authority to make such a decision!"

Sergio didn't hesitate and shot back, "And when the Commandant complains regarding his next meal, I will be sure to tell him it was all because of you," he said, pointing directly at Schultz, "you took my best worker away against my wishes." This made Schultz even angrier, but he couldn't say anything. Fuming, he stormed out of the kitchen.

Sergio looked at John and, with a hint of humor in his voice, said, "Boy, he really doesn't like you, does he?" Both men couldn't help but laugh at the situation, savoring a small victory over the malicious Sergeant.

As the two men continued their work in the dimly lit kitchen, they couldn't help but wonder about the days ahead in this place where each sunrise brought new challenges and uncertainties.

Little did they know the world beyond their prison camp held countless other stories, including one unfolding in England, where Billy faced his own trials and tribulations, a world apart but inexorably linked by the threads of war.

Chapter 17

The Final Mission

In England, Billy was jolted awake by the sharp voice of a fellow crewman announcing the arrival of the mail. The unexpected intrusion pulled him out of a vivid dream where he was reliving his most recent fiery descent into the English Channel. While he and most of the crew had escaped, they had tragically lost their pilot, Captain Joel Morgan, and co-pilot Lieutenant Don Parker.

"Mail's here, boys!" the crewman shouted, a stack of letters clutched in his hand.

Billy acknowledged the announcement with a half-hearted lift of his cap, muttered a thank you, then tugged the cap back over his eyes. He didn't bother to rise. After all, since leaving home, he hadn't received a single word from his parents or his few friends.

You'll be safer in the air, his father had confidently asserted in one of their last conversations. Billy's thoughts lingered on those words, a bitter chuckle escaping him. *Safer in the air?* The irony felt almost laughable, a cruel joke.

He mulled over his father's ignorance of the harsh realities of war, how he had bartered his son's safety for monetary gain. "Asshole," Billy muttered under his breath, his disdain evident even in the solitude of his thoughts.

He knew the life expectancy of a bomber crew was dismally low, with around 50 percent not surviving their tour of duty, and they had to complete a daunting number of missions before they could even consider returning home. The magic number was 35, and he was only at 19, so his odds didn't look good. He had already gone down twice.

The first time had been shortly after he had first arrived in England in support of D-Day. During the mission, their B-17 had been hit by an enemy flak gun. The plane shuddered and lurched, adrenaline surging through him as he braced for impact. He had heard the sound of metal tearing and ripping, and he had felt the heat of flames on his face. Miraculously, the B-17 had stayed airborne, but the damage had been severe. He and his crewmates had recognized they wouldn't make it back to England.

As they flew over the English Channel, the weight of uncertainty pressed on him. Thoughts of Sarah and his crew danced in his mind. Would any of them make it out alive? Amidst the chaos, an unexpected calm enveloped him, bringing peace and acceptance. He had done everything humanly possible; now, his fate dangled on the unpredictable threads of destiny.

Miraculously, they crash-landed on an English beach. Emerging from the wreckage, he was shaken, yet against all odds, alive.

He finally mustered the energy to rise from his bunk, as the time for the mission briefing drew nearer. He could feel the weight of the previous weeks on his shoulders, but he knew he had to keep going. As he slipped on his flight jacket, he noticed the grime and wear on it, a stark reminder of the realities of war.

He stepped out of his tent and into the chilly morning air, making his way to the mess tent. The camp was alive with activity as fellow airmen prepared for another day in the fight against the enemy. The smell of oil and exhaust hung heavy in the air, mixed with the aroma of breakfast cooking nearby.

As he entered the mess tent, he grabbed a tin mug and filled it with steaming black coffee, which was more a necessity than a luxury in times like these. The bitter taste jolted him awake as he took his first sip, and his thoughts turned to the life he'd left behind.

His mind wandered to Sarah. Despite his reckless actions toward her, he remained drawn to her. He acknowledged he might have been careless, but he had yet to be shackled by guilt. He was still the same confident man, but now, he found himself pondering the implications of his past actions more seriously. If given a chance, he would not take her for granted as much as he had.

Then there was his father's money. Before the war, he had reveled in its power and significance. However, facing death had given him a glimpse of life's fleeting nature. While those riches now held a slightly diminished allure, they were still essential to him. He recognized the significance of intangible things, such as the sheer preciousness of life itself.

Yet, his pride remained intact, untouched by the horrors of war. He knew upon his return home, he would pursue Sarah with undiminished intensity, but with a touch of newfound appreciation.

Finishing his coffee, he took a deep breath and readied himself for the mission briefing. He knew each mission brought him closer to going home, fueling his determination to keep pushing forward. He walked toward the briefing tent, ready to face whatever challenge may lie ahead.

During the briefing, the air hung heavy with tension and anticipation more than usual. The intelligence officer, a somber man with a stern expression, addressed the bomber crews as they sat in the crowded, dimly lit room.

"Gentlemen," the officer began, his tone serious, "you've been assigned a difficult but critical mission. Your target," he said, gesturing towards a marked spot on the large map at the front of the room, "is a major munitions factory in Schweinfurt, Germany. This facility is a key producer of the Germans ammunition and artillery rounds."

The crews exchanged uneasy glances, well aware of Schweinfurt's reputation for heavily fortified airspace. They knew anti-aircraft guns and German fighter planes would be formidable obstacles. The officer continued, "You'll be flying in a large formation of B-17s, supported by fighters. Your mission: deliver your payload and return safely. But make no mistake, this will likely be the most dangerous mission you've undertaken."

Afterward the men studied detailed maps of the target area, and they couldn't help but sense the gravity of the task ahead. They knew their success could deal a significant blow to the German war machine, but the cost could be high. The room buzzed with conversation as the crew members quietly discussed their strategy.

Captain Mitchell, a seasoned veteran shaped by countless missions, stood before his crew. His gaze moved deliberately across each member, ensuring a moment of personal connection. "Listen up, guys," his voice steady and firm. "We've faced tough odds before and we're still standing. This mission is no different. Stay sharp, have each other's backs. We're going to get through this and return in one piece, just like we always do." His words, filled with a blend of determination and reassurance, lingered with the crew as they dispersed, each member internalizing the captain's message as they made their final preparations.

The moment of preparation gave way to action. As the crew boarded their B-17, the ground crew hurriedly loaded the bombs onto the aircraft. The engines roared to life, and the heavy bomber began to taxi down the runway, the vibrations reverberating through the fuselage. Billy took his position as the waist gunner. Checking his machine gun and ammunition belts, it felt like the hundredth time. The plane gained speed and lifted into the air. The B-17 formation assembled in the skies over England, their silver bodies glistening in the morning sun. The radio chatter filled the airwaves as the pilots and crewmen communicated with one another, ensuring they maintained a tight formation.

As they crossed the English Channel, the mood in the aircraft grew tense. The first signs of enemy resistance appeared as they neared the French coast. German fighters darted in and out of the bomber formation, their guns blazing. The gunners aboard the B-17s fought back valiantly, downing several enemy fighters in the process.

Meanwhile, the American fighter planes escorting the bombers sprang into action, engaging the Germans in intense dogfights. Their skill and determination were evident amidst the chaos of the aerial battle.

The combined efforts of the bomber gunners and the fighter pilots managed to turn the tide. Despite their best efforts, one B-17 was shot down and another was severely damaged, forcing it to return to England. After a fierce struggle, the remaining Germans decided to retreat, allowing the rest of the B-17 formation to continue their mission, albeit with heightened vigilance and a feeling of loss for their fallen comrades.

As the formation approached the target area near Schweinfurt, the anti-aircraft guns on the ground opened fire. The air grew thick with flak, black puffs of smoke from enemy anti-aircraft fire surrounding them. The B-17s shuddered and rattled as they struggled to maintain altitude.

"Bandit six o'clock high!" The tail gunner's voice unexpectedly echoed over the intercom.

Billy and his crewmates immediately scanned the sky behind them, knowing 'six o'clock' signaled a potential threat directly at their rear. A lump formed in Billy's throat as he spotted the menacing silhouette of a Messerschmitt Bf 109 swooping into view. The German fighter, resembling a predatory bird made of steel and fire, was closing in fast. Spotting the enemy plane diving towards them, Billy yelled out, "There it is!" He frantically attempted to swing his gun into position, but the agile fighter quickly moved out of his line of fire.

"Brace yourselves!" Captain Mitchell's voice cut through the tension, laden with the gravity of the moment. He banked the B-17 quickly in a desperate evasive maneuver, but the heavy bomber lacked the agility of the nimble German fighter. The Messerschmitt, relentless in its pursuit, surged forward, its engine snarling menacingly. A devastating barrage of bullets rained into Billy's B-17, each strike resonating inside the cabin like a death toll.

Flames erupted, rapidly engulfing the wings and fuselage in a voracious inferno. The roar of the engines now drowned out by the anguished screams of his crewmates. Panic and chaos reigned as they grappled with the unfolding catastrophe, each man trapped in his own struggle for survival.

Captain Mitchell's urgent command cut through the chaos, "Everyone, out... now! Bail out! Bail out!" Adrenaline pumping, Billy unhitched his harness and seized his parachute. He strapped it on meticulously. The aircraft shuddered and groaned alarmingly beneath him, a harrowing reminder of their dire situation.

He stumbled towards the exit, the roar of the engines and the screech of rending metal filling his ears. All around him, crew members scrambled in a frenzied search for their parachutes, their movements marked with stark panic. With each step, the reality of jumping into the open sky became more evident, a terrifying yet necessary leap for survival.

He caught a glimpse of the tail gunner, slumped forward motionless - a grim indication that not everyone would make it out. The urgency to act intensified within him. Memories of his earlier crash into the English Channel flooded his mind-the terrifying plunge, the bone-chilling water, the loss. Determined, he had survived once and would fight to survive again. Taking a deep breath, he activated the door's release mechanism and leapt into the cold void.

As he plummeted, the wind and engine noise engulfed him. Mid-fall, he yanked the ripcord; his parachute unfurled, slowing his descent. His eyes scanned the sky for fellow crew members, but despair hit as he saw no other parachutes. Alone, he drifted towards the unknown terrain below. Watching his B-17 crash into the ground and burst into flames, the harsh reality settled in-he was the lone survivor.

Bracing for impact, he descended into a dense forest. The landscape rushed up to meet him, a whirl of lush green and earthy brown. Tree limbs snagged his parachute, jerking him to a stop. The force broke his strap, plunging him through the dense canopy. Leaves and twigs whipped at his face and limbs, while the symphony of cracking branches filled his ears.

A jagged branch pierced his side its wicked edge slicing through fabric and flesh. Gritting his teeth against the agony, he wrestled to free himself. When the branch finally snapped, his free fall resumed. Colliding with the ground, gasping and contorted in pain, he experienced a chilling realization: he was isolated, wounded and in enemy territory.

Before he could get his bearings, the sound of approaching footsteps caught his attention. Drawn by the sight of his parachute, a German patrol had located him. Enemy soldiers encircled him, rifles at the ready. There was no escape.

THE CAMP WAS AWAKENING under the soft glow of the rising sun, its rays doing little to alleviate the pervasive tension. Soldiers and prisoners moved with deliberate intent, their wary glances betraying underlying anxieties. Amidst this environment, a friendship had formed between John and Sergio. Over the past month, among the barbed wire and guarded towers, the two men had found comfort in shared stories.

One day, while peeling potatoes in the quiet of the kitchen, John listened as Sergio casually mentioned his time studying cooking in England.

"So, you can cook, huh?" John said with a smile. "I had no idea."

Sergio grinned. "Oh yeah, I've been told I'm quite the chef." He chuckled, "It's also forever been my dream to go to America and open a restaurant in New York City, which I will do when this war is finished."

"Well, if I ever get out of this place, I'll be your first customer when ya open. And who knows? Maybe even work for ya as a waiter."

"I believe you might have to brush up on your customer service skills first." They both chuckled at the joke, stepping out of the kitchen to unload the newly arrived supply truck.

Under the relentless scorching sun, they unloaded crates of tomatoes, streams of sweat tracing their foreheads. John, muscles straining, hoisted a particularly heavy crate onto his shoulder. In the midst of his labor, his attention was drawn to a group of civilians being herded into the camp under close guard. Among them, he noticed several men wearing armbands identical to those he'd seen at the last depot before his arrival here. He squinted against the glaring sun, trying to discern more details. Mixed within the group were soldiers, some in a dire state, being carried on stretchers towards the infirmary. Others, though weary and battered, walked unaided, escorted by guards for processing.

"Hey, Sergio, look over there, why are they bringing in civilians?" he said, gesturing towards the group of civilians and soldiers.

Sergio glanced over, then looked away. "Don't ask questions. It's better that way," he warned in a hushed tone.

But John couldn't look away. He watched as the civilians were led in a different direction than the soldiers, towards the other end of the camp. There, two tall red brick smokestacks loomed in the distance, continuously emitting smoke into the air, seemingly without end.

As they continued their labor, the sound of whistling cut through the air, signaling the approach of Sergeant Schultz. John and Sergio briefly paused, exchanging wary glances. Schultz strolled past them, his demeanor carefree yet subtly menacing, eliciting tension from both men familiar with his unpredictable nature.

Abruptly, Schultz halted. With a casual flick of his wrist, he pulled a locket from his pocket, holding it up in the sunlight. It glinted briefly before he kissed its surface. This seemingly trivial action was charged with unspoken malice. John's grip on the crate handle tightened, his knuckles whitening, as he involuntarily stepped forward, a tide of anger rising within him. Sensing John's agitation, Sergio placed a reassuring hand on his arm, gently holding him back.

Sergio looked at the locket in confusion, not grasping its significance. But as John's face flushed with anger, it became clear the locket held deep meaning for him. Schultz, with a sly grin, flipped them the middle finger before laughing and walking away, his laughter a cruel reminder of the power he wielded over John.

"What's going on, John? Why did that make you so angry?" Sergio asked, concern etched in his voice as he tried to understand the reason behind John's intense reaction.

John let out a long breath and said, "That there locket's got a piece of my heart in it. Belonged to my girl, Sarah. She gave it to me before I headed off, with her picture tucked inside. That no-good Schultz snatched it when I first got here, talkin' dirty 'bout her and all."

"Bastard! Using it against you is cruel."

"Each time I see the locket in his hands, it's like he's snatchin' away a piece of my heart. The thought gnaws at me, reckonin' I might not get to hold Sarah or hear her sweet voice again."

Sergio placed a hand on his shoulder. "Don't you give up. You'll make it out of here, and you'll see her again. I truly believe it."

As they returned to their work, John smiled and said, "I sure hope you're right."

Their conversation was abruptly interrupted by distant explosions, jolting them both. Plumes of smoke rose into the air, visible even from their position. The German guards nearby became visibly agitated, casting nervous glances towards the horizon and murmuring among themselves.

John squinted at the sky, his gaze drawn to what appeared to be tiny specks far away. He nudged Sergio and pointed upward. "Do you see those?" he asked, his voice tinged with a mix of curiosity and concern. "Are those..."

Sergio strained his eyes, trying to make out the distant shapes. "I'm not sure," he replied, a note of uncertainty in his voice. "It could be, but it's hard to tell from here. Your eyes might be playing tricks on you."

The distant explosions weren't a new occurrence; they had been growing louder and closer over the past few days. The unease among the Germans was becoming unmistakable. It was as if the war was inching closer, step by step. Something was approaching, and it seemed only a matter of time before it reached them.

Sergio turned back to John. "We need to hurry with this truck. Dinner is approaching, and you must deliver the food to the infirmary before we serve the others. We can talk more on this later, but for now, we have work to do."

John nodded, his mind still occupied with the sights and sounds of the distant conflict. Together, they quickly finished unloading the truck, their movements swift and efficient under the looming shadow of the unknown.

Meanwhile, as Billy was ushered into the camp infirmary, the doctor's voice echoed through the space-terse and commanding-ordering, "Clear the beds in the corner, we've got fresh ones coming in!" He didn't lift his head from the clipboard he was reviewing as the new prisoners were brought in.

One of the nurses, a stern woman with a rigid posture, rushed to comply. "Move it, we haven't got all day," she directed, her voice void of any warmth or sympathy.

Another nurse followed suit, barking at a pair of inmates resting on makeshift beds. "You two, out! Make room for the new arrivals."

The atmosphere was charged with urgency and indifference, a stark contrast to the vulnerability of the ailing prisoners. There were no comforting words, no soothing gestures; it was clear in the infirmary, sympathy and kindness were in short supply.

Lying on a stretcher, Billy's body throbbed with pain from the wound in his side. The air hung heavy with the stench of disinfectant and the moans of other prisoners.

As the doctor examined his wound, he muttered to himself in German, seemingly indifferent to whether Billy understood him or not. "Gut, gut," he said while probing the wound with his fingers, causing him to squirm in agony.

"It hurts," he moaned.

The doctor looked at him with disdain. "You assume I care about your pain? You are lucky we are even treating you. We have more important tasks to do, than waste our time on the likes of you."

His teeth ground together, a vain attempt to contain his agony, as the doctor continued his indifferent examination. The nurses carried on with their duties, cleaning and sterilizing instruments, all while casting timid glances and sharing light jokes with the German guards who occasionally strolled in. Their interactions often had a flirtatious edge.

Despite the pain and discomfort, he couldn't help but feel despair. *How could I ever hope to escape this place, with such callous and indifferent people in charge of my care?* As he lay there, he knew he was completely at their mercy, and the thought made him shudder.

Later in the day, John was heading to the infirmary with food for the patients and staff. Before leaving, he paused to chat with a returning work detail. Their faces were smudged with soot and their bodies sagged from fatigue.

"Rough day, eh?" he asked, noticing their exhaustion.

"You can say that," one of the workers responded. "We were sent to the other side of the camp to shovel out ashes from one of those damned furnaces."

John's eyes widened, "The civilians I saw earlier, the... 'Juden' as the Germans call them, they're forced to do the same?"

"Worse. Those poor souls are treated like... like they're not even human."

"But why? What have they done?" A profound silence followed John's question.

The men exchanged weary glances, their expressions a mixture of sorrow and confusion. "No one knows, mate," another worker finally said. "They all keep saying something about the final solution."

"And the numbers I've heard about?" John asked, referring to the peculiar tattoos he had heard mentioned around camp.

The workers shrugged. "Only another way to strip 'em of their identities, I guess," one offered. Listening to their accounts, John grappled with the unfathomable cruelty these innocent people were forced to endure.

While stationed in England preparing for the impending D-Day invasion, he and other soldiers had heard rumors of the terrible conditions faced by the Jews in Nazi-controlled territories. These were largely passed around in hushed whispers, unconfirmed reports which were hard to believe due to their horrific nature.

Details had emerged of men, women, and children forced into ghettos and work camps, stuffed into overcrowded sheds with scant food or basic necessities. Yet, these rumors were often met with skepticism and disbelief. The sheer scale of the brutality seemed so vast and unprecedented, and many found it hard to accept such systematic atrocities were even possible. Some even dismissed these stories as mere war propaganda.

While these thoughts lingered in his mind, John's immediate duties brought him back to the present moment. Carrying the food into the infirmary, he tried to focus on the task at hand. As he dropped off the food, his gaze drifted towards the patients lying on the cots.

One man in particular caught his eye, but he couldn't make out the face in the dimly lit tent. Something about him seemed familiar, though. He hesitated and weighed the idea of moving closer. As he took a step forward, a stern-looking nurse materialized in front of him.

"Place the food over there, quickly!" she instructed, pointing to a nearby table cluttered with medical equipment.

A wave of disappointment swept over John. He had hoped to at least exchange a few words with some of the new prisoners, but it seemed it wasn't going to happen. Silently, he complied with the nurse's instructions, setting the food on the indicated spot.

As he made his way out, John glanced back once more. *Is there something I'm missing? Why does that man seem so familiar?* A peculiar sensation lingered in the back of his mind, gnawing at him. Shaking his head, he tried to dispel the unsettling feeling and returned to his duties. *Something's not right*, he thought, an uneasy feeling persisting as he walked away.

Chapter 18

Whispers from the Past

Back in Georgia, Aunt Jean buttoned her cardigan, casting a worried glance towards the back room before stepping out. With the infant in tow, she made her way to her old Ford, setting off towards town for errands. *I hope Emily finds the strength to pull through*, she thought.

Meanwhile, Emily stepped into her dimly lit bedroom, the floorboards creaking beneath her weight, betraying the history of the old family house. In her hands, she held a small package, wrapped in brown paper which rustled as she placed it on the antique wooden nightstand. The package, with its neat handwriting bearing Sarah's name, looked misplaced amidst the room's stillness.

She settled on the edge of the bed, fingers absentmindedly tracing the embroidered patterns on the sheets. Each thread wove a tale of days gone by, notably the ones she spent with Timmy. Those memories now served as bittersweet reminders of joy once had. The telegram, now tucked away in a drawer, had changed everything. Timmy's absence felt like a void which consumed her daily.

Timmy had entered her life when they were both only ten, bringing with him a warmth and happiness which pulled her out from the murky depths of her troubled childhood. His presence had been a comforting constant, standing by her side even at her alcoholic father's funeral.

Later, as her husband, he illuminated her world with genuine love, a feeling she had not known before him. But now, her world was a cold void without him, a labyrinth of sorrow she struggled to navigate. The weight of raising their child alone, a task which felt insurmountable amidst the overwhelming darkness of her mind, loomed over her. She opened the top drawer of the nightstand and stared longingly at her escape, her soul grappling with despair and solitude.

The pain was made more acute by the memory of her brother, lost in the Pearl Harbor attack. His absence was a wound which had begun to heal, until the news of Timmy's demise arrived.

Now, every reminder of their lives, of their love, was like a knife twisting into the ever-fresh wound, making the solace she sought in the drawer seem ever more tempting.

As Sarah wandered through the town, she momentarily halted to exchange pleasantries with familiar faces. Aware of Emily's plight, they offered her sorrowful nods or shared a few words of encouragement before she proceeded on her path. Cradled in her arms was a basket laden with freshly harvested fruits and an assortment of essentials, commodities she knew Emily sorely required but had probably neglected in her grief.

The memory of that somber day crept into her thoughts unbidden, the day the dreaded telegram arrived at John's parents' home. She could almost feel again the chilling touch of the telegram paper when John's father had handed it to her. The words had seemed to blur before her eyes, each letter a hammer blow to her heart: *The Secretary of War desires me to express his deep regret that your son John has been reported missing in action.*

Her voice had come out as a shaky whisper when she asked, "What does it mean?" Her gaze was a plea for understanding, a desperate search for hope.

John's father met her gaze with an expression lined with deep understanding. "It means there's hope, Sarah," he had replied, his voice a pillar of calm amid the tempest of uncertainty. "John could still be alive. Until we receive definitive confirmation, we cling to the shimmering sliver of hope."

She had nodded, tears etching tracks down her cheeks, her fingers clenched around the fragile thread of optimism which had been offered to her. She had held onto hope each day since, her prayers before bed filled with fervent wishes for John's safety, and his watch gripped in her hand each night.

As she approached the house, a strange, muffled sound caught her attention, its source and direction unclear. Confused, she knocked on the door, only to be greeted by silence. *She might be napping.* Knocking a bit harder, she called out Emily's name. Receiving no response, she tentatively tried the door handle, surprised to find it turned easily. Pushing the door open, she called her name again, this time more softly, as she stepped inside and placed the basket on the dining room table.

Taking a quick look around, she didn't notice anything unusual. *Maybe she stepped out for a bit.* It was then she noticed a sliver of light peeking from the partially open door of the back bedroom. With growing concern, she made her way towards the room. As she pushed the door open further, the unexpected sight before her made her heart shatter.

Emily was slumped to her side, blood oozing from her head. In her lifeless hand, the gun still grasped. Sarah screamed, tears cascading down her cheeks as she stumbled back and raced to the kitchen. Fumbling with the phone, she rapidly dialed the operator, her voice shaking as she struggled to utter the words "police" and "ambulance."

Days had passed, and now Sarah, dressed in black, was a picture of grief. She stared at her reflection in the vanity mirror, her long black dress swaying as she shifted her weight. Her makeup sat untouched as she thought, *What's the use? I'm sure my mascara will run and make me even more of a mess than I already am.*

A light knock on the frame of the open door startled her. "It's about time to leave dear," her mother whispered, her own black attire a mirror reflection of Sarah's solemn mood, before beginning to turn away.

"Mother," Sarah called out.

Her mother paused and turned back. "Yes, my dear?"

Sarah looked back at her reflection, her eyes reddening, fresh tears threatening to spill. "I feel it's my fault."

Her mother approached, placing a reassuring hand on her shoulder. "Why would you think such a thing?"

"It's just... if only I hadn't stopped to chat with Mrs. Thompson in town... maybe I could've been there in time. Maybe I could've noticed the signs earlier, or the deep pain Emily was going through after the baby and with Timmy gone."

"Oh, sweetheart. Emily had been battling more than only the loss of Timmy. Often, we don't see the signs of such deep struggles until it's too late. Even if you had been there, if she was determined... she might've still..." her voice trailed off, the weight of the words too much to bear.

Sarah's eyes met her mother's, searching for some comfort. "But I should have been there, knowing how much she was struggling."

"Life is filled with countless 'should haves' and 'could haves,' Sarah. You couldn't have known how deep her pain was. She hid it well, like many do. The important thing now is to remember her for who she was and the love she brought into your life." Sarah remained silent, knowing deep within, her mother was right. But it didn't ease the pain in her heart.

Recognizing her pain, her mother gave her a comforting squeeze, whispering, "Come now, it's time to go." She helped Sarah to her feet, and together they left the bedroom, side by side.

The air outside was heavy, reflecting the weight in Sarah's heart. As they approached the cemetery, she was surprised by the number of flowers and the turnout at the funeral. Her parents, as well as Timmy's and John's, were present as well.

Although she still felt like crying, she had already shed all the tears she could. She stood there, staring at the headstone reading 'Emily Griffin,' which lay beside the one marked 'Timmy Griffin.' For a brief moment, she found comfort in the thought the two were now together forever. Oh, how she wished John was there with her now.

Her thoughts were interrupted by the soft sound of her name being called from behind. She turned to see Aunt Jean. Sarah hugged her, dry tears trying to flow.

"Aw, my dear, it will all be okay. I know it may take some time, but we'll get through this." She reassured her.

Sarah offered a slight smile before asking, "Where's the little guy?"

"He's with Ms. Bixby. I wasn't sure how he'd cope out here, and you know she wanted to come, but she didn't believe her legs could hold up standing for so long. So, she offered to watch him until I got back."

"Give him a kiss for me," Sarah said.

"I will."

"It was good seeing you again. I guess it's time to head home." Sarah said.

"It was good seeing you too. Don't be a stranger,"

Sarah turned to leave, but Aunt Jean stopped her. "Oh, wait. I almost forgot." She reached into her purse, pulled out a paper-wrapped package, and handed it to Sarah.

"What is it?"

"I believe Emily wanted you to have this, as it's addressed to you."

Sarah stared at the package, wondering what it could possibly be. "Thank you." she said, then turned and walked toward her parents' car, which was parked nearby, waiting for her. The mysterious package occupied a corner of her mind, urging her to unwrap it.

As the night deepened, Sarah lay on her couch, warmed by the fireplace, and finally succumbed to her curiosity. She stood and reached for the package on the coffee table. She paused, then tore off the brown paper and was met with the word, 'Diary.'

As she started to open it, her mother entered the living room. "Sarah, you're still up?"

"Yes," she replied, "I couldn't sleep, so I thought I might read for a few," knowing her mother saw the book in her hands but was far enough away as to not make out the title on the cover.

"Okay, well try and get some rest. Good night," she said, exiting the room.

Once Sarah was sure she was gone, she sat and opened the book, smiling as she read one of the early entries:

Me, Sarah, John, and Timmy spent the day at the creek trying to catch frogs. We didn't get any, but it sure was fun!

But her smile faded as she flipped through some of the later entries:
Daddy's drunk again and slapped me...
He slept in my bed again last night...
I told him no, but he didn't stop...
As she thumbed through the pages, the revelations contained within them stunned her. *Why didn't she ever mention this?* she wondered, feeling unease forming in the pit of her stomach. The date April 19 caught her attention. This was the day Emily's father had drowned. Her heart raced and her fingers trembled with excitement. Piqued with curiosity, she began to read the accompanying entry. After absorbing the contents, she closed the book hastily.

Her eyes widened as she rose from her seat. *How could she and Timmy have kept this from me?* she pondered, her thoughts tinged with bewilderment, startled by the secret her friends had silently carried all these years.

Approaching the fireplace, the temptation to throw the book into the flames grew. *This secret... it could destroy their memory.* The thought of her deceased friends being judged as monsters was unbearable.

Memories of shared laughter, dreams, and whispered secrets came flooding back. *They were more than just this one secret*, she realized. *Their lives, their love... I can't let this overshadow all the good.* Acting quickly, she retreated to her room, seeking a secure place to hide the book and its burdensome secret, a place where it would not tarnish the cherished memories of her friends.

DAYS HAD PASSED SINCE John's visit to the infirmary, but the memory remained vivid. The dimly lit room, the quiet sounds of patients stirring, and above all, the haunting appearance of the man with his disturbing features - his image was etched deeply into John's mind.

Determined to learn more about him, John sought out Sergio. "Sergio could ya find out more 'bout a fellow in the infirmary?" he asked.

Sergio looked at him skeptically. "Why? What do you want to know?"

"His name, where he's from, anything. I jus' can't shake the feeling we've met before."

"Alright, I'll see what I can do," and he soon headed towards the infirmary.

Once there, he approached the nurse on duty. "Hello," he began, aiming to keep his tone casual and unobtrusive. "I'm here to screen the newcomers for any potential food allergies. Need to ensure we don't run into any unexpected issues during meals."

The nurse nodded, giving him a once-over before allowing him access. "Okay, as long as you don't interfere with our work," she cautioned.

"Of course, I'll be as swift and discreet as possible," he reassured her.

Turning his attention to the man John had described, he skillfully weaved his questions into a casual conversation, successfully keeping any suspicions at bay. Once he gathered the information he needed, he exited the room, offering the nurse a nod as he left.

Upon his return, Sergio shared the information he had gathered. "He was part of a bomber crew."

"It's probably nothin' then. I don't believe I know anybody in the air corps."

Sergio added, "He's also allergic to nuts." But this piece of information held no significance for John. "You're from Georgia, right?"

"Yeah, so?"

"He lives in Georgia, too."

John froze, his mind racing. *I have to find out more 'bout this man. Why does he seem so familiar? Have we crossed paths before?* Unable to dismiss his curiosity he asked, "Would it be possible for me to go alone and chat with him?"

Sergio looked at him skeptically. "You still want to talk to him?"

"I know. There's jus' something 'bout it all."

Sergio nodded. "Alright, I'll see what I can do."

The next morning, John found himself outside the infirmary, his heart racing with anticipation. He entered and asked one of the nurses if he could speak to the injured man. The nurse looked at him with disdain. "Ah, you again. Sergio told me you'd be coming today for a follow-up?" she asked, her tone cold and uncaring.

"Shouldn't take long," John replied.

"By all means," she said, rolling her eyes. "Maybe it will quiet him down. His moaning has been getting on my nerves. Besides, he'll be dead soon anyway with his infection."

He thanked her and made his way towards the bed where he had last seen him. "Hey there." he said as he approached the bed. The man rolled his head in the direction of where he stood, and their eyes locked. They both seemed bewildered and confused, as if they were struggling to remember where they had seen each other before.

For a moment, there was a palpable tension in the air as the two men stared at each other, searching for some clue to unlock the mystery of their connection. Then, as if struck by lightning, it hit them both with unexpected and overwhelming force. The memories flooded back, filling their minds with images and emotions from time past.

John turned and quickly exited the infirmary. He walked hastily back towards the kitchen, questions racing through his mind. *How was it even possible? Of all the places in the world!* But there was no denying it. He recognized the face and the crooked nose which never healed right. It was Billy, without a doubt.

Chapter 19

Veiled Vendettas

Walking back, lost in his memories, John's mind wandered to their last encounter. Emotions surged in him - pure hatred for the man and all the turmoil he had stirred up in the past. The memories of their tumultuous history weighed heavily on his mind, threatening to consume him.

He tried to shake off his thoughts and focus as he entered the kitchen. Sergio noticed his return and the speed of his visit to the infirmary. "Short visit," he remarked, looking at him with concern.

He paused, his mind still reeling from the encounter. "Yeah, I didn't stay long," he replied, trying to keep his voice steady. "I don't want to talk 'bout it." Sergio continued his work, while John found it difficult to focus.

Finally, John let out a deep breath. "I do know him. Names Billy Harrington, we lived in the same town."

Sergio stopped what he was doing and turned towards him. "Great! Then what's the problem?"

John hesitated for a moment. "There's a past 'tween us, and it ain't good."

"Oh, is that so."

John recounted the events leading to the dance they'd attended before the war, detailing Billy's behaviors towards him and Sarah. He spoke of Timmy breaking Billy's nose and how he seemed to stalk Sarah. But John held back on one significant detail: the last letter he received from Sarah was before he was captured. It detailed the unspeakable thing Billy did to her in the alleyway. Thinking about it set a fire to his anger.

"Timmy? Who's Timmy? I've not heard you mention him before."

John's face darkened, "Timmy was my best friend. We grew up together, thick as thieves, and faced a heap of troubles side by side. Decided to join the Army together. But in the last battle we were in, he got hurt something bad. Watched him take his last breath right in front of me, jus' 'fore I got captured."

Sergio's expression softened as he listened. "I'm sorry," he replied.

"Seeing Billy after all this time... it stirs up a mess of old memories and a heap of anger," pausing for a moment. "But lookin' at him now, all broken, can't help but remind me of Timmy, lyin' there helpless 'fore he passed."

Sergio listened with patient attentiveness before sharing his viewpoint. "History pertains to past events, does it not?" he proposed. "Yet, your actions now can shape some of what transpires next, possibly influencing your future." Sergio carried on, "The truth is, none of us can be certain about our time on this earth, so why harbor resentment within?" He paused, letting his words linger in the air, before adding, "Purely a thought to ponder upon." Having delivered his piece, he turned back to the task at hand.

John took a deep breath. *Sergio's got a point, at least partly. The past... it's here, staring me in the face. I've got to face it, once and for all. This might be the only shot I've got.* As he prepared to speak again, an unexpected disturbance abruptly pulled him back to the present.

Sergio unexpectedly caught sight of a rat scurrying near the kitchen door. He let out a string of Italian expletives as he glared at the unwelcome intruder. Turning to John, he urged him to head to the storage room to retrieve the rat poison.

"Sprinkle it generously around the doorways. And make sure you wash your hands good afterward, as the poison contains arsenic and is quite toxic." The sense of urgency in Sergio's voice was unmistakable, emphasizing the importance of exercising caution when dealing with such a hazardous material.

John promptly headed to the storage shed, then followed Sergio's instructions. After completing the task, he returned the box of rat poison to the shed and made his way back to the kitchen. He had just returned when he saw Sergio wince in pain. Hot oil had splattered on his arm, causing him to drop the ladle. "Ah, cacchio!" He yelled as he turned off the stove and headed to the sink.

John rushed over to him. "You okay?"

Sergio grimaced as he raised his sleeve without thinking to examine the burn. "Yes, only a little burn."

As John looked at his arm, he noticed a faded tattoo of a series of numbers on his forearm. He remembered his earlier conversation regarding the tattoos they had seen on the men at the other end of the camp, asking, "What's that?"

Sergio followed his gaze and his expression changed, realizing his mistake. He had worn long sleeves inside and outside the kitchen. The guards had sometimes joked with him about it on hot summer days, but he had laughed it off with them, claiming he was cold-natured or wanted to avoid burns like the one he received.

Taking a deep breath, he looked at John. "Now that you've seen what you've seen, I suppose you deserve the truth. I pray I can trust you with this."

John nodded and placed a reassuring hand on his shoulder. "Course you can."

Sergio lowered his sleeve and began to explain. "My mother was Jewish. She moved to Italy from France and it's where she met my father, an Englishman who was working in Italy at the time. So, it makes me half Jewish. It's also how I learned English - from my father. And yes, most of the rumors concerning me are true."

John listened as he shared the difficult truth on his past. He had indeed cooked for the German high command until he was identified as being Jewish by the Gestapo and taken into custody.

"When the Commandant, General Kurt Schneider, was assigned here, he was able to bribe a Lieutenant at the jail where I was being held with a promotion and brought me here with him to be his personal chef and camp cook. He's the only one who knew my secret until now," Sergio continued.

John couldn't believe the Commandant had protected Sergio. "Why would he do that?"

Sergio took a deep breath before continuing. "The General had discovered my secret quite by accident while I was with him in Berlin. He had seen a family photo on my desk with a Star of David hanging on the wall behind us. At first, I thought my life was over, but he only looked at me with a knowing expression and didn't say a word."

He began to unravel the narrative, "He admired my knack for culinary arts and saw the touch of humanity it brought amidst the harsh realities of war. You see, he did not genuinely support Hitler or the Nazi party's values and agendas."

Sergio paused for a moment, choosing his words carefully. "He viewed himself simply as a soldier serving his country, not a fanatic serving a regime. He considered protecting me as his silent act of resistance against the Nazi system."

Seeing the surprise register on John's face, Sergio nodded, "Yes, it's hard to believe, isn't it? But he couldn't fathom why anyone would want to persecute an entire group based solely on their religion."

John reeled in disbelief at this revelation. Sergio merely shrugged, "Not all Germans supported Hitler's ideology, you know. But they couldn't voice it out loud. They viewed themselves as patriots serving their country, and the Commandant was one such person. He just... genuinely enjoyed my cooking."

"So, the Commandant is playing both sides," John said with disgust.

"Yes, he has to keep up appearances for the sake of his position, but he also knows what is happening here is wrong. It's why he has protected me and tried to make life a little easier for the prisoners when he can."

"But why doesn't he do something more to stop it?"

Sergio shook his head, a somber expression settling on his face. "It's not simple, John. The Nazi Party, the Gestapo, and the SS are omnipresent, watching and listening everywhere. If the Commandant were to take any action against their directive, it would risk not only his own life but the lives of everyone in this camp. He's trapped, like all of us. It's a delicate balance he has to maintain."

John found himself wrestling with Sergio's words, struggling to reconcile them with his own perception of the Commandant. "But he's the one in charge, right? Can't he jus' say no?"

Sergio sighed deeply. "Before the rise of the Nazis, the Commandant had been a career military man in the German army. He served honorably, but the rise of Hitler and the Nazi Party changed everything. The man found himself in a position where he was expected to enforce policies he didn't agree with. He's between a rock and a hard place. This isn't a justification for his actions but an explanation of the terrible situation he, and so many others, found themselves in."

John sat back, letting the reality of the situation sink in. The sense of moral simplicity he had held about the war seemed to be evaporating. "So, everyone's... stuck?" he asked, the question hanging heavily in the air.

Sergio nodded, his gaze distant. "In a way, yes. It's survival, John. The ones who wield power are also ensnared in the terror the Nazis have inflicted upon the world. They're forced to walk a treacherous line between survival and humanity. The implications are chilling, and the reality of this era's nightmare is emerging clearer with each passing day."

John sat in stunned silence as Sergio spoke. He couldn't believe his friend had endured so much hardship and had kept such a dangerous secret for so long. "I had no idea," he said. Then, leaning forward, asked the question weighing on his mind. "What 'bout your family? They still in Italy?"

Sergio's smile faded, and his eyes grew distant. "No, I heard they were taken away by the Gestapo shortly after the war began," he said, his voice heavy with emotion. "I decided to stay and cook for the high command because it was the only way for me to survive. My father had taught me everything I knew concerning cooking, and it was a skill I could use to keep myself alive." John looked at him, his heart heavy with sympathy.

"I knew the risks of being discovered, so I took measures to conceal any signs which might give me away. I was constantly afraid someone would find out, but I had to keep going for my own survival."

The conversation continued to unfold, layering complexity upon John's understanding of the war, the world, and the people navigating their lives within it. The realization began to dawn on him - these circumstances were far more intricate than he could have ever fathomed.

A question surged forth from his newfound understanding, catching even himself by surprise. "Sergio," he began, his voice reflecting his struggle with a difficult concept, "Can a good person do a bad thing and still remain a good person?"

Sergio studied John's face for a moment before responding, "A difficult question. History is rife with examples of people forced to make tough choices due to circumstances. Think back to the time of chivalry and knights. Consider the story of Sir Lancelot, one of the most famous knights of the Round Table in the Arthurian legend."

He looked thoughtfully at John as he continued, "Lancelot was King Arthur's most trusted knight and the queen's, Guinevere's, lover. When Guinevere was falsely accused of a crime and sentenced to death,

Lancelot rescued her. But in the process, he killed several of his fellow knights, including Sir Gareth, whom he loved like a brother."

Sergio's gaze held steady as he concluded, "So, was Lancelot a villain for his betrayal and the men he killed? Or was he a hero, protecting the honor of the woman he loved? The truth, John, is often more complex than we would like to believe. Sometimes, the line between good and evil becomes blurred, forcing honorable people into unthinkable situations. It's the circumstances which often dictate such choices. The world is not black and white but filled with many shades of gray."

John locked eyes with Sergio, a determined gleam in his eyes. "Thanks Sergio."

As they conversed, the complexities of war and the world unfolded before John, revealing layers he had not previously comprehended. With sobering clarity, it dawned on him the immense responsibility he bore - to right Billy's wrongs and to confront the harsh realities exposed by Sergio's story. In these tumultuous times, difficult decisions were inevitable. Now, armed with this new perspective, he grasped the gravity of the choices people faced.

"No problem." He then segued into their immediate tasks, "Let's prepare dinner for the infirmary now. I've received the updated list of patients with food allergies. Once we finish, you can deliver the trays and then get some rest." John nodded in and began to assist Sergio in preparing the meal trays.

Sgt. Schultz had been listening to the conversation with his ear pressed against the door, thankful he had decided to step away and get a cup of coffee. He felt satisfaction knowing his suspicions about the Italian cook had been correct. Schultz hated how Sergio seemed to have the Commandant's favor and could do as he pleased, and now he knew why.

Schultz was raised in a family with a long history of military service. His father had served in the German army during World War I, and his older brothers had also enlisted when World War II broke out. He admired his father and brothers for their bravery and dedication to serving their country.

Though he became a skilled soldier, he couldn't shake the feeling he was destined for something greater-specifically, a position in the Schutzstaffel SS. Drawn to the raw power they commanded, he aspired to rise through their ranks, believing being a mere guard was beneath him.

The SS, as Hitler's most trusted troops, was both revered and feared. Adorning oneself with the Totenkopf, or skull and crossbones emblem, and SS insignia was a declaration of authority. These symbols, specifically the lightning bolts in the SS insignia, stood as reminders of Hitler's brutal policies. Moreover, they were notorious for their cruelty in the concentration camps.

Determined to align himself with such power, he saw the SS as his ticket to Hitler's inner sanctum. With the revelation of a hidden Jew in their midst, he believed he had the perfect opportunity to impress them, a thought which brought a sly smile to his face.

With determination in his steps, he made his way across the camp, leaving behind a trail of dust with each stride. The SS headquarters tent loomed ahead, the notorious double lightning bolt emblem clearly visible on a sign out front, even from a distance. As he approached, the sounds of muffled conversations from inside hinted at the power held within those canvas walls.

As he reached the tent, his mind raced with excitement. He imagined how the SS officers would react to his revelation and how they would praise him for his keen observation. He stopped and took a moment to compose himself before entering. He wanted to appear calm and collected as he delivered the news. He stepped into the tent, meeting the stern face of one of the SS officers.

"What do you want?" The officer demanded coldly.

"Sir, I have some information which may be of great interest to the SS and the Reich."

"Well, spit it out then, Sergeant."

"I have discovered there is a Jew hiding right under our noses, working as a cook in this camp. He has been protected by the Commandant himself."

"Are you certain of this, Sergeant?"

"Yes, sir. I overheard a conversation between the cook and an American prisoner. They discussed the cook's Jewish heritage and how the Commandant has been protecting him."

The officer stood, his face a mask of fury. "This is an outrage! However, Colonel Richter is not present at the moment. Report back here first thing in the morning when he returns."

"Yes, sir!" he replied and promptly left the tent, excitement coursing through his veins. Not only would he expose the Jew hidden in the camp, but he would also take away the protection the American prisoner had been enjoying. He smiled as he walked away, rubbing the locket in his pocket, feeling his fortune was about to change.

After delivering food to the infirmary, John decided to make a quick stop at the restroom. He glanced around discreetly while washing his hands. Certain he was alone, he turned his right front pocket inside out, allowing the white powder residue to fall onto the floor. After flushing away any remnants of suspicion, he finished washing his hands, ensuring he left no trace behind.

As he dried his hands and exited, his mind was consumed with thoughts of the following day's uncertainties. Unbeknownst to him, a dangerous storm was beginning to brew around them.

Chapter 20

Freedom's Cost

The following morning, as the first light of dawn broke over the horizon, Schultz, meticulously groomed and dressed in his crispest uniform, confidently strode towards the SS headquarters tent.

The camp was still shrouded in predawn mist, lending an eerie quality as his polished boots left a trail of damp footprints on the ground. He had taken great care to ensure his appearance was impeccable. Today was his day to be recognized and praised for his dedication to the cause.

As he neared the entrance of the tent, the imposing figure of Colonel Richter emerged, standing authoritatively in the doorway. The dim morning light cast sharp shadows accentuating his stern features, while his own uniform appeared equally immaculate. He felt a mixture of pride and anxiety, knowing he had vital information to relay, and his performance could make a lasting impression on Richter.

With his back straight and head held high, he saluted crisply before the officer. "Sir, I have urgent news regarding the cook Sergio." His words rang clear and concise, reflecting the attention to detail he had applied not only to his appearance, but to all his actions that morning.

Richter's expression grew serious. "I have been informed by the Lieutenant you spoke to last night on your discovery. If your information proves accurate, I assure you, you will be well-rewarded for such a commendable deed, Sergeant."

Schultz's chest swelled with pride at the prospect of being recognized for his diligence and loyalty. Within minutes, a group of SS soldiers assembled, ready to carry out their orders.

As the SS soldiers prepared to depart, John approached the infirmary, consumed by thoughts of Billy. He entered and walked towards the area where he had been lying.

However, when he arrived, he found the bed empty, replaced with fresh sheets. Confused, John stopped a passing nurse. "Excuse me, where is the patient who was here?"

The nurse replied coldly, "He's dead. They took him away to the pit last night."

The pit was a mass grave where the dead were disposed of unceremoniously, covered with a thin layer of dirt until the next batch of bodies arrived. The process repeated until the pit was full, after which another would be dug. John stood there, grappling with the reality: *Billy is truly gone.*

Meanwhile, elsewhere in the camp, a different scene was unfolding. Richter, Schultz, and the group of SS soldiers marched purposefully across the camp, their boots leaving impressions in the damp earth as they traversed the dirt pathways. Their destination: the camp's kitchen. The atmosphere was tense, as the soldiers knew an important arrest was about to be made.

Upon reaching the kitchen, the door swung open with a loud creak, revealing the bustling workspace inside. The unexpected intrusion caught everyone off-guard, and the two prisoners working inside froze in their tracks, their eyes widening in fear and confusion.

Richter stepped forward; his gaze fixed on Sergio. His voice boomed, filling the room with an icy chill. "Are you a Jew?" Sergio, visibly shaken, stood there, not uttering a single word. Thoughts whirled in his mind, a haunting question surfacing amidst the turmoil: *Has John betrayed me?*

As the silence stretched on, Schultz spoke up, eager to prove himself. "Sir, I heard him admit it last night. I suggest you check his arms for evidence." In an instant, a bitter understanding dawned on Sergio. *So Schultz is the treacherous viper who exposed me.*

Richter's eyes narrowed. "Seize him!"

His soldiers moved forward, closing the distance between them and their target. "Hold his arms and raise his sleeves," Richter ordered tersely.

The guards complied, grabbing his arms firmly and lifting his sleeves. There, exposed for all to see, was the telltale tattoo. An unsettling silence fell upon them.

"So, it's true!" Schultz said.

Richters voice rang out, cold and commanding, "Clear the kitchen. Now!" His order cut through the room, snapping the kitchen staff out of their shock. With wide eyes and quickened steps, they hurried out, leaving Sergio in the firm grip of the soldiers. The clatter of pans and the shuffle of feet faded, leaving only the ominous silence of the unfolding scene.

A wave of anger washed over Richter's face as he stepped closer, his voice seething with contempt. "You dirty Jew!" he shouted, delivering a powerful blow to the stomach. The force of the impact made him double over in pain, but the guards held him upright, preventing him from collapsing.

Still glaring, Richter continued, "First, we take care of you. Afterward, we will deal with the Commandant." As the soldiers began to drag Sergio away, his carefully concealed secret was laid bare for those last few lingering eyes to see. His fate was now cloaked in ominous uncertainty.

Across camp, Commandant General Kurt Schneider, the seasoned and respected military leader, arrived at his office early in the morning, as usual. The scent of old books and polished wood filled the air, while the morning sunlight crept in through the open blinds, casting a warm glow on his desk.

As he settled into his leather chair, young Private Wilhelm entered, holding a steaming cup of coffee. Wilhelm was a shy, lanky young man, barely 18 years old. He was somewhat simple-minded, but he had a good heart and a cheerful disposition which endeared him to everyone he met.

"Here, sir, as you like it," he said, handing the coffee to him with a proud smile.

"Thank you, Wilhelm."

As the young man turned to leave, he watched him for a moment longer, a protective glint in his eye. *He reminds me so much of my own son.* He had known Wilhelm would have struggled to survive among the harsher soldiers, so he had taken the boy under his protective wing.

As Wilhelm reached the door, there was an urgent knock on the frame. Captain Dietrich Kölb, a distinguished soldier, stood in the doorway, his face lined with concern. "General, may I have a moment of your time?"

"Of course, Dietrich. Come in," he replied, glad to see his trusted Captain. He gestured toward Wilhelm and asked, "Would you like coffee?"

"No, thank you, sir."

Schneider nodded at Wilhelm, who was still waiting for the response. "That will be all for now, Wilhelm. Thank you." Wilhelm nodded, disappointed, and dutifully exited the room.

Now alone, Schneider could sense something serious was amiss. The Captain's usually stoic demeanor was replaced by a hint of anxiety, which only served to heighten his own concern. "What is it, Dietrich? What's happened?"

He hesitated for a moment before speaking. "Sir, we have received new intelligence. It seems the enemy is planning an attack sooner than we expected."

"And no one else knows? Especially Richter, correct?"

"Only you, sir, as you requested," he replied.

Schneider knew the enemy had been closing in from both sides, and he had intentionally kept this information from the SS, as he despised them. The only question which remained was who would arrive first. "Do we know if the Russians or the Americans will be here first?"

"Regrettably, we don't know, sir."

The gravity of the situation was not lost on Schneider. He steepled his fingers, deep in thought, as he contemplated his next course of action. He took a deep breath and looked Dietrich straight in the eye. "Alright, remember the plan and relay it to those we trust."

"Yes, sir'".

"And Dietrich, ensure you take Wilhelm with you and protect him."

"You have my word, sir."

Schneider had long recognized Germany was losing the war. He had witnessed the urgent increase of Jews arriving at the camp and the furnaces burning 24 hours a day.

The murder of innocents sickened him; it was not what he had signed up for, and it disgusted him. Although he was the commandant, the SS really controlled most of the camp, and he had to be careful, as they reported anything going against the Führer's wishes straight to Berlin. He had seen cases where, when such events had happened before, the perpetrator simply disappeared.

The SS's pervasive influence limited his ability to intervene in the camp's operations, but he was determined to do what he could to protect the people under his command.

He knew speaking out against the atrocities would only put him and his men at risk, so he had been biding his time, waiting for the right opportunity to ensure their safety and prevent them from being implicated in the horrors taking place around them.

While stationed in Berlin, he sensed the Führer's rising power. Speaking on his concerns led to his assignment to the camp as punishment. But now, with the end of the war in sight, he was more determined than ever to protect those in his care, particularly young Wilhelm, and to ensure he and his trusted men would not be part of the atrocities any longer.

The SS's pervasive influence restricted his capacity to alter camp operations, yet he remained steadfast in his commitment to shield the people under his charge. Openly challenging the brutalities would endanger both him and his men; hence, he had been discreetly biding his time, seeking an opportunity to safeguard their welfare without implicating them in the camp's atrocities.

His reassignment was the result of voicing concerns over the Führer's rising power while stationed in Berlin. However, as the war's conclusion neared, his determination only grew. He aimed to ensure he and his trusted soldiers, particularly young Wilhelm, would stand apart from the crimes committed within the camp's confines.

Captain Kölb hesitated for a moment before continuing, "There is something else you should know, sir."

Schneider looked at him attentively, "What is it?"

"I have learned Colonel Richter is on his way to the kitchen to make an arrest."

"Do we know who the prisoner is and why?"

"No sir, only it's a Jew."

Schneider paused, a hint of recognition flashing in his eyes. "Thank you," he said curtly. "Proceed as instructed. I have an urgent matter to attend to myself."

Captain Kölb nodded crisply and said, "Yes, sir," before promptly exiting.

Schneider gathered his thoughts; he needed to act fast to protect Sergio. A single wrong move could have disastrous consequences for them. He wondered how Sergio's secret had been discovered after all this time. They had been so careful ever since Berlin, when he had first learned of his secret: he came from a Jewish family.

He had accidentally seen a photo on Sergio's desk while searching for him to discuss a dinner request. When Sergio returned, he placed the photo back, made his request, and left, never mentioning the image again.

He was well-aware of the precariousness of the situation, particularly as reports on the horrific condition's at other concentration camps like Auschwitz and Treblinka began to filter through. It was a grim reality he knew Sergio could face if he didn't protect him.

Schneider had seen similar ominous signs before. He recalled the events of the Kristallnacht in 1938, where violence against Jews surged dramatically across Germany It was then he realized he needed to get his family to safety.

His wife, despite being German born, was of Jewish descent, a fact which put her and their son in danger. He had managed to orchestrate their secret escape, securing them a place on a cargo ship destined for the relative safety of Canada. After the war, he planned to make his way there as well, in hopes of reuniting with them.

Now, learning of Sergio's arrest, a wave of sadness washed over him. He was reminded of the plight of thousands of innocent people who had become victims of their ancestry, people like his wife, like Sergio, whose lives were forever altered by the devastating politics of hate and intolerance.

The night before he had departed Berlin for his new position, he had stopped by the jail housing Sergio. Luckily, a Lieutenant was on duty. He had lied, telling him Sergio was an important political prisoner whom he was to escort to the prison personally. The Lieutenant looked skeptical saying he would need to check with his Captain.

He had responded with a stern rebuke, asking if the Lieutenant dared to question his authority. He further intimidated him with the thought of what his Captain would say when he found out about his insubordination. This managed to unsettle the Lieutenant enough to persuade him to grant his request.

As they exited the jailhouse, he turned to the Lieutenant, a firm note of command in his voice. "Thank you, Lieutenant," he said, "but you will speak of this to no one. If asked, you will say the prisoner has escaped."

Seeing the Lieutenant's unease, he offered further reassurance. "And Lieutenant, your cooperation today won't be forgotten. I'll see to it you receive a well-deserved promotion." This promise seemed to soothe the young officer, alleviating his anxiety about the irregularities of the evening.

With Richter now on his way to make the arrest, he needed to act swiftly and decisively. He opened his desk drawer and removed his Walther P38 pistol. After checking to ensure it was loaded, he stood and holstered it. Grabbing his cap, he took a deep breath and headed out the door.

He hurried through the camp, reaching Richter not long after they had exited the kitchen. He stopped to confront him, asking, "What do you think you're doing?"

Richter sneered and replied, "I'm doing my job, arresting a Jew, like you should have done long ago."

Schneider's expression hardened. "Don't forget who you're talking to, Colonel."

"I know precisely who I'm talking to, a traitor who protected a Jew. And of course, you know what happens to traitors of the Reich." He subtly unsnapped his holster, his hand hovering close to his weapon.

The two men stared at each other, tension filling the air. Richter turned to the other SS men with him and ordered, "Arrest him."

Schneider instinctively reached for his own gun, but Richter was faster. He drew his pistol, extending it and aiming it directly at the general.

As John left the infirmary, he caught sight of the Commandant and Colonel Richter, their confrontation escalating. A moment later, he heard a shot and saw the Commandant fall backwards to the ground.

To his surprise, he noticed Sergio detained among the group, looking shocked and distraught. Panic surged through him, and he sprinted towards them, shouting his Sergio's name desperately.

Hearing the commotion, Richter paused and turned towards the sound of the voice. "Who is that?"

"A worthless cook assistant, the one I overheard Sergio talking to last night." Schultz replied.

While watching him approach, Richter ordered. "Take care of this nuisance."

"With pleasure," he responded, a malicious grin spreading across his face. He stepped in front of John as he neared Sergio.

For a brief moment, John and Sergio's eyes locked, and he could sense the fear in his friend's eyes. Without warning, John was blindsided by a powerful punch from Schultz, knocking him to the ground.

As he lay there, dazed and looking skyward as Schultz stood over him, he noticed a plane suddenly fly low and fast directly overhead. The roar of its engines was deafening, and he could feel the wind from it as it passed so close it seemed as if he could touch it.

Before he could process what he was seeing, the air erupted with yelling and shouting. German soldiers screamed "Alarm! Alarm!" Then, the piercing wail of a siren filled the air, signaling the camp was under attack.

John heard a massive explosion from the front gate and felt the vibration course through his body, followed by gunfire. He rolled to his side and spotted Sergio standing unsteadily, as if in a trance.

He screamed his name, trying to catch his attention. Finally, Sergio's gaze fell upon him. John continued to yell "Get down!"

attempting to be louder than the gunfire, but Sergio could only see his lips moving, unable to hear the words amidst the chaos.

Sergio attempted to make his way towards him, not understanding what was happening. He was 10 yards away when his body abruptly began jerking in contorted ways, as if he was being struck by an unseen force.

"No!" John screamed, watching in horror as bullets tore through Sergio's body and his friend collapsed lifelessly to the ground.

Amid the chaos of gunfire and explosions all around him, he crawled to him. As he reached him, he cried out in anguish, realizing he was once again... alone.

He lay dazed and confused, face buried in his hands. He was oblivious to his surroundings and didn't notice the gunfire had stopped. He barely registered the sensation of a foot nudging him and the voice following. The voice! Could it possibly be true?

As his mind raced and his head cleared, he could make out the words. "Hey! Hey, buddy! You alive?"

He rolled over, and as his eyes cleared from the dust, he saw what appeared to be an American with a Tommy gun. He simply replied, "Yeah."

"We got another live one!" the soldier yelled to someone out of sight. He helped John to a sitting position and offered him water from his canteen before helping him to his feet.

"Let's get you out of here and home," he said, holding him steady as they walked.

As they walked, John saw Sergeant Schultz lying face down. In a quick move, he broke free from the soldier's grip. The soldier, caught off guard, could only watch as John dashed to Schultz's side and dropped to a knee.

Frantically, he searched the Sergeant's pockets under the soldier's bewildered gaze until his fingers closed around the familiar shape.

Withdrawing the locket, he stood and, in a fit of rage, kicked the lifeless body several times before facing the stunned soldier. "Now we can go."

"What was that all about?"

"Had to tie up some unfinished business is all," he replied coldly, his eyes fixed ahead as they walked toward the remains of the camp's entrance. The soldier sensed there was more to the story but didn't press the matter.

He and the other liberated prisoners gathered outside the gate, exhausted from their time in the camp. They sat on the ground, while the Americans cleared the rest of the camp of Germans. The sounds of gunfire and explosions echoed in the distance, gradually fading.

As they sat, two sleek P-51 Mustang fighters flew overhead side by side. The powerful roar of their engines reverberated through them, drowning out all other sounds. The silver-skinned planes shimmered in the sunlight, each emblazoned with the unmistakable blue and white star of the US planes. The pilots dipped their wings, a gesture of solidarity and triumph. The prisoners watched in awe, some too weak to hardly lift their heads, but all understood the heartfelt meaning behind the gesture.

John's mind raced, trying to reconcile the scenes unfolding before him. From the powerful display of the P-51 Mustangs to the stark reality of the prisoners, every moment seemed surreal. And there, amidst it all, was Captain Kölb, a man he recognized, leading the German prisoners. The sight of his smile, in stark contrast to the somberness of their situation, left John perplexed. *It's Captain Kölb. But why is he smiling?*

As the group drew nearer, he watched in disbelief. Kölb's smile was unmistakable, yet as they passed by, it shifted to a look of sorrow. Kölb met his gaze and nodded in his direction before continuing on. *What did that gesture mean?* John sat there, confused and unsure, the question echoing in his mind.

When the fighting above had subsided, Kölb remembered the General's instructions: at the first sound of battle, they were to gather in the bunker and wait until the fighting was over. Afterwards, they should exit with their hands in the air and surrender. Kölb had prayed it would be the Americans they surrendered to, not the Russians. He had read reports from the Eastern Front on the fate of Germans who surrendered to the Russians, whose reputation for brutality and revenge was well-known. Those reports were far from pleasant.

As Kölb, Wilhelm, and the other loyal followers of the General had emerged from the bunker with their hands raised in submission, they were relieved to see they were surrendering to the Americans and not the Russians.

He walked with a sense of freedom he hadn't felt in years. His soldiers were finally free, and he couldn't help but smile.

As he passed by the American cook, he felt a pang of sadness. He had seen Sergio, lifeless, beside the General and recognized the bond they shared, reminiscent of his own with the General.

Gazing upon his former prisoners, he felt a deep sense of shame and regret for the unspeakable atrocities committed by his fellow Germans in the name of his country. He knew history would judge him and General Schneider harshly and not look kindly upon his fellow Germans.

But he was grateful for this opportunity to surrender and keep his men alive as he had also known the war had long been lost. For him and everyone who had occupied the camp, the war was finally over. Like the Americans, he too harbored hope in his heart and wished to see home again.

While Kölb and his men were coming to terms with their new reality, John and the other former prisoners were facing challenges of their own. The camp had been liberated for a week now, and John had finally been checked by the medics. He was grateful to be alive and to have survived the ordeal, but he couldn't shake the feeling of sadness and loss permeating the camp.

As the soldiers searched the camp, they found the storage building where the Germans had stored the prisoners belongings. They began the painstaking task of going through the bags, trying to identify the belongings and return them to the survivors. For those who had died, their bags were loaded onto a truck to be sent back to the states.

His bag had been located and handed over to him. He unfastened it, his fingers deftly working the closures. Inside, his old uniform lay folded. Extracting it, he let the worn fabric unfurl, revealing the emblem and insignia of his now past life. Slipping into the uniform, he could feel it draping loosely around his frame, a stark reminder of the physical toll his captivity had exacted on him.

John's fingers closed around his journal, its worn leather cover a familiar presence. It was a silent witness to his past. It held his many experiences from before his captivity. With careful movements, he opened it, the spine giving a soft creak of protest, as he sought out the last page he had filled with his words.

His gaze landed on the familiar handwriting, a message from his past self captured on the page. The words, once hastily scrawled, served as poignant reminders of the trials endured. Time might have faded the ink, but the raw emotions etched into those pages remained as fresh as ever.

John traced the lines with his fingertips, each word acting as a catalyst for a flood of memories. Visions of the past returned unbidden - the stark realities of war, the lingering fear and despair, the losses sustained, and the shimmering hope of seeing Sarah once more.

One of the supply Sergeants, busy returning the bags, caught sight of the journal resting on his lap, "Noticed you've got a journal there. Have anything to write with?"

"No," John admitted, with a hint of frustration in his voice.

Without missing a beat, the Sergeant reached into his pocket and pulled out a pen. "Here, take mine," he offered, tossing it towards him.

Holding the pen, he stared at his worn journal, pondering where to begin. There was so much he wanted to say, so much he wanted to share, but the words seemed stuck in his throat. Finally, he took a deep breath and looked at the Sergeant. "Thank ya," he said.

The Sergeant replied with a smile. "No problem, you take care now."

He nodded, appreciating the simple, yet significant gesture. A wave of gratitude washed over him as he paused. *The man in these pages - full of fear, timidness, and uncertainty - that's not who I am anymore. I've endured. I've done what I needed to out of love, knowing one day I will be judged for my actions. But I've survived. And now, it's time to move forward.*

Drawing a deep breath, he prepared to continue his narrative in the worn pages of his treasured journal. *But where do I even begin? How can I explain to Sarah, or anyone, all that I've seen, done, and endured? Maybe in time, under the oak, I will tell her 'bout running into Billy. But until then...* His pen hovered for a moment before touching the paper. With a resolute heart, he started to write: *This is my story, in my own words...*

Epilogue

He had spent the afternoon lost in thought, reminiscing under the shade of the old oak. He looked upward at the massive branches with a newfound appreciation for it. He now understood and could see why it was such a special place. He knew he couldn't change the past, but he could make peace with it.

His journey back to Warrenton had been about more than just collecting old belongings. It was about finding answers and closure. He understood now and felt like he finally had both. He read his father's journals and the diaries as well. All of which explained everything. *He now knew all the family secrets.*

Such as how his father had received a letter from his mother not long after the Battle of Saint-Lô. In the heart-wrenching words she'd penned, she recounted her chilling encounter with Billy. It took place in a secluded alleyway, a sinister backdrop for the assault and pain she'd endured at Billy's hands. The revelation ignited a fury within him, kindling a flame of vengeance which was yet to find its path. He had vowed to seek retribution, although the specifics of when and how remained unknown at the time.

He was surprised when he later spotted Billy in the camp infirmary. It seemed like a stroke of luck when Sergio had asked him to deal with the rats that day. It's when the idea had struck him. He had discreetly scooped some of the poison into his hand and slipped it into his pocket. That night, his suspicions were confirmed when he noticed the allergen tag on one of the food trays reading 'B. Harrington.' He realized this might be his only chance.

While preparing the trays for delivery, he took the poison from his pocket and sprinkled it generously throughout the food, subtly mixing it with a fork. After delivering the trays, he went to bed but found sleep elusive, as he couldn't help but wonder how long it would take. The next morning, he was astonished to discover his plan had worked so quickly. A smile had spread across his face, knowing Billy would never bother them again.

Then there was the hidden truth contained within his mother's diary, which emerged a startling revelation: she had suffered a miscarriage after her encounter with Billy. This was a secret she had kept from his father-a pregnancy and its harrowing end which remained shrouded in silence for the rest of her life.

And so, when the opportunity arose to adopt him as a baby from elderly Aunt Jean, his legal guardian at the time, Sarah embraced it. The decision served a dual purpose; it not only alleviated her own fears, but also enabled his father John to fulfill the promise he had made to Timmy. She also understood the weight of the vow he had made on the battlefield, and his adoption became their shared path towards honoring his commitment.

Another secret was nestled within the weathered pages of a second diary, bearing the faded name of his birth mother 'Emily' etched on its cover. One of the entries, steeped in the past, was dated *April 19, 1937,* and read:

Daddy insisted yesterday I go fishing with him today. I told Timmy last night I wouldn't be able to see him because I would be at the river at Dan's Fork fishing. He had already been drinking this morning and asked if I was ready to go. I was afraid to say no.

We went down to the river, and I carried the poles. He started drinking again and said, "Let's go swimming." I said I didn't want to. He came over to me and started to touch me and remove my dress. I wanted to scream and run but I couldn't move and knew what would happen if I did.

About this time, Timmy came down the hill. I think he wanted to surprise me. He saw me scared and ran to my dad, telling him to leave me alone. He pushed Timmy to the ground and told him to mind his business. Timmy grabbed a large piece of broken branch and hit him, causing him to stumble. He was drunk, so he couldn't keep his balance and fell near the edge of the water. He didn't move.

Timmy went over to check him and saw his head to the side and eyes wide open. He saw the blood where his head had hit the jagged rock. We didn't know what to do. He told me he would take care of it and pushed him into the river. As we watched him float down the river, He told me "We can't tell anyone about this. Okay?"

I told him okay, and he made me promise. He told me when they ask what happened, just tell them You were fishing. He was drunk and stumbled and fell in the water. I was never here either, okay. I love you, Em, and you don't have to worry about him ever hurting you again. He kissed me, then said now go find someone and tell them you need some help. He then ran up the hill out of sight.

A profound realization struck him: his biological parents had played a role in his grandfather's demise. The story of an accidental drowning, a narrative he had been told and had accepted as truth all his life was merely a fabrication. Had the townsfolk learned the truth, that a young black boy had caused the death of a white man, they most likely would have lynched him, a harsh reality of the times.

Also, after the traumatic events described in her diary, she wrote about struggling with deep emotional and psychological distress following childbirth, and the death of Timmy, what we would now recognize as postpartum syndrome. In her small Georgia town, such conditions were poorly understood, often misdiagnosed, and rarely spoken about, leaving many women like her to suffer in silence.

Overwhelmed and without support, she tragically took her own life, adding another layer of sorrow to the family's hidden history.

He sat there, momentarily paralyzed by the magnitude of his discoveries. A torrent of emotions cascaded through him, leaving him drained and contemplative. It was as if the earth had shifted beneath him, revealing chasms filled with untold secrets and buried truths. Yet, as he absorbed the revelations, a certain serenity began to envelop him, the calm after the storm.

He drew in a slow deep breath, the fresh air seeming to cleanse the turmoil within him. With newfound resolve, he gently rose to his feet, his hands thoughtfully gathering the weathered journals and diaries. Each of these aged pages had proven to be a doorway into his past, and he treated them with respectful reverence as he placed them back into the box.

Holding the box once again, he walked a few yards away from the old oak, the weight of the box seeming lighter now that it had relinquished its secrets. Carefully sitting the box down, he peered inside once more, his gaze fell upon the old pocket watch and tarnished silver locket.

These objects, familiar yet forgotten, were pieces of his past he'd seen often as a young boy. Back then, he'd regarded them with innocent curiosity, their true significance far beyond his understanding. Now they appeared to him in a new light, transformed into profound relics of a hidden history.

His fingers hovered above the items, the physical connection seeming to deepen the emotional gravity. He thought back to the many times he'd innocently played with these objects, completely unaware of the intricate narratives they held. With this newfound perspective, he carefully lifted them, now seeing them not just as simple artifacts, but as intimate links to his past.

The weight of them felt different in his hands, filled with significance and weighted with revelations. He closed his fingers around them, their cold metal warming to his touch. Gently, he slipped them into his pocket, feeling them settle against the fabric, a tangible link to a past he was finally beginning to understand.

Tearing out a few pages from the journal, he lit a cigarette and then set the pages on fire, tossing the burning sheets into the box. As the box continued to burn, he stubbed out his cigarette and walked to the other side of the tree, where he stopped.

He retrieved the two items from his pocket: first, the watch, which he laid atop the marble, and then the locket. Opening it, he smiled at the picture of the beautiful woman inside before closing it and placing it on the adjacent marble.

He stepped back, a smile on his face. With a mixture of sadness and gratitude, he made his way back down the hill. As he reached the car, he stopped and turned, gazing back at the oak tree and the two headstones of his parents glistening in the sun with newfound appreciation.

He knew the memories and secrets he had discovered would remain with him forever. This realization brought him understanding and closure.

As he prepared to drive away, Jacob now understood why his parents had taken him to the old oak almost every Sunday for a picnic. He also grasped why his father had insisted on burying his mother, Sarah, there after her death, and why he himself wanted to be laid to rest beside her when his time came.

He now understood their love would endure forever in the same place it began. He smiled and stepped on the accelerator, glancing in his rearview mirror as the tree faded into the distance. He recognized, perhaps, *some secrets are best left untold*.

Afterword

As I close the narrative of "Secrets of the Oak," I am reminded of the incredible journey that this novel represents - both for its characters and for myself as an author. It has been a labor of love, of painstaking research, and of deep respect for the time period and the people who lived through it.

The 1930s and 1940s were a time of profound change and challenge, marked by desperation, resilience, and the ever-resilient spirit of humanity. It was these stories of courage and endurance that I sought to capture in the lives of the characters who populate the pages of "Secrets of the Oak."

While the characters and their stories are a product of my imagination, they were influenced by countless real accounts and historical events of that era. My goal was to tell a compelling story. Additionally, I aimed to provide a glimpse into a time marred by segregation, conflict, and hardship, showcasing the strength and resilience of the human spirit.

Writing this novel has been a deeply personal journey. It has been an opportunity to delve into a period of history that has always fascinated me and to share that passion with readers. My hope is that "Secrets of the Oak" provides not just an engaging read, but also a deeper appreciation for the people who lived through such challenging times. Their stories, their strength, and their spirit continue to inspire and teach us valuable lessons about acceptance, love, resilience, courage, and the enduring power of the human spirit.

Thank you for joining me on this journey through "Secrets of the Oak." I hope you enjoyed reading it as much as I enjoyed writing it.

Lynn Whitsitt

Acknowledgements

Firstly, I would like to express my deepest gratitude to my wife, Brandi. Your unwavering support, understanding, and encouragement were the cornerstones of this work. You've been my compass when I've lost my way, and this book would not exist without you by my side.

To my parents, thank you for nurturing my love for stories and history. Your lessons, values, and unconditional love shaped the man and the writer I am today. This work is a testament to the wisdom and strength you've imparted to me.

I wish to extend my heartfelt appreciation to all the soldiers and their families who have served, are serving, or were lost in service. Your courage, sacrifice, and resilience are unparalleled, and this book is but a small tribute to your heroism.

Thank you to Kari Brabander, whose keen eye and insightful comments have made this book better in every way. Your constructive criticism and guidance in this project have not gone unnoticed. Of course, I also want to express my gratitude to Sharon Presock and Krystle Yates who reviewed each chapter as I built it out, pointing out my typos and asking questions about things I missed.

To the wonderful ladies at Museum of Cultural Heritage in Warrenton, GA who took the time to answer my many questions. I am also thankful to authors Tony Perez and Jody Jessica Brody, from whom I've learned a lot and appreciate the advice and teaching they provided.

Lastly, to you, the reader: Thank you. By picking up this book, you've given life to these characters and their stories. It is my hope that you find within these pages a tale that moves you, provokes thought, and reminds us of the strength of the human spirit and the power of love. Thank you all!

Don't miss out!

Visit the website below and you can sign up to receive emails whenever Lynn Whitsitt publishes a new book. There's no charge and no obligation.

https://books2read.com/r/B-A-BNGCB-OFOSC

BOOKS 2 READ

Connecting independent readers to independent writers.

About the Author

Lynn Whitsitt is a retired Army Officer who now resides in Georgia, alongside his wife and four pets. Lynn embraces his passion for reading and crafting narratives. Beyond the written word, he relishes in exploring Georgia's natural wonders and engaging in insightful dialogues with diverse enthusiasts. His zeal for storytelling is reflected both in his life and his work.

Read more at https://www.LynnWhitsitt.com.